JILLIAN HART

grew up on her family's homestead, where she raised cattle, rode horses and scribbled stories in her spare time. After earning her English degree from Whitman College, she worked in travel and advertising before selling her first novel. When Jillian isn't working on her next story, she can be found puttering in her rose garden, curled up with a good book and spending quiet evenings at home with her family.

VICTORIA BYLIN

has a collection of refrigerator magnets that mark the changes in her life. The oldest ones are from California. A native of Los Angeles, she graduated from UC Berkeley with a degree in history and went to work in the advertising industry. She soon met a wonderful man who charmed her into taking a ride on his motorcycle. That ride led to a trip down the wedding aisle, two sons, various pets and a move that landed Victoria and her family in northern Virginia.

Magnets from thirty states commemorate that journey and her new life on the East Coast. The most recent additions are from the Smithsonian National Museum of American History and a Chinese restaurant that delivers, a sure sign that Victoria is busy writing. Feel free to drop her an e-mail at VictoriaBylin@aol.com, or visit her Web site at www.victoriabylin.com.

JILLIAN HART
VICTORIA BYLIN
In a Mother's Arms

Steeple
Hill®

Published by Steeple Hill Books™

STEEPLE HILL BOOKS

Steeple
Hill®

Recycling programs
for this product may
not exist in your area.

ISBN-13: 978-0-373-82809-8
ISBN-10:   0-373-82809-8

IN A MOTHER'S ARMS

Copyright © 2009 by Harlequin Books S.A.

The publisher acknowledges the copyright holders of the individual works as follows:

FINALLY A FAMILY
Copyright © 2009 by Jill Strickler

HOME AGAIN
Copyright © 2009 by Vicki Scheibel

www.SteepleHill.com

Printed in U.S.A.

CONTENTS

FINALLY A FAMILY
Jillian Hart

You have turned for me my mourning
into dancing; You have put off my sackcloth
and clothed me with gladness.
—*Psalms* 30:11

Chapter One

❦

Angel County, Montana Territory, 1884

Molly McKaslin felt watched as she sat in her cushioned rocking chair in her cozy little shanty with her favorite book in hand. The story she was reading had taken her far away to the landscape of England, where the rush of fictional rain drowned out the real sounds of the Montana wind breezing through the open windows. Mr. Darcy's offer of marriage to Elizabeth Bennet vanished like mist and Molly blinked, reorienting herself. What had drawn her out of her story?

The lush new-spring green of the Montana prairie spread out before her like a painting, framed by the wooden window. The blue sky was without a single cloud to mar it. Lemony sunshine spilled over the land and through the open windowsill. The crisp scents from the nearby orchard and grass fields filled the cheerful one-room shanty. The door was wedged open, letting the outside noises in—the snap of laundry on the clothesline and the chomping crunch of an animal grazing. My, it sounded terribly close. This was her cousin Aiden's land. Perhaps he had let his livestock onto the lawn to give the fast growing grass a quick mow?

The peaceful afternoon quiet shattered, right along with a crash. She leaped to her feet, spinning around to see her good—and only—china vase splintered on the newly washed wood floor. The sprays of buttercups and daisies were tangled amid the shards, water pooling on the polished planks. She stared in shock at the culprit standing at her other window. A golden cow with a white blaze down her face poked her head further across the sill, obviously curious where the tasty flowers had gone to. The bovine gave a woeful moo, her liquid brown eyes pleading for help. One look told her this was the only animal in the yard.

"And just what are you doing out on your own?" She set her book aside.

The cow lowed again. She was a small heifer with a sweet innocence about her. Still probably more baby than adult. The cow lunged against the sill and wrapped her long tongue around the top rung of the ladder-back chair, straining toward the cookie racks on the table. She was obviously tame. She cast a plaintive look and mooed softly, perhaps saying the bovine version of "please."

"At least I know how to catch you." Molly had grown up on her family's farm and she knew how flighty cattle could be. This one still might run off on her yet. She grabbed a cookie off the rack and sure enough the heifer's eyes widened with a doe's sweetness. "I don't recognize you, so I don't think you belong here. Someone is going to be very unhappy with you."

The cow batted her long brown lashes, unafraid. Molly skirted around the mess on the floor—she would bemoan the loss of her mother's vase later—and headed toward the door. This was the consequence of agreeing to live in the country when she had vowed to never do so again. Life had happened, and her path had led her to this opportunity, living on her cousin's land and helping the family. God had quite a sense of humor, indeed.

Her bare feet puffed up the chalk-dry dust outside her door. Before she could take two steps into the soft, lush grass surrounding her shanty, the cow came running, head down, big brown eyes fastened on the cookie, all four legs blurring in motion. The ground shook.

Uh oh. Molly's heart skipped two beats.

"No, Sukie, no!" High, girlish voices carried on the wind.

Over the cow's head, Molly briefly caught sight of two identical school-aged girls racing down the long dirt road. The animal was too single-minded to respond. The cow's head was down as she pounded the final few yards, her determined gaze fixed on the cookie.

"Stop, Sukie. Whoa." Molly kept her voice low and kindly firm. It may have been a long time since she had managed a cow, but she knew they responded to kindness better than to anything else. She also knew they were not good at stopping, so she dropped the cookie on the ground and neatly stepped out of the way. The cow dug in with all hooves, skidded well past the cookie and the place where Molly had been standing.

"It's right here." She touched the cow's shoulder, showing her where the oatmeal treat was resting in the clean grass. While the animal backed up a foot and nipped up the goody, Molly grabbed the cow's rope halter.

"Good. She didn't stomp you into bits." One of the girls swiped her hand over her forehead, as if in serious relief. "She ran me over real good just last week."

The second girl stood with her head down, sucking in air. "We thought you were a goner. She's real nice, but she doesn't see very well."

"She sees well enough to have found me." Molly studied the girls. They both had identical black braids and golden-hazel eyes and fine-boned porcelain faces. One twin wore a green calico dress with matching sunbonnet, while the other wore blue. She recognized the girls from church and around town. "Don't you live across the main road? Aren't you the doctor's children?"

"Yep, that's us." The first girl offered a beaming, dimpled smile. "I'm Penelope and that's Prudence. We're real glad you found Sukie."

"We wouldn't want a cougar to get her."

"Or a bear."

"Or a wolf."

What adorable children. Molly knew she was staring, she couldn't help it. She drank in details—the faint scattering of freckles across their sun-kissed noses, the glint of trouble in their beautiful eyes, the animated dearness as the twins looked at one another, as if in complete understanding. The place in her soul, the one thirsty for a child of her own, ached painfully. She felt hollow and empty, as if her body would always remember carrying the baby she had lost. For one moment it was as if the sun blinked out, as if the wind died and the earth vanished.

"Hey, what is she eating?" One of the girls—Prudence?—tumbled forward. "It smells like a cookie. You are a bad girl, Sukie."

"Did she walk into your house and eat off the counter?" Penelope wanted to know.

The past slipped back into place, the sun scorched her face and the grass crinkled beneath her feet as the cow tugged her toward the girls. "No, she went through the window."

Penelope went up on tiptoe. "I see them. The cookies. They look real good."

"Yes, real good. The best I've ever seen." Prudence took hold of the cow.

Molly was captivated by the girls and their identically pleading expression, so sweet and innocent. She wasn't fooled. Then again, she was a soft touch. "You two keep a good hold on Sukie, and I'll see what I can do about getting you some cookies."

The girls exchanged happy looks, apparently pleased their plan had worked out so well.

Yep, she was much too soft of a touch. She headed back inside, keeping an eye on them as she went. "Do you girls need help getting the cow home?"

"No. She's real tame. We raised her from a bottle."

Penelope and the cow trailed after her, hesitating outside the door. "She loves us. We can lead her anywhere."

"Yeah, she only runs off when she's looking for us."

The girls laughed, the merry sound rising like music on the wind and warming the shadows within her. She tried not to count the years, but she knew. She would always know. Four long years had crept by one day at a time, when she had no longer heard that music of her baby daughter's laughter. Her life had become nothing but silence.

"Thank you so much, Mrs.—" Penelope took the napkin wrapped around the stack of cookies. She tilted her head to one side, puzzled. "We don't know your name."

"This is the McKaslin ranch," Prudence said thoughtfully, enduring affectionate licks from Sukie. "But I know you're not Mrs. McKaslin."

"I'm the cousin. I moved here last winter. You can call me Molly."

"So…" Penelope gave her twin a cookie. Beneath the brim of her sunbonnet, her face crinkled with serious thought. "You don't know our pa?"

"You haven't been sick yet?" Prudence asked as she fed her cookie to the cow.

"No, I only know Dr. Frost by reputation. I hear he's a fine doctor." That was all she knew. Of course she had seen his fancy black buggy with the top up speeding down the country roads at all hours. Other times she had witnessed that same buggy going through town at a more leisurely pace. Sometimes she caught a brief sight of the man driving as the vehicle passed—an impression of a black Stetson, a strong granite profile and impressively wide shoulders.

Although she was on her own and free to marry, she paid little heed to eligible men. All she knew of Doctor Samuel Frost was that he was a widower and a father and a faithful man, for he often appeared very somber and serious in church. She reached through the open door to where her coats hung on wall pegs and worked the sash off her winter woolen.

"Oh, he's a real good doc," Penelope went on, looking entirely innocent as she nibbled on the edge of her cookie, as if debating something.

Likewise, Prudence nibbled, too. "Our pa's nice, and you make good cookies."

"*And* you're awful pretty." Penelope was so excited she didn't notice Sukie stealing her cookie. "Maybe you could like Pa."

"I don't know the man, so I can't like him. I suppose I can't dislike him either." The sash came free and she bent to secure it around Sukie's halter. "Do you want some water before we go?"

"You ought to come home with us." Penelope grinned, happy to take hold of the end of the sash. She no longer looked quite so innocent. No, she looked like nothing but trouble. "Then you can meet our pa."

"Well, I don't know. It's Sunday. A family day." Goodness, why would the twins ask such a thing? "Come on, girls, let's get you home."

"Do you want to get married?" Penelope's feet were planted.

So were Prudence's. "Yes! You could marry Pa. Do you want to?"

"M-marry your pa?" Shock splashed over her like icy water. Had she heard them right?

"Sure. You could be our ma."

"And then Pa wouldn't be cross anymore."

"Or lonely. So, do you want to?"

Molly blinked. The words were starting to sink in. The twins wished so much for a mother that they would take any stranger who was kind to them. The poor things. She froze in place with the tops of the grasses brushing her skirt hem, her eyes blinking from the harsh sun. The girls were adorable. Any woman would be lucky to have the identical set of them to love.

She pushed aside that old longing she felt, one that could never be satisfied. There would be no children for her. As for stepchildren—well, that was another matter too painful to consider. "No, I certainly cannot marry a perfect stranger, thank you for asking. But I would take you two in a heartbeat."

"You would?" Penelope looked surprised. "Really?"

Prudence lost her last cookie to the cow. "We're an awful lot of trouble. Our housekeeper said that three times this morning, and that was *before* she left for church."

"We would make Pa get you a nice ring. Would that matter?"

"No, sweetie." How did a child understand that marriage was more than a ring and a simple "I do"? Commitment was a lifelong vow, and love was fragile and endlessly complicated. It could not survive without deep devotion and deeper emotional ties. "Does your pa know you propose on his behalf?"

"Now he does." A deep baritone answered. Heavy footsteps crunched in the grass near the house. Dr. Frost marched into sight, rounding the corner of the shanty. His hat brim shaded his face, casting shadows across his chiseled features, giving him an even more imposing appearance. "Girls! Home! Not another word."

"But we had to save Sukie."

"She could have been eaten by a wolf."

Molly watched the good doctor's mouth twitch, as if he were doing his best to keep his foreboding appearance. He spotted her and she couldn't be sure because his eyes were shadowed, but a flash of humor could have twinkled in their depths.

"You must be the cousin." He swept off his hat and sunshine worshipped his features. The twinkle faded from his eyes and the hint of a grin from his lips. It was clear that while his daughters amused him, she did not. He stiffened, and his deep tone sounded formal. "I had no idea you would be so young."

"And pretty," Penelope, obviously the troublemaker, added mischievously.

Molly's face heated. The poor girl must need glasses. Although she was still young, time and sadness had made its mark on her. She didn't know what to say to that. The imposing man had turned into granite as he faced her. Of course he had overheard his daughters' proposal, so that might explain it. Perhaps he was afraid she would change her mind and accept!

The poor man. She smiled—she hoped not too

much—and took a step away from him. "Dr. Frost, I'm glad you found your daughters. I was about ready to bring them back to you."

"I shall save you the trouble." He didn't look happy. "Girls, take that cow home. Get moving while I apologize to Miss McKaslin."

She was a "Mrs." But she didn't correct him. She had put away her black dresses and her grief. Her marriage had mostly been a long string of broken dreams. She did better when she didn't remember. She breathed in the sweet spring sunshine and held its warmth deep inside. "Please don't be too hard on the girls on my behalf. Sukie's arrival livened up my day."

"At least there was no harm done." She winced and he scowled. "There *was* harm? What happened?"

"I didn't say a word."

"No, but I could see it on your face."

Had he been watching her so closely? Or had she been so unguarded? She blushed, fearing he could see the secrets within her, hiding like shadows. Perhaps it was his nearness. She could see the bronze flecks in his golden eyes and smell the scents of soap and spring clinging to his shirt. A spark of awareness snapped within her like a candle newly lit. "It was a vase. Sukie knocked it off my windowsill when she tried to eat the flowers."

"Was that before the cookies?" His eyes crinkled pleasantly.

"Yes, but it was an accident."

"The girls should take better care of their pet." He drew his broad shoulders into an unyielding line. He turned to check on the twins, who were progressing down the road, passing the bridled horse who stood patiently grazing in the grass between the wagon tracks.

The wind ruffled his dark hair. He seemed distant. Lost. "How much was the vase worth?"

Without price, but how did she tell him? Perhaps it would be best not to open that door to her heart. "It was simply a vase."

"No, it was more." He stared at his hat clutched in both hands. "Was it a gift?"

"No, it was my mother's."

"And is she gone?"

"Yes."

"Then I cannot pay you its true value. I'm sorry." His gaze met hers with startling intimacy. Perhaps a door was open to his heart as well because sadness tilted his eyes and seemed to cover him like a coat. He looked like a man with many regrets.

She knew well the weight of that burden. "Please, don't worry about it."

"The girls will replace it." His tone brooked no argument, but it wasn't harsh. "About what my daughters said to you."

"Do you mean their proposal? Don't worry. It's plain to see they are simply children longing for a mother's love."

"Thank you for understanding. Not many folks do."

"Maybe it's because I know something about longing." It was a living thing within her always yearning, if she would let it, wishing for dreams that could not come true. "Life never turns out the way you plan it."

"No. Life can hand you more sorrow than you can carry." Although he did not move a muscle, he appeared changed. Stronger, somehow. Greater. "I'm sorry the girls troubled you, Miss McKaslin."

Mrs., but again she didn't correct him. It was the sorrow she carried that stopped her from it. She preferred to stand in the present with sunlight on her face. "It was a pleasure, Dr. Frost. What blessings you have in those girls."

"That I know." He tipped his hat to her, perhaps a nod of respect, and left her alone with the restless wind and the place still open in her heart.

Chapter Two

The hot walk on the dusty road beneath the blazing afternoon sun had not put Samuel in a better mood. With every step he took, his emotions strengthened. Even when Miss McKaslin was well out of sight, he could feel the tug of her sadness. One very much like his own.

His feet felt heavy. He had to stop thinking about the woman. She was far too pretty and young for the likes of him. He checked for any signs of traffic on the main road—there were none—and led the horse, his children and their cow across. Dust swirled lazily with the breeze and puffed up in chalky clouds as they went.

"So, Pa." Penelope sidled up to him, as sweet as sunshine and suspiciously innocent. "Wasn't Miss Molly pretty? She's real nice, too. When Sukie almost ran her into bits, she didn't even yell."

Before he could even respond, Prudence chimed in. "She makes good cookies, Pa. That's real important."

He knew about the list the girls had been making,

cataloguing desirable traits for a future mother and praying over them every night. It tore him apart. Life was about disappointment and loss, and learning how to face both with acceptance and trust in God. He thought of Miss McKaslin and her sad, soul-filled blue eyes and the tendrils of her golden hair framing her delicate face. No wonder the twins had proposed to her.

He hated to do it, but he had to be practical. He had to teach the girls how to face life. These childish daydreams and wishes were going to break their hearts and their spirits if they didn't stop. He had to do his best to protect them. To teach them how to live. He cleared his throat, to rid his voice of his own turmoil. "What were you girls thinking?"

"Nothing. Not really." Penny, always the leader, was the first to speak. With the scrunch of her face in adorable lines, she was thinking hard on how to explain her actions. "We didn't plan it. Honestly. It was Sukie! She's why we were there. It's *her* fault we met Miss Molly."

"That's true, Pa," Prudy chimed in. "She's not in trouble? You won't punish Sukie, will you?"

"I hardly think sending Sukie to her stall to think about what she's done will help matters." Honestly, those girls. They were too tender-hearted. "But you two are the reason she got out of her pen in the first place."

"She missed us."

"She loves us. That's why she got out."

He bit his lip. Frustration became a burning pressure behind his ribcage. The girls didn't understand. He didn't know if they ever would. His head began to pound, making it harder to figure out what more to say to them.

"It won't happen again, Pa."

"Yep, we'll make sure Sukie doesn't get out again. We promise."

The cow was hardly the issue. Sam thought of all the hard words he could say about life and hardship, but he didn't. The house came into sight along the rutted road. He would have to finish this discussion later. He had re-sponsibilities waiting. "You shut Sukie into her stall this time so she'll be safe. Since Mrs. Finley is at church this afternoon, you girls will have to come with me. I have a house call to make."

"No, Pa. We don't want to go, do we, Prudy?"

"No, Pa." Prudence joined her sister and their iden-tical voices blended in a chorus of dissent. They could stay here. They could take care of themselves. They would stay up high in the tree until he came back.

None of that was going to work. "You girls need to learn to be sensible. You are too young to stay at home without Mrs. Finley. You take care of your pet and come straight to the buggy. I don't want any arguments. You hear?"

"Yes, Pa." The girls' heads bowed together as if to hide their disappointment.

He knew it couldn't be fun for them to sit in the buggy for often more than an hour at a time, but it couldn't be helped. "One more thing. There will be no more talk of Miss Molly. She's Miss McKaslin to you. That's the proper way to address her. I won't have you going across the road to her shanty again. Do you hear me?"

This time there was no answer. The girls merely blew out a quiet sigh. Two identical heads nodded, black braids bobbing up and down. Disappointment hurt, he knew, and he hated it. It was best never to dream. Eventually the girls would figure that out. It was his prayer for them.

He loved his daughters. He wanted what was best for them. And that was a good solid life right here, in this world, with their feet on the ground and their wishes made of practical things, things that had a chance of coming true.

"Don't be long." His warning carried after them on the restless wind as they broke off to lead Sukie to the barn.

"We won't." Penelope's promise sounded far too sad for an eight-year-old girl.

He hated that, too. He kept them in sight as he led Stanley to the buggy and backed him between the traces. The placid gelding stood patiently while he hitched him up. Sam worked fast, keeping both ears on the rustling sounds and lilting voices coming from deep inside the barn. Why he thought of Miss McKaslin and her gentle voice, he couldn't say. He was not a man prone to daydreams of any kind.

"Are you girls ready?" he called out, checking to make sure his medical bag was on the floorboards.

The stampede of their shoes as they came running was answer enough. The little girls, one dressed in green and the other in blue, tumbled into the yard and climbed up onto the bench buggy seat, scooting over to make room for him. He settled down, released the brake and snapped the reins, his mind firmly back where it belonged. On his girls, on his job and on the ill Mrs. Gornecke in need of his help.

Molly tucked the dustpan between her shoes and swept the last of the shards of china off her shanty floor. There. Her last home chore of the day was done. She knelt to retrieve the full pan, and her gaze wandered toward the window. The grass was still slightly trampled from her visitors.

You could marry Pa. Do you want to? The memory of the little girls' voices chased away the silence in her shanty. *You could be our ma.*

How could she feel both sad and sweet in the same breath? She remembered the girls' cute faces, shining with hope and possibility. They could not know how she had once been a mother, or how no other child could fill the emptiness. Still, they were precious, those twins. Remembering the alarm on the good doctor's face when he'd overheard their proposal, she laughed. The poor man! Oh, he'd been friendly enough, but he'd certainly walked away fast as he could. And without a single backward glance as he'd herded the children and the cow down the road.

"Molly! Was that you laughing?" Joanna, her cousin's new wife, padded into sight through the open doorway. She looked lovely as always with her honey-gold hair neatly coiled up and her sensible tan-colored calico. "Why, you are grinning ear to ear. I can't believe my eyes. What has you shining like the sun?"

"It's nothing, nothing at all." Now she was embarrassed. To be caught daydreaming! Good thing she'd only been thinking and not doing something more embarrassing like talking to herself! She set the dustpan on the table, intending to dispose of the broken china later, grabbed the package of wrapped cookies and her sewing basket. A glance at the little mantle clock told her it was later than she'd thought. How much time had she wasted thinking of the Frost twins and their father? "I'm sorry I've held you up. You had to come looking for me."

"It's not like you to be late. You had me worrying. I wanted to make sure you were all right."

"Oh, I'm as fine as can be." She shut the door and checked the lock. The grass rustled against her skirt ruffles as she led the way along the path. "I won't make you wait again, Joanna. I'm grateful for the work and the shanty. I don't want you to think I'm taking advantage."

"I told you, I've been without a home and a job before. I know how hard it is for a widow alone." Joanna's understanding had helped Molly more than she could measure. While Joanna had never buried an infant, she had sympathized gently and wholly. Her compassion had made the first difficult months here much easier to endure, when she had felt so lost. "Am I wrong, or did I see Dr. Frost and his twins at your doorstep?"

"Yes. There was an incident."

"Oh?" A world of hope knelled in that single word.

Molly's face seared once again. The blush had returned, and it had doubled in intensity. What if Joanna realized the reason for her good humor? "It's not what you think. The girls' pet cow found the shanty and the newly baked cookies."

"So, there's nothing sparking between you and Dr. Frost?"

"Goodness! What a thought." She pictured him hurrying down the road. "I doubt I will see him again. At least I hope not. I intend to stay in very good health."

Joanna didn't say a thing, but Molly feared more comments on the subject could be coming at a future time. Oh, joy. Troubling, yes, but she had more pressing concerns to manage. She worked Saturdays and several afternoons for her other cousin, Thad, and his wife. While she was grateful for the shanty on the family land, her job was at times not an easy one. Cousin Noelle, who was blind, needed help around the house and with their new baby. Taking care of little Graham was a joy, but his sweet weight in her arms could bring up a well of sorrow if she let it.

"If you married, you wouldn't have to work three jobs to make ends meet. Something to think about." Joanna was merely being kind, wanting the sort of future for her that Molly wanted for herself. But Joanna didn't understand—she couldn't understand—as they crested the final rise of the trail and the main farm house came into sight.

"Ma!" Sweet, platinum-haired Daisy hopped up from the porch steps and ran toward her mother, her baby doll tucked in the crook of her arm. "See? Lottie loves her new dress we made her."

"I see, precious."

Molly tucked away her own yearnings. It was enough to see that there was good in the world, that children were treasured, and love reigned. Sometimes the fairy tale came true. Storybook endings were possible in real life.

"You aren't feeling poorly, are you, Molly?" Cousin Aiden ambled into sight from the other side of the surrey. The hint of a grin on his granite face did nothing to lessen his intimidating presence. "I spotted Doc Frost and his girls on the road a bit earlier. Thought he might be calling on you."

"Calling on me? Hardly." Did everyone have marriage on their minds? First the twins, then Joanna and now Aiden. Perhaps it was the beautiful May Day. After a long cold winter, folks were naturally optimistic. She breathed in the sweet, warm spring air, determined to find the good in the day and in the blessings of her life. "I'm a very fussy widow. I'm afraid I won't settle for just any doctor who happens along on the road."

That had her cousins laughing as they boarded the stately surrey, and the horse drew them down the driveway, past her little shanty and toward the main road.

She caught herself glancing at the narrow driveway across the way, the one winding through tall new green grasses. She couldn't stop wondering about the handsome doctor with the shadows in his eyes. And his little girls hungering for a mother's love the same way she yearned for a daughter's.

Sometimes there were no ever afters. Sometimes life

fell far short of a storybook ending. She vowed to put the Frost twins and their family on her nightly prayer list. After all, they had a lot in common.

"How much longer, doc?" Mrs. Gornecke shifted against her pillows, asked a silent question, one she was probably too afraid to put into words. Hers had been a bad case.

Scarlet fever could be a dangerous illness, that was a sad fact. He'd seen the effects more times than he cared to remember. He snapped his medical bag closed. "I can't honestly say, Mrs. Gornecke. Your fever has been high and persistent. This is of great concern. I'm not unduly worried, but I mean it when I say you must follow my instructions precisely."

"I try to, as much as I can. But my little ones—" She fell silent, her gaze trailing toward the open window to where her small children often could be seen playing in the lawn of the backyard. Not today. A mother's love shone, transforming her. "Are you sure they are safe?"

"Not a single symptom. As long as they stay away at your parents' place."

"I can't help worrying."

"Of course. If anything changes, I will make sure you know." He left his shirt sleeves rolled up and snatched his jacket off the arm of the nearby chair. He respected Mrs. Gornecke. She was a devoted wife and mother, one who thought of others first, the kind of woman his wife had not been.

And if a quiet voice at the back of his mind wanted to remind him that there were plenty of women in the world with Mrs. Gornecke's integrity and sense of devotion, he refused to listen to that voice. Or the fact that Molly McKaslin came to mind.

"I'll check on you tomorrow, Mrs. Gornecke."

"Thank you kindly for coming on Sunday. We were supposed to be at church this afternoon, me and my little girls."

For the May Day Tea, the Ladies' Aid put on every year. Paula had been the president of the organization years ago. Samuel nodded, anxious to go before the old sorrow could catch up to him. He wanted to keep moving, for it was the best way to cope with long-standing loss and his personal shortcomings. So he grabbed his bag and gestured to the husband, huddling quietly in the corner. He waited until the door was closed and they were in the parlor of the small three-room house before he gave Mr. Gornecke more medicine and detailed instructions on his wife's care.

"I'll do all you say to do, doc." He held open the door. He looked haggard, torn between his work and the important care of his wife. "About the bill—"

"We'll discuss that when your wife is better. Right now, I want you to take care. Or you will likely be the next patient I visit."

Once outside, he rushed down the rickety front steps, hoping his daughters had followed orders and were right where they ought to be. They were in troubled water as it was.

"Pa!" Penelope's green sunbonnet poked out from between the brackets supporting the buggy top. "We're right here. Just like you told us."

Prudence's blue bonnet popped out next to the green. "We hardly moved a muscle. That's what you said to do, and we done it!"

His biggest shortcomings felt enormous when those two pairs of hazel eyes focused on him. He felt their need like the burn of sun on his back. He had failed on his promise to his wife. He could hear the desperate plea of Paula's voice in memory, the guilt increasing with every step he took toward those little girls. *Promise me you will marry again and soon. I know how you feel, but those girls need a mother, someone who is kind. They are so easy to love. Find a gentle lady who will love them as I do.*

Years had passed, and he had yet to keep that promise. He hadn't even tried to make good on it. He could blame it on his work. He'd been overrun with the demands of his job and of the little ones in his care. There hadn't been time for courting and marrying, not even for looking for a kindly woman. The truth was, he hadn't wanted to.

"I'm thrilled to see that you girls behaved for once." Stern, he set the bag on the floor before climbing up. "I almost thought I was dreaming. I thought those finely behaved young ladies couldn't possibly be my daughters."

"But we are, Pa. And we aren't young ladies. Mrs. Finley says we are wildcats." Penny sounded quite pleased as she bounced over on the seat to make room for him. "But I like wild cowboys better."

"Me, too." Prudy quickly agreed. "All we need is a pony. Can we have one, Pa?"

"You know the answer to that." He settled on the seat and reached for the reins, where they lay on the dash. With a snap, Stanley stopped drowsing and gave a mighty pull forward. All he needed was for his girls to be riding wild instead of simply running wild. Yes, that would surely make fathering them easier. "Proper young ladies do not ride horses."

"They do in the dime books."

Bless Mrs. Finley for reading her adventure novels aloud to the girls. "Books are make-believe, not real life. You two ought to know the difference. Now, no more talk about nonsense. When we get home, I want you both to go count up your pennies and figure out how many extra chores it will take to buy Miss McKaslin a new vase."

Penelope sighed. "I *knew* you were going to bring that up eventually."

"Yeah," Prudence agreed. Both girls were downcast again. "We don't gotta lotta pennies, Pa."

"Then I suppose you two have a lot of work ahead of you." He guided the horse around the bend in the town street, seeing not the road ahead but the image of a blond-haired woman, a vision in a pink calico work dress. For some reason, Molly McKaslin had opened up his emotions and somehow he had to put a stop to them.

"Look at all the pretty things!" The girls' voices rang out in unison, speaking the same thought and drawing his attention back to the road in front of him.

The church with its spire shone pure white in the sunshine, surrounded by lush trees and deep-emerald grass. Cloths in every color of the rainbow draped a dozen tables in the dappled shade. Women and their daughters of all ages relaxed in chairs around the tables, feasting on cake and tea, while others milled in groups on the lawn, deep in pleasant-looking conversation.

"I sure wish we had a ma." Prudy's whisper was little more than a sigh of longing.

A longing he had to ignore. He willed down his feelings, snapped the reins. Stanley obliged by picking up his pace and taking them swiftly away. The lilting rise and fall of women's voices and little girls' laughter carried after them on the wind.

Chapter Three

Three days had passed since the Frost incident, as Molly preferred to think of it. Remembering the little girls and their very naughty cow still warmed her with a chuckle or two. She thought of them this time every day as she guided her trusty mare onto the driveway home. She couldn't see the Frost house from her vantage on the cart seat, and that made her wonder. What sort of trouble were the twins getting into now? Was Sukie securely penned?

There was no sign of girls or heifer as she gave Ruth plenty of rein. The old mare was tender-mouthed and she knew her way home. There was no point in directing her any further. The horse's gait quickened, anticipating a nice restful evening in the shade of the orchard with cool, lush grass for her supper.

Molly didn't blame her one bit. The day's heat was unusual for May, and the hot puff of wind offered not a lick of relief. Wednesday was her toughest day of the week. She'd started at five in the morning at the bakery, helping Mrs. Klaus mix and knead bread dough for hours. A noon stop at the dress shop to work for a few hours and to drop off the piecework she did in the evenings for Cora, the owner. Then off to her cousin Noelle's house to help with the baby and the house chores.

Yes, she had been running for the good part of twelve hours. And it wasn't over yet. She glanced at the two baskets of sewing work she intended to tackle the rest of the week. It would help with the mortgage she had against her dear Ruth, the last of the debt accumulated from her marriage and illnesses. Needless to say, her late husband Fred had not been good with money.

The cart rattled down the lane, bringing her shanty into view. A blur of red and a streak of yellow in the lush green grasses caught her eye. Whatever could that be? She was too far away to see clearly, but it looked like the rounded top of a little girl's sunbonnet. It looked like—

The Frost twins. That could only mean one thing. Sukie was on the loose again.

"Miss Molly!" In tandem, the girls raced through the wild grasses. One in bright yellow calico, the other in bright red, they burst up the rise and through the wild-flowers, panting as if they had run a hundred miles. "You're not supposed to be here—"

"—cuz it's supposed to be a surprise—"

"—'cept we had to pick flowers—"

"—and it took longer than we thought."

Molly reined her mare to a stop and set the brake,

gazing down at the pair of them. How welcome to see their round button faces shining with goodness and life! Their sweetness refreshed her weary spirit, that was for certain. "I'm worrying about Sukie and you girls are picking wildflowers?"

"Oh, we're not here because of Sukie." One of the twins—Penelope?—swiped an ebony curl from her eyes. "She decided to stay at home."

"We're here because of the surprise." The other twin skipped in place, apparently too excited to stand still.

"Surprise?" Curious, Molly hopped down from the cart, landing with a swish of her skirts. "What on earth have you girls been up to?"

"All sorts of trouble," Penelope assured her as she took Molly's hand.

"Lots of trouble," Prudence concurred as she took Molly's other hand.

Was it her imagination that the sun shone more brightly? Or just her lonely mother's heart delighting in this connection with children—even though they were not hers? Molly felt her loss and loneliness like the shadows cast at her feet, but they were small compared to the great sunlit world around her, shimmering with color. The purple foxglove nodded in greeting along the path, the yellow faces of daisies waved and the buttercups smiled as they skipped by. With small hands tucked in her own, happiness seeped into the cracks of her soul.

"We hope you're not mad we came." Penelope smiled up at her, using both dimples.

How on earth could Dr. Frost deny these girls

anything? Molly melted at the sight. "Mad? No, but I am worried about your housekeeper. Does she know you girls are here?"

"She was busy peeling potatoes for supper," Prudence answered.

"Yeah, so we didn't want to bother her with asking."

Molly chuckled; she couldn't help it. "You two are definitely trouble. You aren't going to worry the poor lady, are you?"

"Nope." Penelope stopped skipping, bringing all three of them to a halt. "Mrs. Finley says we have to tell her where we are, and we did. She can't run after us."

"She's got tired bones," Prudence explained seriously. "But she reads to us and she's nice."

"She's almost like a grandma."

"We like her a lot."

"Since we don't have a ma."

"We sure would like a ma."

They walked the last few yards with the grass rustling their hems and crunching beneath their shoes. One question did happen to bother her. Now seemed like a good time to ask the girls. "Why hasn't your pa remarried?"

"He doesn't want to disappoint some nice lady." Penelope's hand gripped her more tightly.

"It's because of us," Prudence confessed. "Nobody wants so much trouble."

"No, that can't be. Where did you hear such a thing?" How could anyone say that to a precious child? Anger blurred her vision. Sympathy for the girls ached within her. She knelt, so she was level with the girls.

"We're a handful. Everybody says it." Penelope rubbed at her eyes and blew out a brave breath. No tears materialized, but her inner pain showed. "We're awful lucky Pa loves us."

"We're a handful for him, too." Prudence hiccupped. "We don't mean to be trouble, Miss Molly."

"That's why we brought you the surprise." Penelope pointed toward the shanty. "So you wouldn't be mad about the vase."

"An' so you wouldn't think we are a whole lotta trouble."

Both adorable faces gazed up at her, tremulous with hope amid their sorrows. The wind caressed the stray strands that had escaped their braids, giving them a windblown look, like unloved ragamuffins in need of a home.

Tears bunched in her throat, making her voice raw and thin. "I don't think you two are trouble, not in the slightest. What did you bring me?"

She must have said the right thing, because their smiles shone more brightly than their sadness. Dimples flashed, and she was tugged the rest of the way to the shanty.

"Come see," the girls called out in harmony.

There, perched on her top step, was a little vase with a bouquet of hand-picked wildflowers. Daisies bloomed, as if in celebration. What a surprise. "You girls brought me flowers."

"We thought—"

"—you would like 'em."

"I do. I love wildflowers." She willed away the

memory of a curly-haired baby sitting up, proud of her ability to do so, gurgling and grabbing at the bobbing daisies while Molly weeded their vegetable garden.

"Did you like the vase?" Penelope ran ahead through the prairie grasses.

Prudence followed, running equally as fast. "We got the one with the most colors."

"We thought you would like it best."

The girls skidded to a halt in front of the bottom step, sunshine kissing them. They vibrated with anticipation. What would it be like to have such energy? Molly felt wobbly as she joined them, hardly able to see for the burn in her eyes. She blinked hard, trying to bring the blur of colors on her step into focus.

"It's little. It won't hold lots of flowers," Penelope explained as she went up on tiptoe. "But it'll hold some."

"Just enough," Prudence nodded her head in agreement, going up on her toes, too. "Do you like it?"

"Do you?"

She could not believe the beauty of the simple glass vase, hand-painted with sprays of sunflowers, foxglove, daisies and roses. Very fine quality indeed. "I've never owned anything so nice."

The twins beamed, hands clasping, joy chasing away their worries.

Charmed, that's what she was, and utterly sweet on the girls. She blinked until her eyes stopped blurring and lifted the vase with both hands. The glass, warmed from the sun, felt delicate, as if it could be easily broken. She had better not put this on her windowsill, just in case

Sukie paid a return visit. "I love it. Thank you. It's mighty thoughtful of you girls to replace the one I lost."

"Pa said to tell you we're bein' responsible for Sukie—"

"—and we're real sorry because it was your ma's." Prudence traced a painted rose with the tip of her forefinger. "Our ma died, too. It hurts real bad, doesn't it?"

"Yes. Very much." All the protection in the world could not save her from the first knell of emotion. Grief for the twins missing their mother. Grief remembering her ma, who would be sad to think of the way Molly's life had turned out. "Come and help me find the right place to put this very special vase."

"It's special?" the girls asked, tromping behind her into the shanty.

"Sure it is, because you two gave it to me." Her shanty was hardly large enough for the three of them to stand side by side in a row. Sunlight streamed pleasantly in through both windows, giving the tidy practical home a golden look. "The table or the bookcase?"

"The table." The two of them trotted over to the small drop leaf table near one window. Two sets of hands reached out to touch the crocheted flowers standing in relief against the lacy runner. "Ooh. It's so pretty."

"Put it right here." Penelope patted the center.

"It's perfect." Prudence sighed in satisfaction after Molly had complied.

"We have a lace bureau cover our ma made." Penelope brushed the petals of the closest daisy. "But that's all."

"Our ma liked to sing songs." Prudence's lightness faded. "She would always be humming and singing."

"Hymns," Penelope clarified, her shoulders hunching with the weight of the memory. "Now all we got is quiet."

"I know just what you mean." Wasn't this the mix of life, the sad and the sweet? "The quiet hurts too, doesn't it?"

"Uh-huh." Both girls nodded gravely. Without their cheer and sparkle, it was easy to see the hardship they had been through.

It was a credit to their father that they still had so much sunlight to them. Thinking of Sam made her feelings sharpen, like a surge in her ability to feel. "It's getting late, girls. Surely you need to be home by supper time?"

"Mostly it's just Mr. and Mrs. Finley—"

"—and us." Prudence traced the edging stitches on one side of the runner.

"What about your father?"

"He comes home late always." Penelope stepped away from the table and out of the bright rays. "He makes sick people better."

Prudence took one last look at the crochet work. "Miss Molly? If you think you can like us now, do you want to think about being our ma again?"

"—now that we fixed things with the vase?"

Molly held out her hands to each girl. "I've never stopped liking you two. I like you both very much."

"We like you, too—"

"—lots and lots."

Small fingers clapped her own, and it was a cozy feeling, like a crackling fire on the coldest day. Like spring after the hardest winter. "You two know why I can't be your mother, right?"

"Cuz Pa hasn't given you a ring?"

"We could get you one."

She laughed, leading them outside. It was the sun tearing her eyes and not the mix of emotions, deeply colored and ranging from bright to dark. "I'm fussy about the man I marry. I want him to love me. That's the reason I want him to propose to me."

"Pa doesn't believe in love."

"He says it's not real, just like a story."

The children's confession troubled Molly all the way to the cart. She remembered the caring father, aware of his blessings in his daughters. Life was endlessly complicated, and she hoped her prayers for him and the girls would make a difference. She wanted God to especially watch over these broken hearts. Sam Frost might not believe in love's power, but she did.

"You mean they haven't come home from school *yet?*" Sam's head was going to explode. He could feel the pressure building in his cerebellum, sending shooting, red-hot pain into his cerebral cortex. Those girls were going to be the ruin of him. He paced the length of the kitchen, his boot heels striking out his anger on the polished wood planks. "It's after six o'clock. They should have been home hours ago."

"If you're going to get all het up, I'll send Abner out on horseback to look for 'em." Mrs. Finley patted a spray of silver hair from her eyes, reached for a hot pad and checked on the boiling potatoes. "I expect they've gone off to look at the Nevilles' pony for sale. They said they weren't going far. Whoa, there. I hear something outside. Probably those rascals now, bless them."

I sure wish we had a ma. Prudy's words had stuck with him for days, reminding him of all his personal failures. He had been a failure at marriage because he had based the foundation of that union on something as foolish and as impossible as romantic love.

He was going to make certain that his girls did not repeat his mistakes. He strode across the porch, straining to hear their high, merry voices and lilting laughter, but the only sound was the wind whispering through the lilac and rose bushes and the paper-like rustle of the corn stalks in the vegetable garden.

His girls. Other young ladies their ages were stitching samplers and learning to sew. When he'd been on his afternoon rounds, he'd seen several girls doing just that. Tidy and proper, sitting quietly in their parlors, happily practicing their needlework. Wasn't that what little girls were supposed to want to do?

Years went by in a blink. Before long, Penny and Prudy would be young ladies being escorted home by their beaus. One day, they would become wives and mothers. They would need to know how to run a proper household and sew for their families.

But how was he going to teach them? Kathleen suffered terribly from arthritis so she could not, and he had no wish to replace her with a younger housekeeper. He pushed open the gate.

You could marry again. He winced, wishing that thought had remained buried in the recesses of his mind.

The clink of shod horse hooves brought him to a dead halt. With the sun nearly blinding him and the rise of chalky dust from the driveway hazing the view, he couldn't see clearly. His first fear was that the girls had found a way to haggle with the Neville family for their ancient pony. But as he braced his feet on the dirt of the driveway, it was no child he saw but a woman. A beautiful woman dressed all in blue coming toward him, gliding on a yellow sunbeam. Molly McKaslin.

He blinked, hoping his vision would clear. But when he looked again, she smiled at him from beneath her dainty poke bonnet.

The rising clouds of dust and the slant of light gave the illusion. As her horse drew closer, it was plain to see she sat in an ordinary country cart, holding the leather reins in her slender hands. The sun remained behind her, cresting the slim cut of her shoulders and burnishing her golden hair like copper. Making her even more beautiful. Even more poignant.

It had been a long, hard day. He was turning fanciful in his exhaustion. Heaven help him.

"Hi, Pa!" To his surprise, Penelope popped into view from the cart floor behind Molly. An identical sun-bonneted head popped up, too. Prudence. "Hi, Pa!"

Unbelievable. Seeing them safe and sound—not that there was much danger in this peaceful countryside— left him relieved. But seeing them in Molly's cart, that was something else entirely. "You two have clearly been bothering Miss McKaslin, against my express orders."

"No, Pa." In unison, the girls hopped out of the cart

the moment it stopped. They spoke, interrupting one another. "We were going to stay out of her way—"

"—but then we remembered what you said about being susponsible—"

"—responsible—"

"—and so we went to the glass shop—"

"—and got a vase for Miss Molly."

"So you would be proud of us."

He drew up, still as steel, so no one could guess at the emotion hitting him. They had *tried* to do the right thing. But in acting on their own, they had made the situation worse. This wasn't only about replacing a broken vase.

It was about the woman beginning to climb down from that cart. The woman who took his offered hand with a subtle smile. The woman whose touch came as softly as spring raindrops against his palm. When her shoes landed on the ground and she moved away, the center of his palm tingled sweetly, as if it would never forget her.

"I brought your wayward girls home." She somehow looked like a story heroine, even with the barn in the background and the old bay mare nibbling at her hat brim. "Thank you for replacing the vase. I know it was costly."

Costly? Normally that would alarm him, but now something like a large bill from the finest shop in town seemed like nothing. Not when compared to how Penny gazed up at Molly as if she'd hung the moon. Prudy, when she sidled next to the woman, did so with clear adoration.

What had come over the two of them? They had never been taken with a lady like this before. It was time to rein in their unruly ways. If he wasn't careful they would have him married by the July Fourth family picnic.

"We owed you a vase, and now our debt is paid." He did his best not to notice the feminine way she pushed a stray curl into place beneath her fashionable bonnet. No, it was best to direct his eyesight to the children ignoring him to cling to her. "The girls will make sure Sukie doesn't bother you again."

"Speaking of which—" She gestured toward the barn, amused. "Unless I'm mistaken, Sukie has gotten loose."

"Sukie!" Penelope held up both hands. "No! Go back to your pen!"

"Bad Sukie!" Prudence scolded, shaking one finger at the cheerful bovine racing across the yard in an ungainly gallop. Her happy moo echoed across the hillside. "She's a runaway stampede!"

"You girls have been influenced by too many novels." That was it. It was decided. These notions of fairy tales, cowgirls and romance had to end. "Put the cow back in her pen—"

The girls were already racing off to intercept their pet, but the heifer turned and led the chase, as if in a merry game. The girls' delighted squeals rose joyfully on the wind.

"You were saying about Sukie?" Molly asked him with a wry tilt to her rosebud mouth.

"I don't know why I try. I'm outnumbered. It's a lost cause."

"Not entirely lost." She laughed, a musical trill that made him think of clear mountain brooks and spring raindrops. "Your girls are delightful. They had me in stitches the entire ride home. I know I've told you before, but they are double blessings. It's a marvel you can keep a straight face."

"It's what I wonder every day." Gazing upon her filled him with questions. Where had she moved from? How old was she? What was she looking for in life? Her fondness for his daughters was unmistakable. Why hadn't she married?

Not that it was any of his business. It was merely curiosity, that was all. As a physician, he knew nearly everyone in Angel County, but he did not know her. This sensible, hardworking lady who watched his daughters race around the field trying to herd their pet cow, who did not cooperate.

"It's an impossible situation. Look at them!" Embraced as she was by the sun, it was hard not to notice her radiant beauty.

A faint, sharp pain arrowed through his chest suspiciously close to his heart. But it couldn't be that organ, since he was not a deep-feeling man. Perhaps his stomach was agitated—he'd been too busy tending a patient to have taken lunch. Surely that was the explanation.

"The more they run, the more Sukie chases them." She laughed, a sound gentler than any hymn. "Now the cow is herding the two of them! What a delightful life you have."

"Yes, delightful." Dryly, the words came off his

tongue, but they felt disconnected from his thoughts and his emotions, which for some unexplainable reason centered on her.

She seemed like a responsible, proper lady. He had noticed her before on his rides through town, working in the bakery in the mornings and Sims's dress shop in the afternoons. Hard not to notice her. As lovely as she was, she wasn't terribly young. He would place her somewhere in her twenties and solidly working on becoming a spinster, he reckoned.

Her words came back to him from the first day they met. *Maybe it's because I know something about longing. Life never turns out the way you plan it.* What did she long for? Why hadn't her life turned out according to her plan? As she watched his twins, that same lonely look returned to her face.

Hard not to understand that. Was she as lonesome as he was? Did she have broken dreams too, ones that could never be made whole or found again?

Perhaps it was the doctor in him, always wanting to fix things. Maybe it was something deeper he did not want to understand. The words came off his tongue before he could snatch them back. "What are you doing for supper, Miss McKaslin? Would you consider joining us?"

Chapter Four

Nothing Sam Frost said could have astonished her more. For one second her pulse lurched in her veins as if the earth had vanished from beneath her shoes.

"I have work to do this evening. I—" The words did not come. She wanted to say she had no time for social engagements, but the look of quiet dignity on his granite face stopped her.

This man could open her up like a door into a room. Standing with him on the verdant lawn, listening to the rush of the wind through the field grasses and the squealing joy of the girls, she felt as if the daylight had never been this vibrant or the air so sweet. Awareness of the man glanced through her like dappled sunshine, awareness that was keenly emotional. Lonesomeness, weariness, regret; feelings much like her own.

"A neighborly invitation," he assured her. "Kathleen is probably done boiling the potatoes about now. You may as well stay. There's always plenty."

"I would be imposing." And looking at what she did not have—and probably never would. Men were not tripping over one another to come courting, that was for sure. Sam did not know what he was asking of her.

"It would be doing me a favor." Humor dimpled the corners of his mouth as they slid upward into a spare grin. "Look at the two of them, running wild. It would do them good to see how a real lady behaves. They look up to you."

"Is there a hidden motive in this invitation?"

"No. If they still run wild when the meal is done, you can stay for dessert."

Why was she laughing? She was not about to be charmed by him. This was not love at first sight. Her world hadn't changed when she'd taken his hand to help her from the cart. Love hadn't sparked like a symphony in full crescendo. He was not her Mr. Darcy. That didn't mean she couldn't be neighborly. She drew in a breath of lilac-scented air. "Then I guess it depends on what is being served for dessert."

"I have no idea."

"You make me an offer without knowing all of the facts? I'm shocked at you, Dr. Frost."

"Sam. Please." He raked his fingers through his thick dark hair, laughing a little, too. His reserved nature fled, and this jovial side of him made her see the man he must have been before sadness changed him.

She knew exactly how that was. "Then you must call me Molly. I'm afraid I have a confession to make. I'm a widow. I should have corrected you when we first met, but—"

"—it was too painful," he finished, the humor fading

from his face, but he did not close up. He remained as if open to her, a stunning, feeling man of great depth.

At least, that was her impression of him. That was what she felt in the silence as it stretched between them.

"Very." She battled to keep the past where it belonged. "I hope you can forgive me."

"There is nothing to forgive. It was my mistake. I assumed."

"It wouldn't be the first time. I've turned down a few courting men who have done the same."

"So, turning down proposals is a habit for you."

"Yes. Is that relief I hear in your voice?" She liked his chuckle, a low pleasant rumbling, a friendly sound she wanted to hear again. How strange. She sidestepped so a tiny butterfly wouldn't get grounded by her skirts, bringing the children into her line of sight. The girls had caught Sukie and were hanging on her, rubbing her neck and face and giggling when the heifer tried to give them swipes with her tongue. "My marriage was not like a fairy tale."

"Neither was mine." His confession resonated with remorse. She did not need to ask if he had done all he could to make his marriage right. She knew because the cost of it was on his face and a weight, like her own, she could feel.

A bell clanged from somewhere behind her. She whirled around to see a plump elderly lady limping away from the dinner bell. Must be the housekeeper.

"We're having apple crisp for dessert," the woman said matter-of-factly, as if she had overheard every word of their conversation and wasn't ashamed for them to know.

"It's the kitchen window." Sam leaned close, his

voice lowered, meant only for her. "Kathleen likes fresh air and to let in the scent of the lilac blooms, but I think she's nosy."

"Good thing for you. If she wasn't, I would be on my way home. Apple crisp is my favorite."

No wonder. Sam tethered the ancient mare in the shade of the barn. A widow. He should have known. She carried a maturity of manner and emotion. She simply appeared so young. Fresh-faced and golden, her features like porcelain. Not that he was noticing.

No, what he noticed was the way she shut the garden gate behind her and disappeared behind purple cones of blossoms, heading to the kitchen to help Kathleen put the meal on the table. He noticed her mare was gentle and white around the muzzle, well groomed and used to kindly care. He noticed the state of the cart—in good repair but not exactly a shining buggy, and the baskets on the floorboards which held pinned up ladies' dresses and petticoats. She must also do piece work in the evenings. A widow's lot could be difficult in these uncertain economic times. Hard not to respect the woman. Hard not to like the first woman in years who had been able to make him laugh.

"Pa?" Penelope skipped into view, a burst of yellow calico in the shady grass. "Where's Miss Molly?"

"I suspect putting the biscuits on the table about now." He gave the mare a pat on the neck and strolled over to the trough pump.

A second calico-wearing girl tumbled into sight. "Is she truly staying to supper?"

"You girls would do well to be more like Molly." He gave the handle a few good pumps. "Do you see her tearing through the pasture like a rampaging cow? No. She's well pressed and every hair is neatly in place. She's helping Mrs. Finley in the kitchen. You might take a page from her book."

Water splashed into the trough and the mare ambled closer for a sip. She would be cool and comfortable here. He left her, aware of two sets of footsteps tripping after him.

"Do you like her, Pa?"

"Do you like her a lot?"

He caught sight of her through the large kitchen window, where she stood beside the table, pouring milk into glasses. She sure could take a man's breath away. Good thing he wasn't looking for the complications of marriage. Because if anyone could interest him, it would be Molly McKaslin.

Here's where things got tricky. He considered his answer as he led the way across the rutted road and into the grassy side yard. "No, girls, I'm afraid I don't like Miss Molly at all."

"Not the teeniest bit?"

"Not even an eensy bit?"

"Nope. Because you two already have all of my heart. There's no room for anyone else." He endured the twins' groan and moans of disappointment as he swung open the garden gate, stunned by Molly staring at him through the window.

The mysterious smile teasing the rosebud softness of her lips and trouble twinkling like stardust in her dream-blue eyes left no doubt. She had heard him quite clearly. Some females he could think of might be unhappy to hear a marriageable doctor did not like them, but she was obviously no average female.

He opened the back door and let his daughters topple in ahead of him. They ran, shoes beating the floor, grass-stained skirts swishing, flyaway hair trailing out behind them. A striking contrast to the proper, tidy, genteel woman turning from the table with the pitcher in hand to offer them a smile of welcome. "I hope you two were able to get Sukie penned and safe."

"Sort of."

"Mostly."

Sam didn't think anyone noticed as he shut the door behind him. The rise and fall of female conversation may as well have been a different language. He leaned against the wall, folding his arms across his chest, simply watching the twins chatter away without giving Molly a word in edgewise. Funny to watch the girls be so polite. They pulled out Molly's chair. They looked like actual proper girls, standing still without fidgeting, listening intently as Molly spoke to them. Each settled into a chair as close to the woman as they could, mimicking her straight posture and ladylike drape of the napkin across her lap.

"I like her." Kathleen swung close on her way by, with a covered tray to take to their quarters upstairs. She threw over her shoulder, "I'll leave you to your courting. Don't scare her away with that cold manner of yours."

"I don't know what you are talking about." He wasn't a cold man and he wasn't a courting one. He didn't have to worry about scaring Molly away. What he did have to worry about was liking the woman too much. That, he feared, was a very real problem.

"Pa!"

He shook his head, realizing there were three females staring at him. He left his thoughts for another time, crossed the room and took his chair. The kitchen was fragrant with the warm smell of roasted chicken, the rich doughy goodness of buttermilk biscuits, steaming potatoes and buttery green beans. But as hungry as he was, every bit of him from the inside out was aware that this was no ordinary supper.

Across the table, Molly took the girls' hands and bowed her head, awaiting grace. Something incomprehensible and powerful flickered to life within him as he felt the impact of her gaze. He did not know what it was. Shaken, he bowed his head, took each of the girls' hands and began to pray.

"Show me Thy ways, O Lord; teach me Thy paths. Lead me in Thy truth and teach me: for Thou art the God of my salvation; on Thee do I wait all day. Father, thank You for Your bounty. Please bless this food on our table, and strengthen and purify our hearts. If it's not too much trouble, please help guide Penny and Prudy toward more ladylike pursuits. Amen."

"Amen." The girls were shaking their heads, apparently not at all surprised by the blessing.

"Amen." Molly released the girls' hands and opened her eyes.

Sam had never seen a more perfect blue. While he had been praying, he should have asked God for help.

Molly had an odd effect on him. He had never been fanciful in the company of a woman before. He grabbed the platter of sliced chicken and forked a few slices onto his plate before handing it to Penelope.

"Miss Molly? Do you like tree forts?" Penelope asked.

"It's really a stump," Prudence clarified, "but we pretend it's a tree fort."

"Yes, my little brother and I had our own tree fort in a cottonwood grove in the Big Bear Mountains." It was as if she were discussing something completely ordinary like the weather, instead of make-believe dwellings. Molly took the platter Penelope offered her and added a thick slice of chicken to her plate. "We fended off attacks from renegade bands and many very bad outlaws."

"We defeated the entire cavalry last week—"

"—and now we are in the middle of a siege."

Clearly, this could not be judicious, endorsing silly stories, but Sam could not look away from Molly as she held the platter for Prudence.

"A siege. How exciting." When Prudence was through dishing up chicken, Molly set the platter in the center of the table. Amusement played across her lovely face as she caught him looking at her. "Sam, I hope you think defending a fort from lawless bandits is a proper way to spend time."

"If you are a soldier or a sheriff."

"Apparently we have differing opinions. It's my mother's fault. She indulged my love of stories at an early age. That's helped with my tendency toward imagination, I'm afraid." She added a biscuit to her plate, again holding the bowl for Prudence. "My earliest memories are of sitting wrapped up in a quilt on my ma's lap. The potbelly stove was roaring, snow was tumbling like a white waterfall on the other side of the windows while Ma read from one of her novels."

"My pa would read Shakespeare." His voice deepened, the tone vibrant with emotion too layered to label. "Every winter evening after supper when the last of the work was done, he would draw his chair up to the stove, light a lamp and open his volume of plays. My sister and I would listen, captivated by the powerful words. We were too young at first to understand, but we would listen. As the years passed, we came to love the plays and, later, read the different parts with Pa."

"It sounds like a wonderful way to grow up." She broke her biscuit in two and buttered it, but her attention remained on the man seated across from her. A man she could see embodying the young Prince Hal, the beleaguered Julius Caesar or the heartbroken King Lear.

She did not tell him that she had read those plays, too. Alone, and only to herself. She did not wish to deepen the tie she felt to him, an emotional link that drew her closer when she should be moving away.

Molly set the last pile of plates on the counter. "Did you know that Sukie is at the window?"

"Okay, troublemakers." Sam set a collection of glassware and steelware next to the pile of plates. "Outside right now and get Sukie into her stall."

"She's out again?" Penelope swiped at her forehead, in exaggerated shock.

"She wants dessert, too." Prudence cut a piece of apple crisp from the baking plate. "Maybe then she'll stop chewing through her rope."

The pair loped out the back door, while the heifer craned her neck farther into the room to keep better sight of them. Her protesting moo expressed her opinion when they—and the apple crisp—disappeared from her sight.

"You really want those two to change?" Molly leaned against the counter.

"Life is hard. I want to prepare them for it." The reserve was back, now that they were alone.

"What was it you thought I could do for them?"

He glanced around, scanning the cleared table and the dirty dishes, which would be left for Mrs. Finley in the morning. "Interest them in needlework. I didn't know you had a disreputable past as a make-believe fort dweller, too."

"The things you don't know about me, Dr. Frost."

"I'm afraid to know more. You looked mild-mannered when we first met."

She couldn't tell if he was jesting or serious. She only knew that the kitchen appeared to shrink as he took one single step closer. He filled her view, making it impossible to ignore his dark, dashing handsomeness, the dependable set of his wide shoulders and his muscled arms that looked strong enough to soothe any pain, if only they would enfold her.

What thinking! She blushed, heat racing to her

cheeks and making her nose strawberry red. Afraid he would notice, she spun away to retrieve her sunbonnet from the peg by the door. Her heels rang loudly, punctuating the silence between them.

"I've offended you?" His question came low and flat, as if without emotion.

But she could see some of the layers of this man, the granite outside, the tender father inside. The scholar, the physician, the widower, the brokenhearted man. Layers that lured her feelings like the moon on the tides, pulling at waves within her, layers of herself she tried to hide.

"No." She shook out the bonnet's ties. "Your daughters are wonderful. If I were you, I would love them as they are. They will grow into more ladylike interests when God wishes them to. Trust me."

"I wish I could."

"You are not a trusting man, are you?" She watched his reserve deepen, taking over. The faint ring of joyful laughter drifted in through the window. "Trust me anyway. I was not so different. I loved climbing trees and riding my pony bareback and helping my pa with the livestock. I managed to learn needlework and become fairly ladylike. They will, too."

"I'm not reassured." He jammed his fists into his pockets, hesitating as if caught between coming closer and staying away. "You are almost as bad as they are."

"I'll take that as a compliment."

"You do have a calming effect on them." He strolled her way. "If they happen into your yard again, would it be too much to show them a stitch or two? Let them see what you are sewing?"

"I would be happy to. Even if Sukie makes another appearance."

"Let's pray she doesn't break anything else." He opened the door to the pleasant breezes. The low slanting sunlight felt welcoming, and the dancing leaves and busy birds almost reminded him there was more to life than work and responsibility. More to living than clinging to the plan and patterns that had gotten him through his grief and raising two small children alone.

"The new vase is safely out of the window's reach," she reassured him.

"Unless Sukie comes in the door."

"Goodness!" She sidled through the threshold, taking care to leave plenty of space between them. As if she didn't want to risk coming too close to him, to the curmudgeon unwilling to trust any female too much. To the man captivated by her wholesome charm and whimsical sweetness completely against his will and better sense.

She passed ahead of him on the brick pathway, her skirts swishing against the overgrown flowers and shrubs. It seemed to him as if the dappled sunlight followed her, and the lark song grew more cheerful as she passed by the apple tree. Lilacs rustled, casting out a handful of tiny purple petals to float behind her on the wind.

You're seeing her with your heart, man. He tried to stop it, to force his mind to see the world as it really was—she, as she really was. Impossible. The squeak of the garden gate did not bring him back to reality. The crunch of his shoe in the grass, the whisper of the breeze against his face or his iron-strong will. Nothing could change the beautiful way he saw her, like first light come to a new world, as she glided through the long pearled rays of the sinking sun, laughing at something he could not see.

"What are you two doing? You are going to spoil my mare even more than she already is." Molly swirled to face him, her movements a graceful waltz. "Ruth loves apple crisp."

Surely he hadn't heard right. "Apple crisp can't be good for her digestion."

"She's used to sweets. I feed them to her all the time."

Why wasn't he surprised? The evening felt surreal as she danced away from him, the music of her alto joining the high sugary notes of his daughter's voices. Dimly he saw the girls and Sukie at the trough, one twin feeding the mare, the other the cow.

"I'm gonna tell Mrs. Finley to make lots more." Finished, Penny washed the stickiness from her hands in the cool trough.

"That way we can come visit Ruth." Prudy stroked Ruth's brown nose with adoration. "She's awful nice."

"Real nice." Penny wiped her hands on her skirt. "It must be *real* fun to have your own horse."

"*Awful* fun."

There was no mistaking the poignant longing in the girls' tones. He wisely chose to remain silent. Not that he could trust his voice with Molly so close. He held out his hand to help her up into the cart. When her long, slender fingers wrapped around his, tenderness flared through him like a comet in the night sky. She may as well have taken hold of his heart.

"Thank you for supper, Sam." Her voice was the loveliest melody he'd ever heard. She settled on the board seat and brushed her skirts into place with no less grace than a goodly princess taking her throne. "I had the most unusual time. I'm sorry to say I had no positive effect on your daughters."

"I'm not even going to ask you to mention the sewing baskets." She had enthralled his daughters and enraptured him. Hardly the steadying, sensible influence he had hoped for. Undeniable proof she wasn't the right woman for him. He released the knot in the rope tethering the old mare. The horse primly nodded as if in ladylike thanks before she stepped forward, drawing the cart with Molly in it.

"Goodbye, girls. Thank you for the vase," she called as she rolled past.

"Goodbye!" The twins sidled up to him, each taking one of his hands. They were so small, frail, clinging to him with unmistakable need.

"I sure like her." Penelope sighed, as if making a wish on the first twilight star.

"I like her, too." Prudence leaned against him, a dear weight at his side.

Together they watched Molly drive down the road, growing farther and farther away from them, taking with her the beauty and the light.

Chapter Five

Spring thunder boomed high above town like cannon fire, startling the horses tethered at the hitching post in front of the dress shop. Molly held tight to her poke bonnet as a gust of wind twisted her skirts and puffed her back a few steps. Enormous raindrops pelted her like buckshot.

What weather! When she had started off to the bakery at fifteen minutes before five this morning, the day had been serene, the wind calm with not a cloud in the pastel sky. Spring was her favorite season, full of temperamental sunshine and exciting storms.

Lightning cracked overhead and she lifted her face toward the sky. Rain patted her cheeks and blurred her vision, but she caught sight of the last tail of a lightning bolt snaking across the turbulent charcoal clouds. Magnificent. She swiped the rain from her face, circled around the agitated horses and bounded up the steps to the boardwalk.

And felt a trickling sensation at the back of her neck. Most peculiar, as she had never felt that exact sensation before. A horse's whinny drew her around and there, veiled by gray rain and the transparent rubber sheets of his buggy, was Dr. Samuel Frost.

The explosion of thunder became silent when Sam's gaze met hers. The rain continued to fall but went mute. The horses neighing and sidestepping at the post made not a single noise. All she could hear was her pulse thump-thumping in her ears.

Sam looked equally as surprised to see her. He remained frozen on his seat, his eyes following her as his buggy sped closer. One moment became eternity as she felt her soul shift.

The rain's fury increased, stealing him from her sight. His black buggy sped on, time leaped back into rhythm and the symphony of rainfall returned.

What just happened? Puzzled, she tripped through the door, dripping as she went. The bell above her jingled, the warmth radiating from the stove wrapped around her like a favorite wool blanket, and she stared out at the street where Sam's buggy had been.

Had he felt the same jolt? She had not experienced anything of that magnitude and importance when she'd been in his house, or during the handful of days since when her thoughts had drifted to him more often than she would have liked to admit. Remembering his sense of humor and his tenderness with his daughters had made her wish he was a different kind of man. The sort to believe in true love.

But she feared true love was the last reason a busy

doctor with two rambunctious children would want to marry anyone, especially her. She caught her reflection in the glass window. While she had never been a beauty, time and hardship had stolen the first blush from her face. The man certainly wasn't interested in her looks.

No, Sam had different hopes. He had hoped she would have a settling impact on his twins. That was important to him. If he chose to remarry, he would probably look for a hardworking and sensible wife, a convenient woman to mother his girls. Love would not be part of the bargain.

In her experience, marriage was far too precious to be anything short of true love. Her life had been one long string of disappointments with Fred, a man she had married hoping deep affection would come later.

She had been terribly wrong.

"Come in and warm up by the stove." Cora Sims, the owner of the dress shop and Molly's boss, set down the pencil she'd been using on the account books and rose from the small table at the far end of the tasteful store. "Why, you are drenched through. That storm is shaking the glass in the panes. There it goes again."

Lightning flashed as if directly overhead, accompanied by thunder. The floorboards beneath Molly's soggy shoes shook while the windows shuddered in their wood casings. The stove lid rattled when a gust of wind sent smoke back down the pipe. Molly peeled off her raincoat and hurried, dripping, toward the back room.

"You'll get a chill back there." Cora held out a dainty tea cup, steaming with freshly poured tea. "I'll hang that up. You sit by the stove. Was that Dr. Frost I saw passing by?"

She took the china cup, surprised that it rattled in its saucer at the mention of Sam's name. "Yes."

"My Holly goes to school with his little girls." Cora tapped through the shop, weaving around the notions display case and the summer silks table in the center of the store. "Am I right in thinking the Frosts live across the main road from you?"

Her cup rattled violently a second time. Goodness, how could one rather reserved man bring forth such a response in her? She hardly knew him. She wasn't sure if she would see him again, or even if she wanted to. Why, then, did it feel as if the storm was raging within her as well?

Because you like him. That terrible truth took the rest of the strength from her knees, so she slipped into one of the wingback chairs positioned comfortably near the stove.

Cora hung up the raincoat and returned with a second tea cup, watching her curiously.

"The Frost property borders my cousin's land, yes." She tried to answer as if she wasn't in turmoil. As if she hadn't just discovered she liked a man who, according to his daughters, didn't believe in love.

"Rumor has it that you had dinner with the doctor and his children the other evening." Cora settled into the neighboring chair, her cup steaming and curiosity sparkling in her eyes. Her smile seemed all-knowing. "Samuel Frost is strikingly handsome, don't you think? Holly came down with a sore throat in March, and he was wonderful. Courteous, brilliant, and kind. I wonder why he has never remarried."

"It is a mystery," Molly agreed, the tea in her cup sloshing over the brim. She did her best to steady her hand. "A widower almost always remarries right away if there are children to raise. That's my observation, anyway."

"I've noticed the same. Dr. Frost hasn't been in any rush to find his daughters a new mother. I believe he's been widowed many years. Five, perhaps more." Cora sipped her tea, leaving a silence between them.

Five years was a goodly length to remain alone with two small daughters. Molly leaned back in the chair, the bracing crisp scent of the tea steaming her face while her mind traveled backwards to the evening spent with Sam. She'd gotten a glimpse of his good humor and tenderness, and how much he wanted what was best for his daughters.

The man had a compassionate heart. Perhaps that was why she liked him. Why her hand trembled and her soul noticed when his eyes had locked on hers. Yes, she liked him more than she should. Much more than was smart.

"I'm nearly finished with the basting work you sent home with me." She firmly changed the subject, took a sip of tea and ignored the regret within her for a wish that could never be.

If only he could get the image of the woman out of his head. Sam paced down the dark hall, restless and unsettled, unable to erase the image of Molly lifting her face to the rain, watching the roiling storm with the kind of joy and wonder he hadn't felt since he was a boy. As a little guy, he remembered spinning with both arms out as the rain pelted over him and thunder crashed overhead. That is, until his mother had called out for him to come in and be sensible.

Why was he remembering such things? There was more—the cave in the hillside he had claimed as his fort, the pony who had been his best friend, his anticipation as Ma and his sister Sara finished the supper dishes while Pa lit his pipe and paged through the big volume of Shakespeare's plays.

Life was not a story. He fisted his hands, arriving at the girls' room, where the lamplight framed them as if with an angel's touch. He froze in place outside the doorway, love creeping endlessly into every place, every fracture, every shadow in his soul. The girls in matching white flowered nightgowns and caps knelt beside their double bed, heads bowed and hands clasped in prayer.

Maybe, he conceded. Just maybe part of life was as fanciful and as captivating as anything made up. His daughters certainly were.

"…and please bless Miss Molly, cuz she's awful nice and pretty and has a horse—"

"—and she said she'd take us in a heartbeat—"

"—an' no one ever says that about us. Amen."

"Amen."

The suspicion that the twins knew he was there was confirmed when both girls opened their eyes and shared unspoken looks. A floorboard squeaked beneath his boot as he shifted his weight. Yep, those two were nothing but trouble, but he was very fond of trouble.

"Into bed, both of you."

"Hi, Pa." Synchronized, they hopped onto their feet, hems swishing.

"Maybe you could put Miss Molly in your prayers, too," Penelope began as she climbed beneath the covers.

"Because we like her," Prudence finished as she dashed around to her side of the bed and jumped into it with a creak of bed ropes.

Molly. She was emblazoned in his mind, an image of purity and elegance standing in the rain. A dream he could not let himself believe in.

"Good night, dear ones." He tucked the covers beneath their chins, brimming over with emotion too tender to measure. "Sleep tight."

He blew out the lamp, sorry when the flame died for it stole his little girls from his sight. As he shut the door behind him, he heard their whispers and a single shared giggle. Emptiness followed him down the stairs to the parlor where the day's newspaper and his Bible awaited him. The fire in the hearth snapped and crackled, echoing in the stillness. He could not deny that his thoughts went to Molly, who was also alone in her house and lonely in her life.

He wished he could keep his thoughts from her, but he could not.

The best thing about a storm was that it did not last. Molly drew back the curtains from her window and took delight in the soft light before dawn. A clear sky turned lavender at the horizon and promised a fair morning. Flowers nodded reverently in the calm breeze and birds sang gloriously in anticipation of the sun rising.

Behind her the morning dishes dried in the drainer and the fire was banked in the cook stove. She swallowed the last of her tea, doing her best to ignore the silence surrounding her and the emptiness. Gone were the mornings filled with a gurgling baby girl chewing on her baked biscuits while Molly hurried to get breakfast on the table. Gone were the sweet times when Merry had beat pots against the floor while Molly had baked bread, or accompanied her to town to shop for groceries, or played with her toes in the clean grass while Molly knelt nearby at the washboard.

God knew best in taking little Merry. That Molly had to trust. But nothing had been able to fill the empty mornings or the hole in her heart. She longed to love again, but would it ever be? There would be no more babies and that meant gone was her only chance for a family.

What a blessing the job at the bakery was. There was no more time to remember. She grabbed her shawl from the row of wooden pegs by the door, slung it over her shoulders and threw open the door.

The shadows and half light greeted her. A lark on the ground gave her a shocked look before taking flight. Something dark on the top step caught her attention. She stopped short, staring at the bouquet of freshly picked flowers, the buds closed tightly. The soft fragrance of lilacs made her smile.

Lilacs. She thought of the garden outside Sam Frost's kitchen door.

Could these be from Sam? She knelt down to gather the long stems. Who else would have given her flowers? The bouquet had been tied with a ribbon. She ran her fingertip over the stems. The leaves felt like dried velvet, the delicate cones of blooms like the finest French silk. Memories assailed her, the lilac bushes outside her childhood home making the house smell luxuriously for most of May, planting a lilac bush outside her shanty with new little baby Merry watching, bundled safely in her basket. The scent of the blossoms reminded her of home, of love, and most of all, of hope.

Sam Frost had left these for her? Tears lumped in her throat and scalded her eyes. The man hardly liked her. She'd seen the look on his face when she'd told him about her long-ago fort. While he hadn't been horrified and she hadn't known quite how to label his confused countenance, she was certain of one thing. Sam Frost had sorely regretted inviting to dinner a woman who knew how to climb trees and fend off pretend bandits.

For a moment, just one long moment as she found a tall jar and filled it with water from the pitcher, she dreamed. What if Sam had been smitten by her? What if he'd cut these flowers with love? What if he'd left them here, hoping it would make her smile? That his regard would brighten her day and lighten her load? That when he gazed upon her, endless love filled him up, real love, the incandescent, perfect kind?

But wasn't that just a wish? Molly set the jar on the counter, closed the door behind her and hurried through the pre-dawn shadows. Sam didn't love her. He had brought his offering to delight her, sure, but because he had decided his girls needed a mother. It was a practical decision on his part, nothing more.

If her disappointment felt as large as the sky and as shadowed as the ground at her feet, she did her best to ignore it. She hurried through sleeping wildflowers and whispering grasses to the barn, blind to the beauty as dawn came.

Sam stumbled into the kitchen, blinking against the too bright light. He felt one hundred years old and soul-weary as he dropped his medical bag on the bench by the door and shucked off his coat. The sun was well up. He had no notion as to the time. Bless Kathleen for the fresh pot of coffee on the stove and the scent of bacon in the air. Must be a breakfast plate for him in the warmer.

"There you are." Kathleen bustled into the kitchen with a broom in hand. "I thought I heard the door close. You've been up since the wee hours."

"Mr. Markus is going to make it. His heart gave him a scare." Sam wrapped his fingers around the back rung of his chair. Maybe it was a trick of the mid-morning light, or his weary mind, but a shaft of sunlight sliced through the window and landed directly on the extra chair at the table, the one Molly had used the other night.

Molly. Thinking of her stirred up all kinds of tender feelings and all sorts of sensible reasons not to acknowledge those feelings. He didn't like her. He wasn't going to like her. He intended to stay in absolute control of his emotions.

Kathleen set a cup of hot coffee in front of him and the plate from the warmer.

"Bless you." He surely appreciated his housekeeper. He felt less exhausted basking in the aroma of crisp bacon, scrambled eggs and blueberry pancakes. "Where are the girls?"

"Out weeding the garden like I told them. They have that vase to work off, although it's my opinion—" Kathleen took a deep breath like a general preparing for battle. "I don't think it's right they work off the vase."

"Their cow broke the vase. They need to learn responsibility."

"Yes, I agree. But it might not look right from Miss Molly's view." Kathleen set the small pitcher of maple syrup and the butter dish on the table. "You just think about that. There hasn't been one woman in these parts brave enough to have supper with you. Those twins are a blessing, but a passel of trouble, too. A wise man wouldn't ask questions. He wouldn't hesitate. He wouldn't look left or right. He would marry that woman. Because if you don't, it might well be an eternity before another woman comes along who's partial to your girls."

Yes, that was exactly what he needed right now. Now, when he was too tired to think straight. He was seeing double. He blinked again. Maybe triple. "I don't want to get married."

"You might consider those young ones. Out there trying to impress you and Miss Molly. They need a mother's love."

He reached for the sugar jar and tipped it into his

coffee. The fog in his head cleared a tad. "The girls weren't out in the garden."

"Sure they were. They were right—" Kathleen peered out the back window where the vegetable garden was visible beyond lawn. "Where did they get off to?"

Not again. Sam pushed away from the table. "Keep that warm for me. No telling how long I'll be."

Tired to the bone, he climbed to his feet. A father's work was never done. If a tiny voice in his head reminded him that Kathleen was right, that his girls obviously needed more than he could provide, he didn't want to admit it. He had been denying that voice for years.

He stumbled out of the back door and hadn't gone two feet before he realized something was different. No overgrown branches smacked him as he marched down the walkway. The overgrown lilacs had been trimmed.

Excellent. The girls were showing some improvement, after all. Maybe what they needed was time and firm, loving guidance. Kathleen was wrong.

She had to be.

"Miss Molly!"

Startled, she glanced up from her work at the bakery's front counter, wrapping dinner rolls, bread and a dozen cookies for Mrs. Worthington's afternoon pickup. She lost count of the cookies. The Frost twins tromped through the doorway, dressed in matching pink calico dresses and innocent faces. *Too* innocent faces. What were the girls up to?

"This is a pleasant surprise," she greeted. "What are you two doing here?"

"Oh, we got real hungry for a cookie."

"Real hungry."

At ten in the morning? Quite unusual. She considered her little customers. "I can't remember you two coming by the bakery before this."

"That's because we didn't know you."

"We do now."

"Uh-huh." Not that she wasn't delighted to see her little friends, but she had learned a thing or two about the pair. "What about your pa? Does he know where you are?"

Both girls shook their heads slowly. Puppy dog eyes and downcast faces.

Adorable. She did her best not to let them see her smile. "Did you girls come to town on your own?"

"It wasn't much of a walk—"

"—it didn't take much time at all. We can go back—"

"—if you want us to."

"You don't, do you?"

What did she do with them? As cute as two peas in a pod and twice as dear. She thought of the flowers at home on her kitchen counter, a gift from their father. A courting man left flowers. No doubt about that. Her stomach tightened, as if filling with too many conflicting emotions. Hope and despair, wishes and reality, faith and fear.

"We were weeding the carrots—"

"—which is really hard."

"We have to get every single weed in the whole garden—"

"—except we got hungry."

Was Sam Frost going to come courting her? Why did that question make the children standing on the other side of the counter suddenly more precious to her? Her hand shook as she recounted the cookies in the bakery box and added two more to make a baker's dozen.

They cannot be your children, Molly. She had to be careful. She had to remember that a child could not fill the void in a marriage when love did not thrive. With a flick of her wrists, she closed the box lid and secured it tightly. "Let me understand this. You two are so hungry you had to walk a quarter of a mile into town instead of going to the cookie jar in your own kitchen?"

"Oops." Penelope blushed.

Prudence bowed her head. "Maybe we wanted to see you, Miss Molly."

"Maybe I want to see you, too, but promise me something." She swept around the counter and brought both chins up to meet her gaze. "You tell Mrs. Finley or your father before you surprise me again. All right?"

"Yes'm." Both girls smiled, little beauties with hearts of gold.

Okay, so she was sweet on them. She nodded toward the table at the large front window, where the day's delicious specials were on display. A chocolate layer cake, a pan of cinnamon rolls, fresh loaves of rye bread and big plates of iced cookies. "Now, each of you pick out one thing. It will be my treat."

"Thanks, Miss Molly." They chimed together, twice the sweetness as they raced ahead of her. They had wanted to see her. Enough they had walked all the way here on a Saturday, when they had any number of fun activities to keep them amused at home.

Their question from the first day they met flitted into her thoughts. *Do you want to get married? You could marry Pa. Then he wouldn't be cross anymore. Or lonely. So, do you want to?*

Longing filled her, the longing of a mother who had empty arms and no child to love. The floor felt shaky beneath her feet. She grabbed onto the counter, holding on. It would be so easy to start caring too much. To let her affection for the girls influence how she felt about their father. She wanted a family with all of her soul, so much she ached with it.

More than that, she did not want to make a mistake. To trade the dream of true love and happiness for the reality of uneasy silences and discord.

Do not start loving them, Molly. She willed strength back into her knees and resolve into her heart. Still, it was hard not to adore the girls. Penelope and Prudence in their matching pink dresses and bonnets, their straight black braids and shiny black shoes leaned carefully over the pretty table covered with delicious treats, considering their choices.

The door swung violently open, sending the jingle bell over it ringing with alarm. A man's dark frame filled the doorway, wearing a black Stetson, black attire and a granite-set look of disapproval. Sam's gaze collided with hers and she felt the wave of his unhappiness like a sucker punch as he pounded into the bakery, his boots striking angrily on the floor.

"Girls! What did I tell you?" His hazel eyes darkened, a formidable man of steel and cool temper.

Molly watched in horror as the startled twins turned from the table, Penelope's shoe caught the table leg, she stumbled and there was a deafening crash.

Chapter Six

Dread cascaded through him at the boom of exploding glass. Wood crashed to the floor. A porcelain plate hit the ground with a ring. One sugar cookie rolled like a wheel toward him, hit the counter and broke into three pieces.

His girls—his adorable, troublemaking girls—were in the middle of the shattered glass, splintered wood and ruined baked goods. Prudence stood with her hands to her face, her eyes round with horror. Penelope was in the rubble down on one knee, cradling one hand with her other. Fresh blood seeped between her fingers.

He didn't remember crossing the floor. Suddenly he was crunching across the debris, fear driving him.

"We're real sorry, Pa." Penelope's bottom lip trembled.

"We didn't mean it." Tears pooled in Prudence's eyes.

"Don't move. Not a step." He lifted Penny from the

rubble, hating the sight of that blood. It didn't look too bad. With a kiss to her forehead, he set her safely away from the shards of glass. "I'll be right back, sweetheart. Let me get your sister."

Penny sniffed and nodded, cradling her cut hand, and he swooped Prudy into his arms. Glass and cookies ground beneath his boots as he turned, and the sight greeting him nearly toppled him. Molly knelt in front of Penelope, examining her injured hand. He lost awareness of everything—the child against his chest, the adrenaline coursing through his veins, fear that his daughter was in pain. He felt weightless, buoyant with emotion.

"It's not bad at all. I'll get some water to wash this with." Pure concern shone like a pearl's luster as she gently wiped a tear from the girl's cheek. "Come over here and sit for me, okay, love? It's going to be all right."

Penny nodded with another sniffle. "It only hurts a little bit."

His good girl. Chin set, more tears hovering but not falling, trying so hard to be brave. Vaguely he was aware of lowering Prudence to the floor. Somewhere in his befuddled mind he knew he should be the one to tend to the wound, but for the life of him he could not seem to move. Two things became crystal clear. The gentle tug against his hand as Prudence wrapped her fingers in his, and Molly as she returned with a bowl, pitcher and cloths.

"Come sit over here." Pure compassion, the woman took Penny's elbow and guided her the few steps to the long bench meant for customers. She helped Penelope to sit, her murmur spoken so low, the words were lost to him.

The little girl relaxed, her gaze taking in every detail of the woman's face. Molly held the little hand to the basin, poured water over the wound and dabbed carefully, checking for bits of glass and debris.

He felt a tug on his hand and met Prudy's worried face and plea-filled eyes. She hadn't been harmed by the broken glass, but she was hurting from something different, something harder to see.

"She's just like our list, Pa." She whispered, sidling up against him, so it was just the two of them. "She's nice in every way."

She certainly is. His windpipe thickened, but it was no medical malady that made it hard to draw in air. It was this woman kneeling before his child, with her delicate golden curls and kindness. There was no pretense. No social decorum. Nothing but concern for the child. Like a mother, she inspected the raw edges of the small cut, speaking soothingly in low tones, trying to tease a smile from the girl to reassure her.

It was almost as if Molly were a mother, for she knew just what to do, how to comfort, how to care.

"You hold that still for me, okay, darling?" Molly took the bloody cloths and rose with a rustle of her skirts. She cradled Penny's chin with her free hand. "I'll look to see if Mrs. Kraus has a salve in the medicine cabinet. Then we'll get that wrapped up good so you can have a cookie. Maybe you had better have two cookies. It will help you heal faster."

He watched, amazed. As she smiled down at his daughter, she changed in the same way a bud opened into a blossom. The same way dawn became morning. Everything about her bloomed. Her eyes, her face, her spirit. Pure radiance. In that light he saw something kindred, the sorrow he'd read in her before. But this held a joy, too, a memory and a love so powerful, he knew. He knew.

Bless her, Lord. Please look after her, for all she has been through.

Sorrow beat at his carefully controlled will. His resolve not to like or to care about Mrs. Molly McKaslin crumbled like a cookie, leaving strong, vibrant emotion. He wanted to think it was sympathy for her lonesomeness he felt, and that's what he was going to tell himself. He could not love her. He *would* not love her.

"I've got some salve in my medical bag in the buggy." He moved woodenly toward the door, his emotions oddly disconnected as he grasped the brass knob and bolted into the warm, bright day, refusing to let himself wonder why he was running so fast.

As Molly wrapped up two cookies each for the girls, she tried not to watch the girls and their father. The girls sat side by side on the bench while Sam knelt on the floor, bandaging Penelope's hand.

She gathered up both little packages and by the time she'd circled the end of the front counter, she made sure she had a smile on her face.

"This should make both of you feel a little bit better." She presented the bundles to Prudence. "Perhaps you could carry this for your sister?"

"Yes'm. Thank you so much, Miss Molly."

"Yes, thank you." The intensity of Penelope's smile had changed.

Everything had changed. Molly swallowed hard, trying to ignore the rawness in her midsection. She gave a tug on each girl's sunbonnet brim. "It was a pleasure seeing you two, but I hope the rest of your day is less eventful."

"Me, too. I only got one other hand." Penelope wiggled her good fingers. "I can't climb into our fort."

"Or lasso Sukie if she runs off."

"Or climb over the rocks at the creek."

"I guess you two will have to stay home with Kathleen for a few days until this heals up right." Sam winked at them. "You'll have to be proper. Maybe learn needlework."

"My hand, Pa?" Penelope showed him the bandage as a reminder.

"I know. Sewing is out of the question, but a father can have hope. Maybe you can sit with me in the library."

"You could read the plays to us." Prudence, hopeful, sidled close to her twin, gazing adoringly at her strong, gentle father. "The one with Viola—"

"—the girl that dresses up like a boy." Penelope finished, all hope.

"*Twelfth Night* it is." Sam rose to his six-foot height. Hard not to be impressed by his dependable shoulders and stalwart kindness. "Molly, thank you for all you've done for my daughters."

He may have been talking about cleaning Penelope's

cut and comforting the girl, or perhaps sweeping up the mess in front of the window, but she suspected he was thanking her for more. Much more.

She felt a pang of hope in her heart. A hope she could not simply give in to. Maybe there was a chance his courting was sincere. Maybe.

"Helping your girls was my pleasure." She opened the door. Fresh May sun streamed in like a celebration of life and love. "I hope you feel better, Penelope."

"I do. Now." Although the child walked by and did not reach out, her need was like a small hand grasping the strings of Molly's heart.

"I'm real sorry my shoe got caught on the table leg."

"I'm real sorry about the cookies."

Impossible not to love those darling girls just a little bit more. "I'm glad you both are all right."

"I apologize." Sam hesitated, taking the weight of the door, close enough that she could see the texture of his morning stubble whiskering his lean jaw. "Calamity finds them."

"Those two are catastrophes in calico." And the dearest. She steeled her mother's need to love those girls, refusing to catch a glimpse of the two through the window, where they waited on the boardwalk for their father.

"If the money I left with you doesn't cover all the damage, you will have Mrs. Kraus bill me?"

"She isn't going to be happy about it. Just a warning." Molly forced her thoughts to the incident, a safe topic, one that would not tear her emotions apart. "I'll do what I can to calm her."

"I appreciate it." Again, it seemed as if he was saying

more as he tipped his hat. "I would hate for the girls to be banned from the bakery."

"I would, too." They shared a smile, but it felt like more. It felt like a tender recognition, like two lonely souls finding their match. "Goodbye, Sam."

"Goodbye, Molly." When he said her name, his tone deepened, as if with great meaning, with high regard. No longer reserved, no longer frosty, no longer keeping his distance, Sam brushed by her, and she felt the weight of his shadows and the spark of hope.

You will not fall in love with him, she ordered. She closed the door, watching as the man she did not want to love caught each girl by the hand. They walked toward his awaiting horse and buggy together. Their shadows trailed behind them, as if there was nothing but sunshine and good days ahead.

Alone, Molly turned her back, feeling every drop of emptiness in her soul and every impossible wish.

The image of Molly kneeling before his daughter and tending her wound stayed with him through the afternoon. So did the picture she had made in the bakery's window, with her arms wrapped around her middle, forlorn and lost as he'd untethered Stanley from the hitching post.

Sam set two glasses of lemonade on the table next to the back porch swing. It had been a good day. He had read to the girls early on. His afternoon rounds had gone well, and if no one needed a doc for the rest of the day, he would have a quiet evening at home. "Mrs. Finley says that's all you get before supper."

"Pa?" Penelope's toy horse, clutched in her good hand, froze in mid-gallop on the flowered cushion. "Do you know what?"

"We've got it all figured out," Prudence added, all innocence as she trotted her wooden mustang across the arm of the swing.

"I'm afraid to know what you girls have planned now." He leaned against the porch railing and crossed his arms over his chest, braced for the details of their next scheme. "Does this have to do with the Nevilles' pony?"

"Well, we would like to have Trigger as our very own—"

"—we surely would."

"But this is more important."

"—a *lot* more important."

More than the Nevilles' pony? This ought to be good. He braced himself for it. Perhaps it had something to do with how doting they had been to Molly's mare. Most likely the girls wanted a little more excitement than a placid old pony could bring to their lives. What else could make the girls study one another, as if silently bolstering up their courage to ask? They had never had a problem asking for what they wanted before.

Penelope squirmed, put her horse down and laid her bandaged hand on her lap. She looked vulnerable, as she had after the bakery display table had come crashing down. "Miss Molly was awful nice to us."

"She didn't yell." Prudence swiped the flyaway strands from her braids out of her face with a nervous brush. "Not even once."

"And when I almost cried, she wiped away my tears. She didn't even scold, because I'm too big to cry." Penelope's voice thinned, and on her dear face showed a world of hurt. Of need. "She's awful nice, Pa."

"And she gave us cookies after—"

"—after I wrecked everything." Tears pooled in Penelope's eyes.

Prudence's lower lip trembled.

A terrible feeling gathered behind his solar plexus. A tight coil that would not relent. His daughters were hurting. So little and delicate. "What are you two trying to say?"

"We like her, Pa."

"A whole bunch."

"We want you to marry her."

"With a ring and everything."

He squeezed his eyes shut, attempting to hold more emotions than he could handle. *Oh, Lord, help me say the right thing. Please guide me now because I'm afraid I will make a mess of this.* His girls, for all their bluster and charm, were frail at heart, as anyone was. Love made everyone vulnerable, especially children. He opened his eyes, trusting that God would help him find a way to make this right.

"We were praying too, Pa."

"So that maybe you would like Miss Molly."

"Really like her."

"So she could be our ma."

This is where he had always failed before. Sam pushed away from the railing and knelt before his daughters. The wind chose that moment to gust, sending the most lyrical scent of lilacs, as soothing as any lullaby. A few stray purple petals floated by.

He had spent so much time keeping everyone at an emotional distance. Necessary for a doctor, but it had become his way of coping. First when his marriage felt like a battleground and second when he'd found himself a grieving widower with a pair of three-year-olds to raise. He'd been terrified of failing again. Of letting his girls down. Of not raising them right.

But something had changed. Someone had changed him. He thought of Molly and her loss, the richness of her heart that had known great love and great sorrow. He brushed a tear from Penny's cheek and a stray curl from Prudy's face. "I thought you two understood. I'm not likely to get married again."

"But it's what Mrs. Finley says you need."

"She says it all the time."

He saw right through their words to the needs of two motherless girls. They were the ones who needed him to marry. They were the ones in love with Molly McKaslin. How did he handle that? He couldn't deny the woman's beauty and kindness or the fact that he liked her.

Truth be told, he more than liked her. But marriage? The tightness coiling in his gut twisted taut. No, he could not build a marriage on love again. His heart hadn't recovered from the last attempt.

At a loss, he dug deep for the right answer. He felt the Lord's reassurance like a touch to his soul, and understood. He gentled his voice, although it remained scratchy, letting his shields down instead of putting them up, letting the wash of emotions hit him instead of denying them. "Do you really want to do that to Miss Molly? Look at me. I'm old."

"Not that old, Pa. You don't have gray hair yet."

"Or wrinkles."

So sincere. He tried again. "Sure, but I'm hardly handsome. Molly might not want to marry an almost-homely man."

"Nun-uh. Your nose isn't *too* big."

"And you have all your teeth."

"That I do." He bit his lip. His adorable girls. "I'm sure Molly wants to marry someone with all his teeth. But you know I tend to be surly."

"You don't scowl nearly as much, Pa."

"You only got cross once today."

"But I work all the time. A lot of nice ladies don't like that in a husband. They want them around to have supper with and to read alongside in the evenings."

"You could find another doctor to help you, Pa."

"That way you could have more suppers at the table."

"You girls have this all figured out, don't you?"

"We've got a list, Pa."

"Not just for us, but for you, too."

A list. He should have expected that. They had always been precocious for their age. Perhaps he would leave the rest of the argument for another time. "I'm going out to help Abner with the barn work. You girls want to come—"

He didn't get to finish his question. A cow mooed behind him near the fence, perhaps announcing a newcomer. The squeak of a wheel and the clop of horse hooves brought him to his feet. He was already striding through the garden without thought, expectation filling him. The rising dust obscured the driver from his sight, but he didn't need to see her face to know it was Molly. He knew because of the rise of emotion moving through him like the tide through the ocean.

"Miss Molly!" The girls clamored behind him through the garden gate and onto the lawn. Sukie rushed up, charging on all four feet, mooing in delight. The excitement was nothing compared to the riot of feelings within his heart for the woman who gave her first smile of greeting to him.

Chapter Seven

"Miss Molly! You came!" In unison, footfalls padded against grass. With Sukie tailing them, Penelope and Prudence hurried toward the cart, bright and shining.

"I had to come see how you were, Penelope." Molly didn't bother to hide her delight as she eased Ruth to a stop in the Frosts' driveway. "How's your hand?"

"Lots better. I can't believe we get to see you twice—"

"—all in the same day!" Prudence finished breathlessly, wrapping her fingers along the top rail of the cart. "Did you come to see me, too?"

"Absolutely. I can't adore one of you without adoring the other." Molly laughed when Sukie skidded to a halt behind the girls, and Ruth gave a low nicker of disapproval. What decorum! She patted Ruth's flank reassuringly. "It's very good to see you, too, Sukie."

The bovine lowed, lifting her head to sniff and gaze dotingly at the bakery box on the seat. Smart girl.

"You smell cinnamon and apples, don't you?" Aware of Sam staying back against the white garden fence, she handed the bakery box to Prudence. "I made this during my lunchtime just for you all."

Penelope leaned against the cart, careful of her bandaged hand. "Apple crisp. I can smell it."

"It smells good." Prudence carefully took the box. "Thank you, Miss Molly."

"Do we have to wait for dessert time—"

"—or can we open it now?"

"It's up to your pa." She allowed her gaze to find him and to linger, and offered a small smile. He clung to the shadows against the house, looking stoic and reserved and handsome. Decidedly handsome. Without a hat, his thick black hair swirled over his forehead to fall at his collar. His pensive look made his angled face appear stronger and deeply masculine. Gone was the morning's stubble, and his smooth jaw was set as if in stone. Her fingertips tingled with the urge to trail the cut of his jaw line.

You are not going to fall for this man, remember? She steeled her spine, determined to be strong. Just because her emotions for him had changed and her regard for him deepened did not mean she had to be sweet on the man. She did not intend to set her cap for him. She could hold back her need to be a part of a family again, to love and the hope to be loved.

"You girls take that into the kitchen first, so you don't spill whatever it is."

"Pa, we'll be careful."

"Real careful."

"Sure, but look at what happened this morning. Calamity strikes when you two are near." He stepped into the fall of sunlight, coming closer. "Go to the kitchen and have Mrs. Finley help you."

"Yes, sir." The two trotted off the way they came, and Sukie trailed them through the garden gate and disappeared from sight.

"Is she going to follow the girls into the house?"

"It's been known to happen." He held out his hand to help her down. "When Sukie was a calf, I would find her in the house at least once a day. She would find her way in through a door or a window."

"She does love your daughters." Molly placed her fingers on his palm, the lightest of brushes. This time it felt significant, like a bolt of lightning in a blue sky. As she swung off the seat, the sensation jolted through her spirit and soul, and for one brief moment she was airborne, buoyed as if by love. Then her shoes touched the ground, Sam withdrew his hand and yet the feeling of lightness remained.

"One morning I came in from a late night call, and there she was, sleeping in the kitchen next to the warm stove." Sam did not look in the least affected as he walked slowly at her side. "Sukie was curled up looking as pleased as could be with herself, and the cinnamon rolls Kathleen had baked for the morning were gone and the pan on the counter licked clean."

It took all her discipline to focus on the words of his story. Her hands had gone damp. Her limbs tremulous. Her entire being quaked as if she would never be the same again. "And what was your reaction?"

"I lit the stove, boiled a pot of tea and took the calf outside. She was back in the house by the time Kathleen started breakfast."

"She was letting herself into the house?"

"A mystery that was never solved." Sam appeared different. Warmer, less guarded. He stopped at the gate and held it open, but shook his head when she went towards it. A hint of dimples framed his grin. "It's my theory the calf used the pass-through hatch for the coal. She grew bigger and couldn't get in anymore. I thought letting the girls get a pet cow would teach them responsibility, but I was wrong. You already knew that, didn't you?"

"Maybe because I grew up in the country. I've had a few pet cows of my own." Yes, that was it. Concentrate on anything except Sam Frost.

"So, you've always lived in the country?"

"No. Scarlet fever took my baby daughter four years ago. Then it took my husband, and I fell sick. My mother came to tend me and she died. After that, I couldn't keep the farm running by myself. I lost the house and the land, so Ruth and I moved into town. All the hustle and bustle made me forget. It was the noise. I was always reminded I was among other people, that my old life had vanished and things were different. Somehow it made it easier to move on. At least partly."

"I'm sorry for your loss, Molly." Rich, his words, deeply intimate his tone. His sympathy touched her, as if they shared that in life and more. He moved closer, and not merely physically. "I pray there will be more children for you one day."

"I had a very hard time having Merry, and my doctor assured me there would be no more babies. Now you know why I think your twins are a blessing. I don't understand why God chose to take my only child, but in losing my daughter I know the value of a child's life and the richness of a child's love." She changed the subject. "How did you lose your wife?"

"Cancer. I did a similar thing when Paula died. I moved from the town into the country. I worked so much, so I could stay numb from any more pain life had to offer."

"It's no way to live. Eventually you have to rise to the challenge of living and loving again, or miss what is greatest in life."

"Wise words." He had recently come to understand that.

Kathleen's voice carried from the open window. "Get out of my kitchen! Shoo! You girls take that cow outside right now."

"But she loves us, Mrs. Finley—"

"—she wants to be with us."

"Honestly! Does my kitchen look like a barnyard to you? Shoo!"

Beside him, Molly's laughter was part amusement, part tears. Was she remembering her losses? He wanted to ask her about what had happened, about her buried child. But he could not hurt her in that way.

"What a good life you have, Sam." Amusement chased away the traces of sorrow from her lovely face, the loveliest he'd ever seen.

"I know that, too." She made him different. He

wanted to thank the Lord for sending the lustrous sunlight because when it glowed, it turned her blond hair to pure gold. He wanted to give thanks for the way his heart came to life, full of melody and harmony and notes in between. For the frightening vulnerable feeling of trusting a woman again.

A clatter arose in the flower garden. A lilac bush rustled and Sukie emerged on the path, a daisy hanging from her mouth. Liquid brown eyes twinkled with mischief as she loped just ahead of her little girls. Molly hopped out of the way, bringing her dangerously close to his chest and to his arms. She smelled like sugar cookies and icing and spring. Being near her was like waking up and finding a dream.

The girls dashed past, pink sunbonnets hanging down their backs by the strings, their black braids bouncing with their gaits. "Sukie!"

The heifer, as if eager to play tag, took off into the field, her tail swishing. Penny and Prudy followed, their laughter like merry bells.

"As you can see, neither is worse for the wear. Everything is back to normal." Everything except him. He sidestepped, resisting the urge to pull her against his chest, to hold her sweetly enfolded in his arms. She definitely appeared more beautiful than when he had last seen her and somehow ever more precious and wholesomely feminine. Stubborn tenderness took root within him, refusing to do anything but flourish.

Don't love her. That would be an enormous mistake. But what he heard was his daughters' pleas. *We were praying, too, Pa. So that maybe you would like Miss*

Molly. Really like her. So she could be our ma. What he felt was their unquenchable need. It could not be his own need to love and care for her that made him reach over the picket fence and pluck one long stem of fragrant lilacs.

His voice was raw and gruff when he spoke, his throat oddly aching as he picked another spray. "Was Mrs. Kraus very upset?"

"I believe she will recover once she receives the rest of the payment for the bill she intends to send you."

"In other words, yes."

"I'm glad Penelope is feeling well enough to play. It could have been more serious." She grew radiant, lustrous from the inside out. The sunshine followed her and the wind moved just to caress her hair and rustle her skirt hem. "Your twins are—"

"—trouble?"

"No. I'm searching for the right word."

"—calamitous?"

"Perfection." She almost won his heart with that one pronouncement.

"I think so, too." He plucked one more cone. *Do not fall in love with her. Do not read too much into this. Do not start making a list of all her amazing attributes.* No doubt, a woman like Molly wanted more than he could give.

And if a tiny voice within him wanted to argue, he refused to listen. He held the flowers out to her, the lush green leaves, dainty purple flowers and romantic fragrance. "Stay. Come join us for supper."

"I can't. I'm expected at my cousin Noelle's house

within the hour." Her fingers closed over his, as soft as sun-warmed silk.

"Maybe another evening?"

"Perhaps." She studied him, as if seeing him for the first time. "Yes, I think I would like that."

"Excellent." He drew back his hand but did not step away. "Thank you for the apple crisp. I'm glad you came by."

"Yes." She breathed in the lovely aroma, the velvet petals tickling her chin. It seemed to her there was a deeper meaning to his words, a deeper meaning in her feelings for him. She clutched the lilacs in one arm and let him help her into the cart. The door to her affections opened wider, as she placed her hand in his.

You cannot love him, she told herself.

She feared it was too late.

Sam could not sleep. Having a headache hadn't helped him to drift off, and it didn't put him in a better temper now. He felt as dark as the night, as troubled as the shadows. The lamp's single flame tossed a pool of light on the kitchen table as he pored over his Bible. He had need of wisdom, but not one verse he read seemed to guide him in the direction he wanted to go. He flipped the thin pages, stopping in Ecclesiastes.

Two are better than one; because they have a good reward for their labour. For if they fall, the one will lift up his fellow: but woe to him that is alone when he falleth; for he hath not another to help him up.

Molly. She was the reason he had tossed and turned, unable to make his mind calm down. He kept seeing her everywhere, even on the back of his closed eyelids, her lustrous kindness, her enthralling gentleness, the silken softness of her face. She loved his girls. They loved her. He trusted her, and he believed she trusted him. Wasn't that enough?

His throat felt scratchy, almost sore and he took another sip of honeyed lemon tea. The tart-sweetness made him grimace, but soothed the discomfort. When it came to Molly, how did he stop seeing her beauty as something lyrical, like a romantic sonnet or a tender hymn? How did he stay sensible, for whenever he looked at her it was with the eyes of his heart?

He drew his finger down the page. Maybe an answer here would guide him.

…how can one be warm alone? And if one prevail against him, two shall withstand him; and a threefold cord is not quickly broken.

Fine, so he would try another book. He thumbed back a few of pages and pressed the book open.

Hope deferred maketh the heart sick: but when the desire cometh, it is a tree of life.

That wasn't reassuring him. He rubbed his forehead, aching from too much thought and worry. Was Molly the right woman for his girls? He believed she was. He could make a list a mile long of all the ways she would be good to his daughters and for them. He could make another equally long list of all the qualities Molly possessed that would make her a good wife. She was hard-working, honest, fair, compassionate and loyal. She was also the only woman who could make him fall in love with her, completely, totally.

How did he keep that from happening? Could he be strong enough? And if she was good for his daughters…

What do I do, Lord? He bowed his head, reaching out for the right answer, for leading he desperately needed. *Show me Your purpose in all this. It can't be to lead me back to an unhappy marriage, can it? Or is my girls' happiness of far more importance?*

No answer came in the still of the night. Just a panicked knock at the kitchen door. Work, always work. Wearily he pushed away from the table, leaving his troubles for another time. When he saw Mr. Gornecke on his doorstep, he grabbed his bag without a word and expected the worst.

"Aiden, stop the surrey." Cousin Joanna touched her husband's arm and stood to get a better look through the tall grasses. "Molly, I believe there is something on your doorstep."

"Oh?" She resisted every urge to leap to her feet and see. Had Sam left another bouquet of flowers? And why was she so blissfully happy about it? A woman ought to be wary of a widower's motives, especially when he had young girls needing a mother. He might be starting this courtship because he needed a wife, not because he was in love with her. Although, last night did make her hope.

Maybe there was a good chance Sam loved her. The spark of his touch was as if to her soul, and—

"Molly, perhaps you would like to be left off here." Joanna's voice interrupted.

She shook her head, realizing she had drifted off in thought. Her cousins were watching her with delight. The children on the cushions beside her were curious as to why they had stopped.

"If I were you, I would want to know what that note says." Aiden nodded toward the shanty.

"Note?" She had to ease off the seat in order to see what her cousins were smiling about. She spied the spray of lilacs tied with a ribbon on her top doorstep, anchoring a blue piece of parchment.

"Yes, perhaps I'll get off here. Thank you for the ride to church." Woodenly she turned around, angling her hoops between the seats, and dropped too hard to the ground. Dazed, that's what she was, remembering the intimate warning of Sam's tone. *Maybe another evening.*

She had not expected an invitation so soon.

The surrey jostled away, and she hardly noticed the dust rising up around her. Every step took her closer to the note. Closer to the wonderful, maybe terrible truth. Her right toe bumped into a rock. She stumbled, unable to take her gaze from the flowers, exactly like the bunch Sam had cut for her, exactly like the bouquet left on her step before.

Please, Lord, let him be in love with me. The prayer lifted from her with all the hope she had left. She knelt on the bottom step, her hands trembling.

This was it, what she had been dreading and hoping for. Sam's image filled her mind, his capable shoulders, his gentle hands, the closeness she'd felt in his presence. Ribbons of affection curled within her as she gathered the lilacs into her arms and shook open the note.

Come dine with me tonight.

Happiness lifted her off the doorstep. She felt as airy as those pure puffy clouds sailing across the crystal blue sky. Maybe this was what it felt like when the most disappointed hopes were on the verge of coming true, when impossible prayers were about to be answered.

Chapter Eight

Sam. The moment she saw him rising from the front porch, where shadows dappled the fresh-cut lawn, her affections took flight like a butterfly. Never had she known such a yearning to see a man. To wait with anticipation for his smile to brush his lips. To be eager for the gentle caring in his voice, in his eyes, in his touch.

She drew Ruth to a halt and didn't wait for Sam to come help her. She practically floated to the ground. Her skirts swished around her ankles and she wobbled, finding her balance. Fine, she may be excited but she was nervous, too. This was the start of a dream come true—maybe.

Please let this be my dream. She hoped and prayed, waiting while he closed the thick volume he'd been reading and set it on the bench.

Delight tasted like sugar on her tongue. How good it was to see him. She'd missed the low rumble of his voice, his easygoing humor, his dependable honor. As he came toward her, her soul seemed to lean toward him, as if a sign that they were meant to be together. That true love was already blossoming between them. She wanted nothing more.

"Good evening." Sam strode toward her, appearing rather informal for a dinner date. He did look striking in a white muslin shirt and denims. "This is a surprise."

"A surprise?" No, that couldn't be right. "You're joking again."

"Uh, no. If you've come to see the girls, they were in the house a while ago charming apple crisp from Kathleen." His smile dazzled her. When he gazed upon her, he made her feel as lovely as a princess and twice as precious.

Was she blushing? She pressed her gloved fingertips to her cheeks. Yes, she was definitely overly anxious. Being courted was no easier the second time around. She drew in a calming breath. "I didn't know the girls would be dining with us as well, but you know that's fine with me."

"Dining?" His brow furrowed. "I didn't know you were coming to supper. No one said anything to me."

"No, that can't be right." She couldn't have heard him correctly. Then again, she hadn't imagined the note. She had re-read it a dozen times since she'd come home from church. "You invited me to have dinner with you. You left the flowers."

"The flowers?" He rubbed at his forehead. Why did he look so confused?

"The lilacs on my doorstep."

"I didn't leave anything on your doorstep. I gave

you lilacs when you were here yesterday, but—" The confusion slid from his face. He shook his head once, scattering his thick dark hair. "You have a suitor."

A suitor? Wasn't it him? No, she realized, her mind spinning. He would have remembered leaving the note and flowers.

"No, I think I have no one interested in me." The first strike of disappointment hit. She set her chin and fisted her hands, but that didn't stop the hurt. He hadn't left anything for her. He had not been courting her. He was not courting her now.

The second beat of disappointment hit harder than the first, but she kept her head up. Tried with all her might to keep the pain from showing. "I was mistaken about supper. Please tell the girls hello for me. I'll head home."

"But, wait—"

Her vision kept blurring regardless of how fast she blinked. She spun on her heels, focusing on the brown blur that was Ruth and the cart and kept going. His footsteps padded behind her, but she ignored them. How could she turn to him now? She had been wrong. Desperately wrong. Sam wasn't falling in love with her. He hadn't even been beauing her. He had no notion how deeply she cared about him—

No, she didn't simply care about him. She loved him. That's why when the third blow hit, it hurt enough to have cleaved her soul in two. To leave her in pieces forever. She tripped over her shoe, and Sam's hand curled around her elbow, keeping her up, holding her in place.

"What's wrong, Molly?" His tender tone cut her to the core. "Please tell me why you're crying."

"It's nothing." There were no truer words. She sniffled, remembering she'd left her reticule in the cart. Great. She had no handkerchief to dry her tears. Her stupid, revealing tears.

His grip felt like iron on her arm, holding her in place. Any moment he was going to put the pieces together and know how foolish she'd been. How romantic and foolish, wishing for a man's love, a man who did not love her in return. Humiliated, she swiped at her eyes.

"Here. Let me." Could his voice be any more caring?

She squeezed her eyes shut so she wouldn't see him drying her tears. She felt the soft cotton dab against her skin, drying her cheeks, catching each tear as it fell. It was not sweetness she felt, really. Nor did she feel an iota of tenderness. This wasn't a loving gesture on his behalf. This was one neighbor being kind to another. Friendliness, nothing more.

"Are you going to be all right?" he asked, his voice raw and wounded.

His kindness felt like torture. She broke away, wiped her remaining tears with her sleeve and tried to take a step.

"It was the girls, wasn't it?" His words were roughly spoken, heavy with regret. "They made you think I was courting you, didn't they?"

She nodded. The temperate winds stirred around her, swirling her skirt ruffles, tangling the curls around her face, perfuming the air with flowers and sunshine. How could she be breaking and the world be so perfect and whole? She couldn't speak. She didn't trust her voice. She fought back her last tear.

"I see it now. The proposal. The disappearances. They mysteriously prune half the garden. Their list. They keep a list with all their qualifications for a new mother. You meet every one."

A dagger to her already wounded heart. The girls. She would never be their stepmother now. Loss crashed through her, taking her last drop of hope with it. She'd had too many losses already. "Goodbye, Sam."

"No, Molly, wait." He stood between her and her cart, barring her escape. "Everything the girls did, the flowers, inviting you here, trying to bring us together, that was wrong. But I can't say I'm sorry. I care for you. More than I think is safe."

"I know what you mean."

"Maybe you should stay." He rubbed the pad of his thumb on her cheek, but no more tears fell. "Let's see what's for supper. It's my suspicion Mrs. Finley is aware of this plan and perhaps has aided and abetted. There might be a very good meal waiting for us."

"Oh Sam, I've been in this exact position before, mistaking caring for love." Sheer pain twisted her features. "I can't stay."

"Not even if I ask you to?" He hated every single tear she had shed. He despised that she was hurting. Molly, gentle-mannered, caring Molly did not deserve this. The valiant tilt of her chin, the steel of her spine, the dignity she struggled to keep broke him apart. Tenderness drowned him, and helpless, he took her hand.

"The girls haven't done anything I haven't thought to do myself." Honesty, opening himself up to rejection, took the last of his pride. He felt like he'd jumped off nearby Angel Falls, the highest waterfall in the territory, and was tumbling to certain death. But he kept going. Her hand felt fragile within his own, trembling with broken disappointment and needs. He could feel every one of them. She needed to be cared for. She needed to care for others. She had deep love to give with no one to give it to. She would make a very fine wife.

Just do it, Sam. Head pounding, throat tight and achy, fear beating at him, he got down on one knee, watching her gasp in realization. Yep, that was just about how he felt, too. Surprised and scared and afraid of another marriage hurting more than it helped. But this time, it would be different. He would make sure of it.

"Molly, I'm hoping you would do me the honor—"

"Oh, Sam, please don't ask me this." Her bottom lip was trembling, and she looked suddenly too young and vulnerable. He had never seen her so clearly. Her goodness, her love, her wounds. She tore her hand from his and dashed around him, skirts swaying.

He didn't remember hopping to his feet or following her. Only that he was by her side. "Please don't go until you hear me out. Until you know what you mean to me."

"Oh, I can see it." She looked angry now.

Even he could tell that was only a mask. She was hurting beneath. He was, too, feeling the strike of her rejection. "You won't marry me?"

"I can't marry you." She looked ready to break apart. "You are thinking about your daughters. That's why you are proposing to me. You think I'm useful. That I'll be a solution to your problems."

"I'm thinking about my girls, yes—" He caught her in his arms. She was so tiny, for the great power she had over him. He would climb mountains for her, swim the ocean, leap to the moon if that's what she wanted. Affection filled him up like a wellspring, refreshing and overflowing. Heaven help him. It could not be love in his heart. This was a convenient proposal, nothing more. "Penny and Prudy are getting older. They will be young ladies in a matter of years. They will be putting up their hair and letting down their hemlines. What good will I be to them, then? They love you, Molly. You love them. I've seen it. Go ahead and deny it."

"But you don't love me."

I don't want to love you. How could he say the words that would hurt her? That would drive her away forever? "What I'm offering you is security. You'll have a comfortable life here."

"Security and comfort? That's wonderful, but a marriage has to be more." Her voice broke. "I need it to be more."

"I'll respect you. I'll treat you right. I'll do my best by you, Molly, if only you would honor me—"

"No." She shook her head slowly, sadly. "That's not what I want."

"I care very much. That has to be enough."

"It's not even close." She choked on a sob, waiting for her words to sink in. Realization swept across his face and he released his hold on her. Freed, she stumbled, unable to orient herself. Even though she was standing upright, she felt as if she were falling down. Maybe it was because of the pain of loss and longing she'd seen in his eyes. She still felt it as she turned from him.

"Doc!" A man's voice broke the silence between them like a gunshot. A horse and rider galloped into the yard, the horse lathered, the rider panicked. "You've got to come quick. It's Mr. Gornecke. He's taken with scarlet fever now and it's real bad. Hurry."

"All right, Jerry." Sam hung his head, his frustration palpable. "Molly, I want to talk about this some more."

"No, I can't bear it. Your heart isn't going to change. It's over, Sam." Aware of the stranger watching, she ducked her head, heading in the direction of her cart. His voice haunted her. *What I'm offering you is security. You'll have a comfortable life here.*

She was walking away from a real chance for a family. To be a mother again. Part of her wanted to go back. She hated such weakness, that she would consider his offer, even secretly, even against her better judgment.

But what about accepting his proposal? No. She did not want to live the rest of her days watching and counting all the ways Sam did not love her. Because she loved him. She had the shards of her foolish heart to prove it.

Ruth nickered in comfort. Molly patted her old friend's neck before climbing onto the seat. She felt drained, hollow. As if the emptiness that had shadowed her for years had become permanent. She gathered up the reins and cast one last look at the man she loved, the man she feared she would always love. He stood with his shoulders straight, his hands empty, the apology plain on his face.

It had been her mistake, nothing more. She snapped the reins and let Ruth carry her home.

It was near midnight when Sam locked the kitchen door behind him and dropped his bag on the bench. At least Mrs. Gornecke was improving, and he had hope for her husband. A rustle in the darkness told him he wasn't alone. A second rustle told him the twins had tried to wait for him and had fallen asleep on the window seat.

Ignoring his pounding head, he paced to the table. Every muscle he owned ached something fierce. Probably from having his heart broken. Worse, he had not faced the truth. He had stayed on the sensible path instead of telling Molly that he was in love with her.

Not that he could do anything about it now. She would be asleep, and he didn't know if she would still want him. He didn't want to build a marriage and a life on a flimsy foundation. Yet the love he felt for Molly was stronger than steel. But was it strong enough?

Maybe the real issue was his fear. He was afraid to let her close. He was afraid to trust in any woman's love, even hers.

"Pa?" Penelope sounded sleepy.

"What are you girls doing out of bed?"

"We tossed and tossed."

"We couldn't get to sleep."

"I'm not surprised." He felt hot, so he shucked off his jacket. "Where did you two go off to when Molly came?"

"Our fort."

"So you could fall in love."

Love. There was that word again. He groped around on the shelf for the tin. When he struck a match, the flame cast a dancing glow on the table set for two with the good dishes and the crystal candlesticks.

Another piece of the puzzle revealed. He lit one of the candles, listening to the drag of the girls' stockinged feet as they came to face him.

"You girls know what you did was wrong." His voice croaked, sounding harsher than he intended.

"We know, Pa." They chorused mournfully. "When we came back and Mrs. Finley said you had a house call—"

"—we figured it was ruined." Prudence sighed, a sorrowful sound if there ever was one.

"Could we have Miss Molly for supper tomorrow?"

"Mrs. Finley could serve the pot roast again."

His head pounded. Sweat broke out on his forehead. He'd never felt so terrible. Maybe because he had lost more today than he'd had in many, many years. Maybe because he was more in love with Molly than he cared to admit even now, when he had hurt her terribly. When he feared he had destroyed any faith in him she had.

A droplet of sweat hit the table as he poured his tea. His hand wasn't steady. Something was wrong. A sore throat. Possible fever. Headache. He set the pot on the table and unbuttoned his sleeve cuff. He only had to roll the fabric once to see the tiny red bumps on the inside of his arms. No, it couldn't be.

He sank heavily into the nearest chair. The bumps hadn't disappeared. They were still there, proof of his illness. He'd never had scarlet fever. He'd been around patients suffering from it since medical school. Why now? Why tonight? His head thrummed too painfully to think anymore.

"Girls, I want you to go straight to Mrs. Finley's room and wake her. You stay there. Have Abner come to me right away. You hear me?"

"Yes, sir." Wide-eyed, the twins froze for one moment, perhaps sensing his fear before they broke into a run, clattering down the hall and up the stairs.

If he had been paying better attention, if he hadn't been so enamored with Molly, he might have caught this earlier. *Before* he had exposed his daughters. Heartsick in more ways than he could count, he lowered his head, clasped his hands and prayed.

Chapter Nine

"Rumor has it you've been spending time with our local doctor." Aunt Ida's nimble fingers plucked at the weeds among the green beans in the pleasant evening light. "Is it merely a rumor, or is there more to the story?"

Days had passed since she had driven away from Sam. She had returned to her empty home, tucked away her devastation and gone on with her obligations. One of them was right here, helping out her extended family, which she intended to do as if Sunday evening had never happened. As if Sam Frost had never admitted that he didn't love her.

Hardly a simple thing. She ignored the sting behind her eyes and the hollow feeling within her and tugged a dandelion seedling from among the little lettuce plants.

What did she say to Aunt Ida? The woman was patiently waiting for an answer.

"I'm certain the rumor is much more interesting than the truth." She patted the earth back into place and used the hand trowel to uproot a thistle start. "I met Sam's daughters when their cow ran away and decided to visit me."

"Those girls are as cute as buttons." Ida wisely did not ask anymore about the rumors she had heard. "Molly, when the Good Lord closes a door, He always opens a window. The trouble comes when we forget to believe in the window."

Just how much had Aunt Ida guessed? She tossed the thistle and the dandelion into the waste bucket. "It's over now, and it's for the best. I've had a marriage without love. I don't want another."

"Yes, the greatest is love." Aunt Ida stopped weeding to study her a moment. "I know you well enough to wonder why you're here, as calm as could be. Helping with the bread baking and the cleaning and washing little Graham's diapers."

"Why? Where else would I be?" Speaking of the baby, Molly could see mother and child as they walked in front of the windows, crossing through the parlor. Cousin Noelle looked blissful as she cradled her son, just as it should be. She was happy for her cousin. She would not think of the family she could have had. The man she still loved. "I'm here to help. It's why I have the shanty to call home."

"That's not what I meant, child." She took off her gardening gloves. "Surely you heard about the doctor? About the illness?"

"No. Are the girls sick? Are they all right?" Alarm

shot through her. She loved those children. If anything happened to them—

"No, dear, it's not the twins."

Not the twins? Her brain stuck on those words, as if unable to move past them, because then that would mean—

"Doc Frost came down with scarlet fever. Don't know when. I only heard it in church this morning. His case must not be severe if you're here. That's all I meant."

"Scarlet fever?" The trowel dropped from her fingers. Scarlet fever. Now her mind couldn't move past that terrible thought. She tore off her gardening gloves, suddenly unable to draw in enough air. No. Not Sam. It couldn't be. Aunt Ida had to be wrong. "Surely he's been ill with that before. He's a doctor."

"Molly." The older woman left her weeding, stepped over the baby beans and into the potato row. Her hands were gnarled from age but warm with love as they cradled Molly's face. "This morning at my Ladies' Aid meeting, we said a prayer for his recovery."

Then it was true. The strength seeped from her bones. The thought of Sam lying in bed suffering— She closed off that image. It was one she couldn't stand. She reached out in prayer. *Watch over him, Lord. Please spare him. Please see him safely through.*

"Are you all right, Molly?"

"Yes." She had to be. "What about the girls?"

"As far as I know they're fine. Kathleen Finley was at the meeting and she said they were showing no symptoms. I believe they are all staying at a hotel."

"Then who is caring for Sam?" She wasn't aware of the tears on her face. Only the fear that she would never see him again. The man she loved. The man who had proposed to her, offering her everything he had—family, marriage, home, hearth and children—everything except his heart. Scarlet fever was a serious illness. If she lost him. If he died with the way things were between them—

"I have to go." She bounded to her feet, in a dither, panic thick in her blood. The sun was setting. It was all she could think. Time was running out.

"Then go, dear. I'll finish here. Go to him, this man you love."

She thanked her aunt and ran for the barn amid the darkening shadows.

He was caught in shadows. They clung to him like smoke, blotting out everything. He couldn't see the trees or the sky or one single color. Where were the girls? He worried about his daughters. Were they lost, too? Feverish, he tossed and turned, searching for them. The smoke thinned, and he was able to see them, running merrily through gray fields. But he was still worried. He couldn't stop searching. There was someone else lost in the shadows.

A cool cloth brushed against his brow, dabbing blessed relief against his fever. He wasn't sure if he opened his eyes or if it was part of the dream. A beautiful woman gazed down at him, her rich golden hair down in braids, her sculpted oval face wan with exhaustion, and her eyes the most beautiful blue he had ever seen. Perhaps because of the love he saw there, pure and true, as sincere as a Shakespearean sonnet.

It seemed to him the shadows disappeared. The smoke released its hold on him and slinked away. The world around him became fuzzy. He lifted his head from the pillow, trying to see more. He recognized the blurry shape of the bedside lamp, and his four-poster bed. The opened curtains let in a blinding splash of sunlight. Had the sky ever been that clear? The grass so green? He could not remember noticing before.

"Lie back, Sam." The tone of her voice was his most cherished sound. He drank in the notes of it. He hadn't realized how much he would miss her gentle alto.

He let her push him into the pillows, the effort to lift his head had exhausted him. He panted, his body trembling with weakness. "You're here."

"Yes, I had to help." Sadness dimmed her like a candle in a harsh wind. "The doctor from Newberry says you are going to be all right. The worst has passed."

"Good to know." It didn't feel past. He hated he was too weak to do more than lay his hand on hers. The simple touch enriched him. She was the reason for the color in his life. She was the reason to believe in love again. "You came."

"I had to. The way we left things—" Regret marked her pretty features. She shrugged her slender shoulders, a gesture of helplessness or maybe, just maybe, despair. "Abner needed help tending you."

Yes, he saw her clearly. This time without the shadows of his experience and the smoke of his fears. He wrapped his fingers through hers, holding on tight.

"There's something I didn't tell you before. When I asked you to marry me."

"Sam, I nearly lost you." Tears pooled in her eyes. "But for the life of me I cannot marry without—"

"—love," he finished for her. His throat hurt, his head pounded, he could barely breathe. But he had to say this. He did not want to close his eyes and become lost in the shadows again. He did not want to live without her. He wasn't afraid anymore. A woman who would sit by his side through the illness that had taken her daughter and her loved ones was someone who would stay beside him forever.

"I love you, Molly," he rasped. "I have loved you all along. I will love you through all the days of our life together if you let me. If only you will—"

"—marry you?" She finished his thought, his question. A single tear rolled down her soft cheek. "I'll only do it for love."

"For love," he agreed. He closed his eyes with a smile on his face and love in his heart.

Epilogue

One year later.

Molly McKaslin Frost felt watched as she sat in her cushioned rocking chair in the sunny parlor with her latest book in hand. She paused in the middle of Edward's offer of marriage to Elinor and looked around for the cause of the disruption.

A cow with a white blaze down her face poked her head further across the sill, reaching as far as she could with her tongue. Her gentle brown eyes focused on the half-eaten apple crisp on the end table just out of reach.

"Do the girls know where you are?" Molly set down her book and held the plate for the cow. Two slurps and the dessert disappeared. Sukie licked her lips and gave a moo, presumably a bovine word of thanks.

"Sukie! There you are!"

"Bad Sukie! You got away again."

Molly set the plate aside just as the twins rode into

sight on their pony. Trigger sniffed the air, apparently unhappy he was a few seconds too late for the apple crisp. Love filled her up until she glowed as she studied her daughters. Penelope wore a blue calico dress and Prudence wore green. Happy, the girls waved at her.

"Ma! Can we get more apple crisp?"

"We're preparing the fort for a siege."

"Then it's important you have adequate dessert. I'll bring some out to the garden gate."

"Thank you!" The twins chimed in unison. Prudence grabbed Sukie's halter lead, Penelope snapped the reins and they rode off together, her little band of soldiers.

In the kitchen, Mrs. Finley looked up from her church paper. "The pot roast ought to be done soon. I suppose I should put on the potatoes."

"If you want to wait a few minutes, I'll be free to help you." She quickly found two plates, choosing ones that had already been chipped on previous fort sieges, and sliced into the apple crisp pan. As she worked, she could hear the girls through the open window.

"Pa! Pa! You're home."

"Surprise. Having a second doctor around these parts sure does help." Sam sounded chipper, as if his rounds had gone well.

A lot was going well these days. They had married last June, and every day of their marriage had been bliss. True love made the difference, for it was the kind of love that endured.

She hopped outside into the lilac-scented air. She felt weightless as she bounded down the garden path. When

Sam came into sight, her heart soared, her soul uplifted. Her husband was home. "Hello, handsome."

"Howdy, pretty lady." He tipped his Stetson in greeting. "Any chance that apple crisp is for me?"

"It's for us, Pa!"

"Us and Sukie and Trigger."

The twins thanked her for the dessert and rode off, bouncing on the pony's broad back. Sukie followed happily, tail swishing.

"Come here, beautiful. I missed you." He unlatched the garden gate and held out one hand.

"I missed you, too." She laid her fingers against his broad palm, and the connection that sparked between them was pure loving sweetness. Just as in all the books, this was her ever after, her storybook ending. She let her husband draw her into his strong arms and hold her against his iron chest. She savored the comfort and joy. She tipped her face up to look at him, this man of her dreams.

"Have I told you lately how much I love you?" He brushed a kiss to the tip of her nose.

"Not lately, no. This morning, yes. After lunch, yes. But not since."

"I'm remiss." Tenderly, he kissed her, sweet and slow. "I love you, Molly."

"I love you." She went up on tiptoe to kiss his chin. What an amazing man. His love had changed her life. He had given her his heart and his daughters. He had made her a wife and a mother again. He had given her more happiness than she could hold. God was truly gracious indeed. "I think we are going to be very happy forever."

"I think so, too, my love." He kissed her again, as gently as any romantic hero.

My love. She held him tight, savoring the sweetness and the joy.

* * * * *

Dear Reader,

When I was asked to write for a Mother's Day anthology, I was delighted. I had been safekeeping Molly's story in one of my notebooks for a special occasion. And I knew this was my opportunity to dust off the notebook, flip through the pages and step into the shoes of a young widow bowed by hardship and loss, and walk with her from her sadness to great joy.

The thing I love most about Molly is her ability to see the bright side of things: beauty in a dark storm, a kindred soul in a lonely widower, and the ability to love even in the aftermath of unbearable loss. Now that is faith. Hers is a mother's heart without a child to love. I thought it just that she find not only a man with a good heart to love, but worthy children, as well. I hope you adore the twins as much as I do, along with Sukie, the cow, who was modeled after my childhood pet calf, Juice.

Thank you for choosing *Finally a Family*.

Wishing you the best of blessings,

Jillian Hart

QUESTIONS FOR DISCUSSION

1. At the beginning of the story, how would you describe Molly's character? What strikes you most about her?

2. When Sam first meets Molly, he overhears his daughters proposing to her. How would you describe his reaction? What does that say about his character?

3. When Molly first meets Sam, he has a strange effect on her heart. What is it, and how does it affect the rest of the story?

4. How would you describe Sam's method of parenting? How does it change, and why?

5. The girls play a significant role in the story. How do they influence the growing romance? How do they change Sam's view of marriage?

6. How does learning of Molly's lost child change Sam's view of her?

7. How does God open both Molly's and Sam's hearts to love again?

8. Mark 10:15 says: *Unless you accept God's kingdom in the simplicity of a child, you'll never*

get in. How is this evidenced through the twins'
faith? How does God answer the prayers of these
children?

HOME AGAIN
Victoria Bylin

For my mother,
Darlene Bylin McLeary.
Mom, you're the best...I love you lots!

Sons are a heritage from the Lord,
children a reward from him. Like arrows in the
hands of a warrior are sons born in one's youth.
—*Psalms* 127:3–4

Chapter One

Guthrie Corners, Colorado
May 1890

Cassiopeia O'Rourke had been named for a constellation, but Heaven couldn't have been further away as she stepped inside the Guthrie Corners sheriff's office. Behind the steel bars sat her twelve-year-old son, looking not the least bit sorry he'd thrown a rock through a window. The *church* window, Cassie reminded herself. She couldn't think of a better way to fan the fires against them.

Since coming home a month ago, she'd wondered every day if she'd done the right thing for Luke. They'd been living in a poor Chicago neighborhood in a tiny flat, one she could barely afford on a bookkeeper's salary, when she'd received a letter informing her she'd inherited her father's mercantile business. The day before, she'd caught Luke in the alley lighting trash on fire. The day before that, he'd been disciplined at school for foul language. Where he'd learned such words, she couldn't imagine. And before that… Cassie sighed. The list went on for a mile.

She'd hoped that moving to Guthrie Corners would give Luke a second chance, that by taking him away from his so-called friends she'd find the sweet boy who'd enjoyed her hugs. Judging by the visit she'd received from Pastor Hall a few minutes ago, she'd been wrong…again.

As she looked around the sheriff's office, her regrets were legion but none were greater than the regrets concerning Deputy Gabe Wyatt. He stood in front of her now with a glint in his eyes and his arms loose at his sides. Dressed in brown trousers, a dark blue shirt and a leather vest, he seemed stronger than ever. His face had a familiar calm, but his hair, wavy and the color of tarnished gold, looked as if he'd raked his hand through it. If he'd been dealing with Luke, he probably had.

Cassie forced herself to hold his gaze until his eyes darted from her face to her toes, then back up. There was nothing personal about his perusal, no sense of the past and kisses they'd shared. He'd taken her measure as if she were a stranger. With her son behind bars, he'd doubtlessly found her lacking as a mother. Fine, Cassie thought. Let him judge her. Others had. Right or wrong, everyone in Guthrie Corners had an opinion on Cassie Higgins O'Rourke.

What kind of mother lets her child run wild like that?
As if she could keep Luke in a cage.
What kind of mother doesn't volunteer at church?

One who ran her own business, a failing one thanks to gossip and grudges.

What kind of woman would leave Gabe Wyatt at the altar?

A stupid one.

As Cassie raised her chin, Gabe crossed his arms over his chest. Fourteen years ago she could have had those arms around her. She could have been his wife. She wouldn't have traded Luke for anything, but she deeply regretted her marriage to Ryan O'Rourke. A long time ago she'd chased after a lie. Instead of settling down with Gabe, she'd run away to Chicago to become an actress. The stage…excitement…freedom. She'd found two of the three. She'd acted in one play and had been swept off her feet by Luke's father, but freedom had eluded her.

Between her wretched marriage, empty pockets and troubled son, Cassie felt as trapped as the constellation for which she'd been named. A vain queen, Cassiopeia had been chained to a chair in the night sky. No matter how the earth turned, she sat with her neck bent in shame. Cassie lived with the same disgrace. She didn't want to look Gabe in the eye, but she had to be strong for Luke.

As she raised her head, he lowered his chin. "Hello, Cassie."

"Good afternoon, Deputy." It didn't seem right to call him Gabe. She'd lost that privilege.

His eyes narrowed with irritation. "I take it Reverend Hall spoke to you."

"Yes."

"So you know why Luke's here."

"I do." Her insides started to shake. The longer she looked at Gabe, the more she wanted to beg for his forgiveness. She'd tried to apologize when she'd first arrived. She'd sent a note asking him to come by the store, but he'd ignored it. Looking at him now, she saw a rock wall. She would have blurted her apologies, but she couldn't speak to Gabe in front of Luke. Gabe deserved as much privacy as she could give him, and Luke needed her undivided attention. She turned to the cell where he lay sprawled on the cot with his hands behind his head, one leg bent and the other stretched as if he didn't have a care in the world. The pose struck her as vain. The boy had inherited Cassie's looks, but he had his father's arrogance.

She doubted he'd obey, but she had to try. "Luke, sit up. This concerns you."

He made a snoring sound.

Cassie made her voice stern. "This *isn't* a request."

Luke grunted. For an instant she thought he'd obey, but instead he switched the position of his legs and sighed.

Her cheeks flamed with embarrassment. What could she do? Take away his allowance? She'd already cut it to nothing. Resort to spanking? Hardly. Cassie knew how it felt to be hit and couldn't abide violence. Besides, Luke had grown four inches this year. He could look her in the eye and probably outweighed her.

With her mouth in a firm line, she turned to Gabe. "I apologize for my son. Of course we'll pay for the window."

"Fine," Gabe said. "But there's no 'we' here."

Cassie stiffened. "What do you mean?"

"Luke broke the window. He's the one who has to pay."

"Of course, but he's a child."

Gabe eyed her thoughtfully, then shot a glance into the cell. Her son made another snoring sound.

Cassie's cheeks flamed. "Luke! Stop that."

As soon as the order left her mouth, she regretted it. She'd just waved a red flag in front of a bull. Just as she feared, Luke let out a belch that would have made Henry VIII proud. Embarrassed to the core, she looked at Gabe. Instead of judgment in his eyes, she saw a twinkle. Cassie saw no humor in the situation at all. She started to speak, but Gabe gave a tight shake of his head.

Winking at her, he called out to Luke. "Nice job, kid. But it's going to cost you."

She opened her mouth to ask what, but Gabe put his finger to his lips to silence her. Cassie bristled. She didn't take orders from anyone, especially not from arrogant men, but she sensed Gabe's wisdom. Besides, she had nothing to lose. The situation with Luke couldn't get much worse.

She nodded her agreement, then looked at her son lying like a lump on the gray blanket. He drummed his fingers on the wall, then burped again. Cassie bit her lip. Twenty seconds later, Luke belched a third time. Mortified, she turned to Gabe. Before she could speak, he silenced her with a look.

Cassie didn't like being treated like a child. Even

more upsetting, she couldn't bear the quiet. Growing up in the Higginses' household, she'd endured family meals where no one said a word. She'd learned to despise silence, especially at night when she looked at the stars. She'd long ago stopped praying for herself, but every night she asked the Lord to look after her son. In those dark hours, she heard nothing.

Now, to her amazement, she heard a wealth of sound…the rasp of Gabe's breath, the beat of Luke's fingers on the wall. The clock ticked and a wagon rattled by. Calmer, she risked a glance at her son. To her amazement, he'd raised his head and was staring at Gabe. The lawman didn't move a muscle.

Luke finally broke the silence. "What's it going to cost me?"

"On your feet, kid."

To Cassie's amazement, he complied. He moved like a snail and he didn't look happy, but he stood up.

"That's good," Gabe said. "Now apologize to your mother."

More silence.

This time Cassie enjoyed it. She knew how patient Gabe could be. The only time he'd rushed her had been about their wedding. She'd been seventeen and had wanted to wait a year. He'd been eager and had pushed for June. She'd said yes to please him, but in most matters Gabe had the patience of Job. The thought sent a pang from her head to her heart. How long had he waited for her at the church?

Luke must have sensed Gabe's stubbornness, because he turned to her. "Sorry, Mother."

Her heart ached with fresh pain. She didn't want to be *Mother*. She wanted to be "Mama" again, or "Ma" because it fit his age. The way Luke said "Mother," she felt like a shrew.

Gabe glowered at the boy. "You got the words right. Now say it like you mean it."

Cassie saw the hard set of Gabe's jaw and knew he'd stand here all day.

Luke must have realized it, too. He looked at his feet, then raised his head. His hair, dark and lanky, hung across his eyes. She'd tried to take him to the barbershop, but he'd fought her on it. He'd insisted he was too old to have his mother take him and that he'd go himself. He still hadn't done it.

To her relief, he looked sheepish. "I'm sorry, Ma."

In a five-minute standoff, Gabe had worked a miracle. Cassie's heart soared as she looked at Luke. "I accept. We'll talk more at home."

The boy, expecting to be released, looked at Gabe.

Instead of opening the cell door, Gabe hooked his thumbs on his belt. "Sit down, Luke. We're not done."

"Of course," Cassie said. "We—Luke—has to pay for the window."

"That's not enough," Gabe said.

"*And* he has to apologize to Reverend Hall," she added.

Gabe ignored her.

Confused, she followed his stare to Luke and saw what she'd come to call "the look." The boy stood with his neck slightly bent and an innocent expression pasted to his face. He looked as sweet as pie, but a smirk lurked behind his eyes. She'd seen that arrogance in Ryan O'Rourke when he'd come home after a night with another woman. She'd seen it in Luke, too. If her son thought he could get away with breaking the window, he was dead wrong. She had to make him understand, but how? What more could she do?

She was searching for an answer when Gabe faced her. "I'd like a word with you, Mrs. O'Rourke. In private."

"Of course."

She gave her son a look that promised a talking-to later, then followed Gabe out the front door.

She still smells good.

That was Gabe's first thought as he led Cassie to a patch of grass behind the jailhouse. He'd have preferred speaking to her out of public view, but he didn't want Luke to hear what he had to say. Neither did he want to be alone with her, but it couldn't be helped. Until now, except for an occasional glance through the window of Higgins Mercantile—part of his job, he told himself— he'd steered clear of Cassie O'Rourke.

The visit from Reverend Hall had changed everything. The minister had caught Luke throwing rocks at the church. He'd broken just one window, but judging by the arsenal at his feet, he'd planned to break them all. Luke had outrun Reverend Hall, but by a stroke of luck, fate or God's hand—Gabe believed in the third— the boy had plowed into him. The Reverend had caught up to them and Luke had landed in jail.

Now here he stood with Cassie. One look at her told

Gabe the truth he'd fought for fourteen years. She'd wounded him to the core, but he hadn't stopped loving her.

Blinking, he flashed back to their so-called wedding day. He'd worried for a full hour before Reverend Hall had pulled him into his office and told him that Cassie was missing. When he'd gone to the house he'd built for her, he'd found the note she'd penned on fine stationery.

I'm sorry, Gabe. I just can't do it.

Why he'd kept the note, he couldn't say. But he had it tucked in the Wyatt family Bible, the one where he'd already written their names. Looking at Cassie now, he asked the question that had plagued him for fourteen years.

Why, Cassie? What couldn't you tell me?

The question hung in his mind like a hawk soaring against the wind. It just hung there, working hard but going nowhere. He wanted to ask it now but he wouldn't. Only a fool stuck his own head in a guillotine. He'd have ignored Cassie forever if it hadn't been for Luke. Gabe had a soft spot for fatherless boys. He'd been one himself…which got him to wondering. What had happened to Mr. O'Rourke?

Don't ask.

For the second time that day, he raked his hand through his hair. He couldn't let Cassie get close, but neither could he turn his back on her son. It would cost him to befriend Luke, but so would doing nothing. If he didn't do his best for the boy, Luke would keep getting into trouble and Gabe would have to deal with even bigger problems. He'd also be up all night with a guilty conscience. When push came to shove, he didn't have a choice in how he treated Luke. He hoped Cassie would go along with his plan.

When they reached the grass, he indicated the bench under an oak. The spot was next to the town library and a well-meaning soul had made it inviting with daffodils now in bloom, the stone bench and a swing hanging from a thick branch.

Cassie stayed on her feet. Either she hadn't seen his gesture or she'd ignored it. Looking nervous, she faced him. "Luke's not a bad boy. He's just—"

Gabe held up a hand to stop her. He heard the same speech every time he dealt with a fatherless kid like Luke.

He's really a good boy.

He didn't mean to do it.

Gabe didn't begrudge Cassie's defense of her son. That's how mothers loved their children. They saw the best and believed the best. Only now, with Luke throwing rocks, she had to face facts. Broken windows led to bank robberies, prison, even death at the end of a noose. He had to get her attention.

"Mrs. O'Rourke, your son's in trouble." He thought of her as Cassie and always would, but earlier she'd called him "Deputy." It had rankled him.

She looked put off. Gabe wondered if the formality irked her the way it irked him, then chastised himself for the thought. It didn't matter how she reacted. She clearly didn't love him. If she had, she wouldn't have left him at the altar twiddling this thumbs with a gold band in his pocket. He didn't mean to scowl at her, but he'd never gotten over the embarrassment. Half the town had been in the pews. The pity had just about killed him.

Cassie looked down at the grass. "Luke has problems. I know that."

Her voice dropped so low, he barely heard her. "When did the trouble start?"

"A while ago."

"Before you came to Guthrie Corners?"

"Yes."

She was still staring at the grass. He wanted to tell her to look him in the eye, but he feared the shine of tears. He settled for looking at the crown of her head, where her dark curls were twisted into a knot. In the sunlight he saw strands of red and remembered thinking she had pretty hair. She still did.

Fool! He had to keep his mind on Luke and off the boy's mother.

Cassie dropped down on the bench. Instead of meeting Gabe's gaze, she stared at the bars marking Luke's cell and spoke to the wall. "Luke's the reason I came home instead of selling the store."

He'd figured as much, though part of him had wondered if—even after all this time—she'd come for him. Did she think of him at all? Apparently not.

"We lived in Chicago," she continued. "Luke made new friends—the wrong kind, if you know what I mean."

Gabe knew very well. "It happens."

"Maybe, but not to *my* son." Cassie finally raised her

chin. "I'll do anything for Luke. I know he's in trouble. I see it in his eyes. He's—" She looked down, pressed her hands to her cheeks and gulped air. As her shoulders swelled and shook, he thought of a flustered bird trying to protect itself.

In his line of work, Gabe dealt with lots of crying women. He knew the power of a strong shoulder and often played the big brother. It came with the job, but this was Cassie and he didn't feel the least bit brotherly. Even so, how could he leave her to weep? He couldn't. Wise or not, he sat next to her and put his arm around her shoulders. The next thing he knew, she'd pressed her cheek against the top part of his vest. Nothing but leather, muscle and bone separated her tears from the very heart she'd broken.

She was trying to talk, but Gabe couldn't make out the words. Nor did he want to. She'd broken his heart once and could do it again. He had to keep his distance. He had to remember that day in church and the months that followed. They'd stretched into long, lonely years. He wanted a wife and had done some courting, but no one had measured up to Cassie. He'd loved her that much. He still did, but he hated what she'd done to him.

Forgive her.

The command came from his conscience. He knew that Jesus had died for him. Like every other sinner on earth, he was an imperfect man with imperfect thoughts. Christ had died for Cassie's mistakes, too. Gabe knew that truth in his marrow, but common sense told him to let sleeping dogs lie. As the saying went, "Once bitten, twice shy."

He waited until her sobs eased, then he lifted his arm from her shoulders. As he stood and walked to the cottonwood, Cassie removed a hankie from her drawstring bag and dabbed at her eyes. "This is embarrassing. I don't usually cry."

I know. Before today she'd never cried on his shoulder. During their courtship, he'd admired her strength. Now he wondered what she'd been hiding from him. He clamped his jaw tight and leaned against the smooth bark of the tree. He had to focus on the business at hand. "It's understandable. You're worried about your boy."

"More like panicked," she said ruefully. "I've disciplined him every way I know, but nothing works."

"That's because he's mad at the world."

She sighed. "And especially at me."

"That's a good sign," he replied. "It shows you're trying."

"I am, but nothing helps. I'm at a loss."

"I'm not," he said confidently. "Luke wants to be a man. He just doesn't know how."

Her eyes widened with understanding. "I hadn't thought of that."

Gabe didn't want to ask the next question, but he needed to know for Luke's sake. "It's none of my business, but where's the boy's father?"

"I don't know and I don't care." She bit off each word. "He's not a part of our lives."

Questions swirled in Gabe's mind, but only one answer mattered. Whoever he was, this O'Rourke character had hurt Cassie. For years he'd taken comfort in the notion she'd found happiness. Apparently not. O'Rourke had left her with a son and a mess to clean up. Gabe knew all about boys, messes and broken glass. He crossed his arms over his chest. "Luke broke the law. That means I'm involved."

"Of course."

"Here's the plan." He spoke with deliberate authority. If Cassie reacted like most mothers, she'd cringe at what he had to say. "Luke spends tonight in jail."

"Jail!"

"That's right," he insisted. "Locked behind bars with nothing to do but think."

"But—"

"He needs a taste of the future he's chosen."

Cassie's breath whooshed from her chest. "But he's so young—"

"He's old enough to break windows," Gabe said dryly. "My deputy usually stays the night when we have a prisoner, but if it makes you feel better, I'll stay myself."

Her eyes clouded. "I just don't know—"

"Cassie." Her name slipped out unbidden. "Luke isn't a boy anymore. The more you baby him, the angrier he's going to get. If he wants to play rough, fine. We'll play rough."

Her brows snapped together. "What do you mean by *rough?*"

The question irked him. "Nothing physical. You know that."

"I do." She twisted the hankie. "I just wish—"

"Don't waste your breath." He didn't want to go

down any road that led to the past. "Tomorrow's Saturday, so there's no school. I'll have him apologize to Reverend Hall, then we'll fix the window. I'll show him how, but he's going to do the work himself."

She looked resigned. "I should pay for the glass."

"I'll get it from the hardware. Luke can do chores around the church to pay me back."

Her eyes filled with relief. "How can I ever thank you?"

By telling me why you left. Except he didn't want to know. "I'll tell Luke he's been sentenced to a night in jail, fixing the window and chores, but there's something important *you* have to do."

"What's that?"

"Stay away from the jail. Don't bring him supper or even his school books. Nothing. Do you understand?"

She looked miserable. "He's growing like a weed. He'll be hungry."

"I'll see that he eats." He'd get meat loaf at Millie's. Dessert, too. If Luke behaved, he'd eat like a king. If he didn't, he'd miss out on the best chocolate cake in town. "Don't interfere, Cassie. It's called jail for a reason."

When she nodded with understanding, he wondered what jails had held *her*. Those places might not have had bars, but he felt certain they'd been dark and cold.

He indicated the building. "I better get back."

As they left the grass, Cassie walked at his side. It would have been the most natural thing in the world to put his hand against her back to guide her. Instead he kept his arms loose at his sides…loose and ready, though he didn't know for what.

Chapter Two

Cassie walked the four blocks to Higgins Mercantile with her head high, but the effort made her neck ache. People stared as she passed, but no one smiled or said hello. She knew why. She just didn't know what to do about it. Maude Drake, an old rival, had been spreading rumors. Cassie had her faults, but she didn't cheat her customers. Neither had she lived in sin with Luke's father as Maude had implied.

The thought made her furious. She'd been innocent when she'd married Ryan O'Rourke. Stupid, too. She'd confused charm with character, a mistake she'd never repeat. Gabe had both. Once she'd seen his reasoning, leaving Luke in his care didn't worry her at all. Her reluctance came from a sense of debt. She already owed him amends for jilting him. Today, when she'd broken down, she'd tried to apologize but he'd cut her off. How could she put the past behind her when it weighed on her every thought?

Sighing, she unlocked the front door of her shop. When she'd first arrived, the display areas had been full of the same clutter she recalled from her childhood. She'd moved it to a storeroom and written to the merchandiser at Russell's Department Store in Chicago, the place she'd worked as a bookkeeper. The buyer for Russell's had been enthused about her venture and had approached Jacob Russell himself. The end result had been a business arrangement where Cassie sold Russell goods on consignment. If she succeeded, she and Luke could live comfortably.

Looking at the displays—pretty dishes, shiny cookware—she had dark visions of having to return it unsold. She'd had two customers in a week, but only if she counted both Pastor Hall and Thelma, his wife. Out of habit, Cassie looked at the window where her father had put a chalkboard showing the time he'd be back whenever he left the store. With business so slow, she hadn't thought to put it up. She ached to go upstairs to her apartment, but instead she took a feather duster from behind the counter and headed for a display of thimbles.

As she swished the ostrich feathers, the doorbell jingled. She looked up and saw Thelma. The minister's wife had been like a sister to Cassie's mother. When Bonnie Higgins had died of apoplexy, Thelma had taken Cassie under her wing.

The older woman paused at the dish display. "These are beautiful."

Cassie loved the fine china. With only Luke at her table, she couldn't justify buying a set for herself, but she sometimes closed her eyes and imagined a table set for the husband and children she'd never have.

"They're practical *and* pretty," Thelma added. "If the women in this town had a lick of sense, they'd ignore Maude and look for themselves."

"I wish they would." Cassie gave the shelf a last flick with the ostrich feathers, then faced Thelma. "I'm sorry about the church window."

"Of course, you are."

"Luke will make it right, I promise."

Thelma's lips curved into a sad smile. "It's not easy being a mother, is it?"

"No." Cassie choked up. To hide her eyes, she went back to dusting.

Thelma came to her side. "I know you love your boy, Cassie. Deep down, he knows it, too."

With anyone else, she could have managed a brazen lift of her head. With Thelma, she could only be herself. "I'm so ashamed."

"You shouldn't be." The minister's wife put iron in her voice. "You're doing your best."

"I don't understand," Cassie continued. "He *knows* what he's doing is wrong."

Thelma squeezed Cassie's shoulders as if she were little again. "You're not alone, sweetie. There's not a mother in the world who hasn't lost sleep over a child. I hear the boy's spending the night with Gabe."

"Yes."

"That'll be good for him," Thelma said. "Now we need to take care of *you*. Let's go to Millie's for tea."

Cassie nearly wept at the thought. She couldn't

remember the last time someone had made her a meal or poured her a cup of something hot. She steeped her own tea with the cheapest leaves, but it usually went cold while she did other things. The idea of sitting at a table and being served touched her to the core, but she saw a problem.

"I don't know," she said. "Millie and Maude are friends."

Thelma got a glint in her eye. "Never mind them. I want tea and you need it."

She also needed to talk. Seeing Gabe—speaking with him—had filled her with questions. Why hadn't he married? Was he happy? When she'd come home, she'd expected to find him with a wife and children. Instead she'd found a bachelor living in the house meant for her.

"Tea sounds good," Cassie replied.

She left the feather duster on the shelf, followed Thelma out the door and locked it behind her. Like before, she left the chalkboard blank. As they walked to the café, they passed a dozen people who'd been her father's customers. Most of them had been in the church when she'd jilted Gabe. She forced a few smiles but gave up after the third cold stare. Thelma greeted every person they met. A few remarked on the weather, but no one treated Cassie with warmth. As much as she wanted a cup of tea, she wished she'd stayed in the store. That feeling doubled when they walked into Millie's Café and Thelma made a beeline for a table in the front window.

"Let's sit in the back," Cassie said.

"Nonsense," Thelma answered. "It's a lovely day and you need the sun."

"But, Thelma—"

"Cassie, trust me. People need to see you."

But Cassie didn't want to be seen. She'd had enough hard looks today, but how could she say no to Thelma? By taking Cassie for tea, the minister's wife was waving a banner of love for the world to see. Determined to be worthy of the kindness, Cassie sat in the chair facing the door. She'd smile at everyone who walked by her.

When the waitress approached, Thelma ordered tea and a tray of petit fours. Cassie's mouth watered. Millie could be mean, but she knew how to bake.

"Now," Thelma said with an arch of her brow. "Tell me about the past fourteen years."

Cassie had visited with Thelma twice since coming home, but she'd been vague about her life in Chicago. She gave a rueful smile. "That would take all day."

"Then start with Luke," the older woman said softly. "Where's his father?"

Cassie blinked and recalled the night she'd left Ryan O'Rourke. He'd come home drunk and smelling of perfume. When she'd protested, he'd struck her. She'd fallen and hit her head. Barely conscious, she'd seen him heading for Luke's room and had cried out. The distraction had worked and Ryan had beaten her instead. Hours later, when he'd passed out drunk, she'd packed one bag and left with Luke in the middle of the night. It wasn't the first time Ryan had struck her, but it was the last. The next morning she'd hired an attorney and petitioned for divorce.

"It's an ugly story." She lowered her eyes. "Ryan

turned violent. I left him for my sake but mostly for Luke's."

Thelma's mouth thinned to a line. "You did the right thing."

"I hope so, but Luke doesn't understand." Cassie felt a headache coming on. "We divorced seven years ago. Luke's never had a father and he blames me."

The waitress brought the tea and two pretty cups. Thelma filled the first one for Cassie, laced it with sugar and handed it to her. "You're strong, Cassie. Your mother would be proud."

As Cassie raised the cup to her lips, she thought of mornings she'd sat at the breakfast table, drinking tea with her mother after her father had gone to the store. She'd been Luke's age when Bonnie Higgins fainted in the kitchen and died a day later. Cassie had been too young to know her mother as a woman. Now, as a woman herself, she missed her more than ever.

"I don't know," Cassie said as she pondered Thelma's question. "What would she say?"

"She'd tell you to hold your head high." The older woman sounded sure. "She'd also love Luke to pieces and spoil him rotten."

Cassie could see it. "She'd have read him Bible stories at bedtime."

Thelma smiled. "Boys like the ones about Pharaoh and frogs falling from the sky."

Cassie made a face. "Not me."

"You would if you heard Gabe tell it."

At the mention of his name, Cassie curled her fingers around the warm porcelain and thought about the day she'd clapped eyes on the handsome new sheriff. He'd come to town from Texas, a former cavalry officer and a bachelor to boot. They'd met at her father's store and she'd been smitten. She'd also been seventeen, practically a child. She'd loved him, but she had wanted to wait to get married. Her father—and Gabe—didn't see the point. Shuddering she recalled the night before her wedding. She'd been a wreck. Then her father had brought the journal written by her mother…

"Cassie?"

She looked up and saw a tray of petit fours. Thelma put a bite of cake with white frosting on a plate and handed it to her. "You looked a hundred miles away."

"More like fourteen years." She lifted her fork. "Gabe never married, did he?"

"No."

Cassie feared the answer, but she had to ask. "I wonder why."

Thelma's brows lifted. "Until now, I figured he hadn't met the right woman."

Until now… To avoid the trail of Thelma's thoughts, Cassie took a bite of cake. Their wedding cake would have tasted exactly like the frosting melting in her mouth. Millie had already baked it and friends had left gifts at the house Gabe had built for her. She knew from the one angry letter from her father that Gabe had returned each one personally. No wonder he'd never married…she'd hurt him that deeply.

She wished she hadn't gone down this road, but she couldn't turn around. Thelma was watching her like a hawk.

The older woman put down her fork. "Do you know what I think now?"

She couldn't bear the memories. "No, and I don't—"

Leaning closer, Thelma whispered so that only Cassie would hear. "I think Gabe's been waiting for you."

"Don't say that, Thelma."

"He loved you, Cassie. I know him. He's loyal."

"But I hurt him terribly."

"You were a scared, motherless girl," she said gently. "How old were you? Seventeen?"

"Old enough to know better." Cassie set down the fork. Her tea had gone cold and the cake made her sad.

"It *was* awful," Thelma replied. "But Gabe doesn't hold grudges. I saw his face when he learned Luke belonged to you. He seemed—"

"Bitter?" Cassie said.

"I was going to say tender."

He had been tender with her on the bench. He'd been wonderful with Luke, too. If he'd let her apologize, maybe they could be friends. But he'd slammed that door shut. She felt buried alive.

"I don't know what to do." She felt trapped at the table, stuck to her chair. "I've tried to talk to him, but he won't listen."

Thelma freshened Cassie's tea, then her own. "That's the problem with apologies. They're hard to make and hard to accept."

"Maybe," she said. "But I feel so guilty."

Before Thelma could reply, the door to the café swung open. In walked Maude Drake with her husband

and son. William Drake owned the bank. Billy Drake had a new haircut and a smug gleam in his eyes. The meeting couldn't have occurred at a worse time. Talk of Gabe had left Cassie reeling.

Thelma turned to the Drakes. "Maude, William. It's nice to see you. You remember Cassie, don't you?"

Bless her good intentions, but Thelma was out of her mind. Next to Gabe, Cassie had hurt Maude more than anyone in Guthrie Corners. They'd been the same age, competing for the same boys. Cassie had been a beauty and she'd flaunted it. Maude had a simple prettiness, but Cassie had called her "Mule Face." For a while, the name had stuck. She'd have blurted an apology now, but she felt certain Maude would cause a scene.

The Drakes gave Thelma a curt nod, exchanged quiet words and left the restaurant. Millie let out a loud sigh, put her hands on her hips and glared at Cassie. "What you did in Chicago ain't none of my business, Cassie Higgins. But—"

"It's O'Rourke now," Cassie said. "*Mrs*. O'Rourke."

Millie snorted. "It should have been Mrs. Wyatt! What you did to Gabe—"

Thelma intervened. "Millie, stop it."

"And that boy of yours! He's a *brat*."

Cassie pushed to her feet. "You can insult me all you want, but I will *not* tolerate you calling my son names."

"Fine," Millie declared. "But whatever you do, keep him away from my café. *Windows* are expensive."

So the news had already spread. Cassie felt weak in the knees. Thelma stood and put an arm around her waist. "Both of you," she said. "Shouting doesn't help anyone."

"It helps me," Millie declared. "Why that—"

The door opened again. When Cassie saw Gabe, she thought she might be sick. Ashamed and trembling, she ran for the door.

Twenty minutes later, Gabe set the picnic hamper on his work desk. It held covered dishes from Millie's cafe, but what he wanted most—answers—didn't fit in a wicker basket. Why had Cassie run away at the sight of him? It was none of his business, but he'd smelled trouble the instant he'd opened the restaurant door. When he'd asked Thelma and Millie if anyone needed help, they'd clammed up. They'd also given him two distinct but familiar looks. Millie had given him the "poor Gabe" look. It usually came with whispering behind his back. *Poor Gabe… Did you hear? That foolish girl jilted him!*

Thelma's eyes had held pity, too. But she'd been focused on Cassie. When she'd turned to Gabe, he'd seen what he called the "Mama" look. That particular spark belonged to mothers of marriage-minded daughters. Thelma didn't have a daughter of her own—she'd raised three boys—but she kept an eye out for the single women at Guthrie Corners Church. She'd given up on Gabe a long time ago, but today she'd looked inspired again.

He refused to think about why. Neither did he want to think about Cassie fleeing the café with her face in a knot. She was none of his concern. Luke, on the other hand, needed his full attention. Tonight he'd get it.

Gabe had left his deputy, Peter Hughes, filling out

the daily journal while he fetched supper. He turned to the desk across from his bigger one. "Go on home, Pete."

The young man shoved to his feet. "Don't mind if I do. The wife's making chicken and dumplings."

A newlywed, Pete bragged every day about his wife's cooking. He'd invited Gabe for supper a few times, but those evenings had been tedious. Married couples, especially young ones that gawked at each other, reminded him of Cassie and the life he'd been denied.

As Pete walked out the door, Gabe looked into the cell. He saw Luke on the cot on his back, still staring at the ceiling. Gabe had often thought of writing a message up there, maybe a Bible verse or just "Caught you looking." He had a plan tonight. If Luke minded his manners, he'd get dessert. If he acted like a mule, he wouldn't. Gabe wanted to make it easy for the boy to behave, so he used his friendliest tone.

"Hey, Luke," he called. "Are you hungry?"

"Nope."

So the boy wanted to play tough… Fine, Gabe thought. He was older, wiser and he'd once been a twelve-year-old boy with a bottomless pit for a stomach. Luke was armed with only a bad attitude. Gabe had an arsenal of meat loaf, mashed potatoes, gravy, corn and chocolate cake. He spoke to the boy through the bars. "Let me know if you change your mind."

He opened the basket, put the food on his desk and unwrapped the napkin from his plate. In the drafty jail, the aroma would reach the kid in seconds.

Next he jangled the silverware. "If you get hungry,

Luke, you need to wash up. There's a full pitcher on the shelf and a washbowl under the cot."

His own hands were clean enough, so he sat down and took the first bite of meat loaf. He usually read the Guthrie Corners Gazette while he ate, so he snapped it open now, folded it back and set it down so he could eat and read at the same time. Three bites later, he heard the trickle of water from the pitcher, looked up and saw Luke filling the washbowl. The sight of the kid's narrow shoulders and gangly arms filled Gabe with memories.

I want kids, Cassie.

Me, too.

She'd looked solemn as she'd replied. He'd attributed her reaction to shyness at the thought of babies being conceived. Now he wondered if something else had made her reluctant.

Fool!

He had to stop wondering about the past. With Cassie's son ten feet away, the challenge bordered on impossible. In order to help Luke, he had to get to know the boy. The effort meant listening to him, even asking questions.

How did you like Chicago?

Tell me about your friends.

What happened to your father?

No way would Gabe ask that last question. It was the most important, but the answers needed to come from Cassie, not a confused boy.

When Luke finished washing, he faced Gabe. The boy had his mother's dark hair, the shape of her face. His eyes, though, had come from his father. They were

brown and held a glint. Judging by Luke's age, it hadn't
taken long for Cassie to latch on to another man. Had
O'Rourke charmed her? Or had she truly been in love?
He didn't know which would be easier to forgive—
foolishness or sincerely loving another man.

Gabe thought of inviting the boy to sit at the desk but
decided against it. Freedom would taste sweeter after a
full night behind bars. He put Luke's meal on a tray—
no cake yet—bent down and slid it through an opening
in the grate at the bottom of the cell. The boy looked at
the food on the floor and glowered. No man liked to
bend down. Neither did twelve-year-old boys, but
humility was part of Luke's lesson. Even so, Gabe
didn't believe in embarrassing a man. To give the boy
some dignity, he turned his back and walked to his desk.
As he sat, he heard Luke lift the tray and carry it to the
cot.

Some jailhouses fed prisoners gruel as punishment,
but Gabe didn't see the benefit. He'd locked up men of
the worst kind, but most were trail trash who hadn't
eaten a square meal in days. A full belly reminded a man
of what he'd traded for thievery, whiskey and bad
habits. He kept a Bible in the cell, too. More than a few
hardened souls had cracked it open. One had wept like
a baby and asked Gabe to pray with him. It had been a
humbling experience for them both.

As he ate his supper, Gabe scanned the newspaper.
The words blurred into nonsense, mostly because he
kept hearing Luke's fork against the tin plate. Judging
by the eager scrapes, silence and hunger had softened the
boy's attitude. Gabe had already told him about his

Get 2 Books FREE!

Steeple Hill Books,
publisher of inspirational romance fiction, presents

Love Inspired
HISTORICAL
INSPIRATIONAL HISTORICAL ROMANCE

A new series of historical love stories that promise romance, adventure and faith!

FREE BOOKS!
Get two free books by acclaimed, inspirational authors!

FREE GIFTS!
Get two exciting surprise gifts absolutely free!

2 FREE BOOKS

▲ To get your 2 free books and 2 free gifts, affix this peel-off sticker to the reply card and mail it today!

GET 2 FREE BOOKS!

HURRY!
Return this card today to get **2 FREE Books** *and 2* **FREE** *Bonus Gifts!*

Love Inspired

HISTORICAL
INSPIRATIONAL HISTORICAL ROMANCE

YES! *Please send me the 2 FREE Love Inspired® Historical books and 2 FREE gifts for which I qualify. I understand that I am under no obligation to purchase anything further, as explained on the back of this card.*

affix
free
books
sticker
here

102 IDL EVLA

302 IDL EVNM

FIRST NAME

LAST NAME

ADDRESS

APT.#

CITY

STATE/PROV.

ZIP/POSTAL CODE

Steeple Hill®

◀ **DETACH AND MAIL CARD TODAY!** ▶

® and ™ are trademarks owned and used by the trademark owner and/or its licensee. © 2008 STEEPLE HILL BOOKS

(LIH-LA-09)

Steeple Hill Reader Service — Here's How It Works:

Accepting your 2 free books and 2 free gifts places you under no obligation to buy anything. You may keep the books and gifts and return the shipping statement marked "cancel." If you do not cancel, about a month later we will send you 4 additional books and bill you just $4.24 each in the U.S. or $4.74 each in Canada. That is a savings of at least 20% off the cover price. It's quite a bargain! Shipping and handling is just 25 cents per book. You may cancel at any time, but if you choose to continue, every other month we'll send you 4 more books, which you may either purchase at the discount price...or return to us and cancel your subscription. *Terms and prices subject to change without notice. Sales tax applicable in N.Y. Canadian residents will be charged applicable provincial taxes and GST. Offer not valid in Quebec. All orders subject to approval. Books received may not be as shown. Credit or debit balances in a customer's account(s) may be offset by any other outstanding balance owed by or to the customer. Please allow 4 to 6 weeks for delivery. Offer available while quantities last.

If offer card is missing write to: Steeple Hill Reader Service, 3010 Walden Ave., P.O. Box 1867, Buffalo, NY 14240-1867

BUSINESS REPLY MAIL
FIRST-CLASS MAIL   PERMIT NO. 717   BUFFALO, NY

POSTAGE WILL BE PAID BY ADDRESSEE

STEEPLE HILL READER SERVICE
3010 WALDEN AVE
PO BOX 1867
BUFFALO NY 14240-9952

NO POSTAGE
NECESSARY
IF MAILED
IN THE
UNITED STATES

"sentence," but they hadn't talked about putting in the window.

He pushed his plate aside. "So Luke, what do you know about carpentry?"

The boy shrugged. "Nothing."

"Ever build anything?"

"Like what?" He sounded suspicious.

"I don't know." Gabe had built lots of things. He'd been the man of the family from the age of ten. "I made a rifle rack when I was your age."

Luke scraped the last of his gravy, then looked up with a scowl. "I don't know how to do nothin' like that."

"*Anything* like that," Gabe corrected.

"I know." The kid sighed. "My ma's always telling me stuff like that."

"She's a good woman." He hadn't meant to go down that road, but Luke had gone first.

"She's all right," the boy said. "It's just…"

"Just what?" Gabe prodded.

"I miss my pa."

Gabe did *not* want to hear about the man who'd given Cassie this child. Anger coursed through his veins—at her, at O'Rourke—but he tamped it down. Only Luke mattered. If he had to bear a few lashes from the whip of jealousy, so be it.

"What happened to him?" he said quietly.

The boy shrugged. "I don't know."

As much as Gabe wanted to let the subject drop, he couldn't leave Luke twisting in the wind. The boy had a haunted look that Gabe knew all too well. The "whys" of life couldn't always be answered, but neither could they be forgotten. For Luke's sake, he decided to push.

"Did he leave you and your ma?"

The boy shook his head. "We left in the middle of the night. I didn't get to say goodbye."

So Cassie had left her husband the same way she'd left him, suddenly and secretly. He wondered how long ago she'd left, but he had no business quizzing Luke about his parents' marriage. On the other hand, Cassie had answers… all of them. She also had a son who bore scars. Luke, he decided, had been in jail long enough.

Gabe shoved to his feet, fetched the key and opened the door. "We've got chocolate cake for dessert. Want some?"

"Yeah!"

Just as he'd hoped, he'd taken the kid by surprise. Even four hours in a cell was enough to make freedom sweet. Luke put his plate on the tray and carried it out of the cell. He could have been at home clearing the table after supper. Gabe had no doubts about Cassie's commitment as a mother. Luke was a troubled boy, but he knew right from wrong. He had good manners and spoke as if he did his homework.

Gabe indicated the chair across from his own. As the boy sat, Gabe passed him the cake and a fork. As they ate, they talked about hammers and nails, glass, glue and how to use a saw. Gabe had a good time, but he knew that tonight, as he dozed on the cot and listened to Luke's soft snores, he'd be thinking of Cassie. Until now, he'd denied his need for answers. He'd learned to live without them, but for Luke's sake, he needed to ask about her husband.

For his own, he had to know why she'd left him at the altar. This Sunday after church, he'd ask.

Chapter Three

The last place on earth Cassie wanted to be on Sunday morning was the church where she'd jilted Gabe, but she had to bring Luke to the service. As part of his "sentence," he had to put away the hymnals and sweep the floor under Reverend Hall's supervision.

Getting Luke up for church had been a battle, but she'd had an even harder time getting herself ready. After Friday's embarrassment at the café, she'd stayed hidden in her store. Today she'd have to face Millie, Maude and worst of all, Gabe. She had to thank him for helping Luke. She dreaded getting a cold shoulder, but it had to be done. By doing the repair on Saturday, he'd spared her the humiliation of sitting in church with a broken window covered by boards.

As she and Luke walked into the sanctuary, her son pointed to the window he'd repaired. "There it is."

Cassie knew the value of praise. "You did a good job."

"Gabe showed me what to do."

Cassie could have wept at the pride in her son's voice. Even if Ryan O'Rourke had been a decent human being, he wouldn't have taken the time for Luke. He'd been obsessed with his stage career…not to mention young actresses. In an afternoon, Gabe had given her son more than Ryan ever had.

With her head high, she guided Luke to the pew next to the new glass and sat. Sunlight fell across her green dress, turning it as pale as dry grass. The warmth loosened the muscles in her neck and she wondered if someday she'd feel forgiven for her mistakes. As she studied the altar, she saw a heavy table carved with grapevines and an empty cross high on the back wall. If she hadn't been desperate to avoid hostile stares, she'd have looked away. It was too easy to picture Gabe in a suit, standing in front of the table with a ring in his pocket…her ring.

Her cheeks flamed with the memory. What would it be like to hold up her head without an effort? To stop being Cassiopeia pinned to the sky with her neck bent in shame? Her throat tightened. She wanted to pray but didn't know where to start. Instead she listened to the murmur of voices as the congregation took their seats. Behind her, she heard the tap of boots coming down the aisle between the pews and the window. She didn't dare look up for fear of the man wearing them. She wanted to be composed when she faced Gabe, not struggling for an even breath.

The boots stopped at the edge of the pew. As a shadow fell across her lap, she heard Gabe's deep voice. "Good morning, Luke. Hello, Cassie."

"Good morning," she said.

"Hi, Gabe." Luke scooted over to make room for him. The boy had assumed Gabe wanted to sit with them. Cassie had no such presumption. Instead of moving closer to her son, she looked at Gabe.

He indicated the pew. "May I?"

"Of course." As she slid across the wood, Gabe lowered his tall body on to the seat. He had a well thumbed Bible in hand, the same one he'd owned for years.

He leaned forward and spoke quietly to Luke. "The window looks good."

"Yeah," said the boy.

Cassie searched for something hopeful to say. "It's a lot cleaner than the others."

Luke grimaced, but Gabe smiled. "Luke's next job is cleaning the rest of them. Isn't it, partner?"

The boy groaned. "I need a ladder."

"I'll get you one," Gabe said easily. "Rags, too."

Could reaching Luke be this simple? She'd known for years that he needed a father, but she'd learned a valuable lesson from Ryan's abuse. No father was better than a bad one. Sometimes she thought about remarrying for Luke's sake, but how could she? Deep down, she still loved Gabe. She always would, but she'd learned another lesson from her marriage. Never again would she depend on anyone. People changed, sometimes for the worse. Sometimes, like her mother, they died unexpectedly.

As the pianist struck the first chord of a hymn, Gabe tipped his head to the side and murmured so only she could hear. "I'd like to speak with you, Cassie. Right after church."

"About Luke?"

"No." His breath touched her ear. "It's about us."

Her stomach did a flip. At last she could apologize to Gabe. She couldn't think of a more fitting place for making amends than the church where she'd left him waiting. She nodded, then faced straight ahead. So did Gabe. The hymn, an old one called "Peace In The Valley," calmed her nerves. She had no hope that the slate could be wiped clean, but maybe today she could find peace of her own. Maybe they could be friends.

Gabe sang the hymn and read the Bible verse aloud with everyone else, but he didn't hear a word of Pastor Hall's sermon. It could have been about the weather for all he knew. Sitting next to Cassie had shot him back in time to the day she'd left. He'd stood in the church for an hour before Pastor Hall pulled him into his office and told him Cassie had gone missing. When the Reverend left to tell the congregation, Gabe's best man, a fellow deputy, had offered to buy him a drink. Gabe had said no. Whiskey numbed a man's misery, but it didn't cure it. Instead he'd gone alone to their future home where he'd found the note she'd slipped under the door. Sitting next to her now, he thought of the question he'd wanted to ask for fourteen years.

Why, Cassie? What made you leave?

Soon he'd have his answer, but what happened then? Her presence stirred the embers of an old dream, but he'd be a fool to breathe life into those feelings. If she ditched him again, he'd be the town laughingstock. Gabe had his pride, but he also loved Cassie and always would. He cared about Luke, too. They'd worked shoulder to shoulder fixing the window and he'd enjoyed himself. At times, he'd felt as if Cassie had never left and Luke were his son.

When Reverend Hall gave a loud "Amen," Gabe came to his senses. He'd made arrangements with the Reverend to watch Luke while he spoke with Cassie in the man's office. It seemed fitting.

At the end of the last hymn, the three of them remained seated until the crowd cleared. When the sanctuary was close to empty, Gabe stepped into the aisle. Cassie, looking nervous, passed him. He put a hand on Luke's shoulder. "Reverend Hall will show you where the broom is."

The boy furrowed his brows but didn't fight.

Cassie paused and murmured to Luke. "I need to speak with Deputy Wyatt. I'll find you when we're done. Don't leave without me."

"All right, Ma." The boy turned and rolled his eyes at Gabe, as if to say, *See, she treats me like a baby.*

Disrespectful or not, the gesture was an improvement over outright rebellion. Gabe knew boys. They reached an age where, now and then, they needed to be treated like men. He clapped a hand on Luke's thin shoulder. "I know how it is," he said. "But mind your manners."

Grinning, Luke followed his mother.

Cassie reached Reverend Hall first. After praising the sermon, she thanked him for helping Luke. The

Reverend clasped her hand. "My pleasure, Cassie. Please come back."

Instead of replying, she stepped into the vestibule. Reverend Hall greeted Gabe with a handshake, then led Luke to a closet to fetch a broom.

Gabe pointed Cassie down the hall to the Reverend's office. When they reached the closed door, he opened it and guided her inside. He'd been in the room a few times since their wedding day—when a man stumbled, he did well to admit it and move on—-but today the space looked exactly as it had all those years ago. Dust motes floated in the light coming through the window, and the bookcases were still bursting with odds and ends in addition to leather-bound volumes of wisdom.

Gabe indicated one of the two chairs in front of the desk. "Have a seat."

With her back to him, Cassie touched the arm of the chair. As he moved to pull it out for her, she turned abruptly. Their eyes met across a distance of inches. Neither moved. Neither breathed. Fourteen years melted like ice in July.

"Why, Cassie?" The words rasped from his lips. "Why did you leave like that? Not even a word—"

She pressed her hands to her cheeks. "I'm so sorry, Gabe. What I did to you is unforgivable. It was the worst mistake of my life. I—"

"Don't do this," he said with a rumble. "I just want an answer."

"But—"

"*Why,* Cassie? What did I do wrong?

"It wasn't you, Gabe. It was me. I…" She dropped down on the chair and looked at the rug. "I was stupid."

"That's not good enough and you know it." He didn't mean to sound harsh. He'd promised himself he'd be matter-of-fact, but looking at Cassie now—smelling her hair, seeing the tiny mole high on her cheek—his blood pounded in his ears.

As she knotted her hands into fists, her knuckles turned as white as his anger. If he'd been alone, he'd have punched the wall. Instead he walked to the window and looked at a field of swaying grass. He thought of the Shepherd's Psalm and lying in green pastures by still waters, valleys and shadows, and finally goodness and mercy following him all the days of his life. At the moment, he felt neither good nor merciful.

Behind him Cassie took a breath. "I didn't plan to leave. It just…happened."

Gabe clamped his jaw. "I need more than that. I *deserve* more."

"Yes, you do." Her skirt rustled as she stood. He felt her eyes on his back but didn't turn as she cleared her throat. "The night before the wedding, I was scared."

He'd been scared, too. "Everyone gets cold feet."

"Mine had turned to ice." Her voice wobbled. "What happened next didn't help. My father gave me my mother's diary. I felt as if she'd walked into the room, but then I started to read."

They were getting somewhere. "What did it say?"

As she peered over his shoulder, the glass caught a faded image of her face. She bit her lips, but they stayed gray as she spoke. "When I opened the book, I expected to hear my mother's voice in stories, maybe prayers. Instead she'd written in verse. Poems I guess, except they weren't pretty. She wrote about how much she regretted her life. She poured her misery into that book."

Gabe frowned. "That diary was personal. Your father had no business giving it to you."

"Maybe not, but he meant well."

"So you read the book and got scared," he said simply.

"Not exactly." Her eyes found his on the glass. "I read the book and realized I was seventeen years old. I'd lived here my whole life. Like my mother, I felt trapped. I had dreams, silly ones but they mattered at the time. Getting married felt all wrong. It was too soon, too…everything."

Gabe dragged his hand through his hair. How many times had Cassie suggested they wait a year? At least three that he recalled. Instead of listening to her worries, he'd cajoled her into a short engagement. And why? Because he'd been tired of waiting for the privileges of marriage. Like most celibate men, he knew all about the burning coals in the book of Proverbs. Instead of waiting twelve months, his impatience had cost him fourteen years.

"I should have told you to your face," she said. "But I was afraid you'd talk me into staying."

He turned and looked into her blue eyes. "I would have tried, that's for sure."

"And I'd have crumbled."

In more ways than one… She'd have stayed and felt forever trapped. She'd have stopped being Cassie and he wouldn't have understood.

Standing straight, she held his gaze. "Thelma expected me to get dressed at the parsonage. My father wanted to walk me to the church, but I told him I was meeting my bridesmaids first. Instead of going to Thelma, I left that horrible note at the house and took the next train."

There it was…a pushy groom, a nervous bride and a bad case of cold feet. From the distance of time, he saw his part in it. "It wasn't all your fault, Cassie. I pushed you too hard."

"Even so—"

"Don't punish yourself," he said gently. "It's over."

She swallowed hard. "Can you ever forgive me?"

He already had. "We both made mistakes. I'm sorry for being impatient. Let's forgive each other and move on."

"Thank you, Gabe." She dabbed at her tears with her sleeve. "It doesn't matter now, but I want you to know… Leaving was the stupidest thing I've ever done."

Leaving Guthrie Corners or leaving *him?* He didn't know, but he wanted to wipe her tears with his thumb. Before he could decide what to do, she squared her shoulders. "You've been great with Luke. I can't thank you enough."

Mention of the boy pulled Gabe back to the problems at hand. "He's a good kid. I've been wondering what happened to his father."

Her eyes blazed. "He's not in the picture."

"I figured that." He counted it as good riddance. "For Luke's sake, I'd like to know more. The boy misses him."

"How do you know?"

"He told me."

Cassie frowned. "I don't want to talk about it."

Neither did Gabe, but he needed the whole story. According to Luke, she'd left O'Rourke the way she'd left Gabe—in secret and without a goodbye. Had she been justified, or did she always run at the first sign of trouble? Gabe had to know. If she'd changed, they had a chance at a future. If not, he'd be her friend and nothing more. He didn't like using Luke to pry, but the boy had a stake in her answer.

He kept his voice low. "I can't help your son if I don't know what happened."

With a quiet dignity, she raised her chin. "Ryan O'Rourke was a philandering two-bit actor. He charmed me like a snake and I fell for it. We got married at City Hall and I count it as the second worst mistake of my life."

They both knew what the first one had been. "You left because he cheated on you?"

"No," she said, drawing out the word. "I left because he hit me."

"Oh, Cassie—"

"He threatened Luke, too."

When she walked to the window and touched the glass, he imagined a moth trapped in a jar, spent and still. He wanted to pound Ryan O'Rourke into the ground. The man wasn't fit to walk this earth, let alone claim Cassie for his wife. A good woman was God's most precious gift. A smart man cherished her. He lived for her and he'd die for her, too. And Luke… What had the boy witnessed?

Two steps brought Gabe to Cassie's side. Without a second thought, he put his arm around her shoulders. "You were smart to leave."

"Was I?"

"*Yes.*" Adultery. Assault. Ryan O'Rourke had thoroughly broken his vows. "How can you even doubt?"

A shudder raced up her spine. "Even with the infidelity, I'd have stayed for Luke's sake. You can see how much he needs a father."

"How old was he when you left?"

"Barely five," she said wistfully. "Ryan didn't fight the divorce, but only because I didn't ask for alimony. I worked as a bookkeeper to make ends meet. A neighbor watched Luke after school, but then he made new friends."

"And you came home to get him away from them."

"Exactly."

With his arm still around her, she tilted her face up and to the side. At the same instant, Gabe looked down. When her mouth parted in surprise, he trailed a finger down her cheek. Her breath caught and so did his. He wanted to kiss her… He wanted to go back to a week before the wedding and do things differently. Did Cassie share the same hope? He didn't know, but a kiss would reveal her answer.

Slowly, giving her time to say no, he angled his head above hers. When she stayed still, he cupped her chin. When her eyes drifted shut, he knew…then, suddenly a rock shattered the window.

Chapter Four

Broken glass…shattered dreams. Cassie pulled away from Gabe with her heart pounding and her eyes wide with shock. She'd almost kissed him. For a moment she'd gone back in time and been young and unencumbered. The broken glass at her feet was a sober reminder of Luke, why she'd come home and the sorry state of her reputation. She had nothing to give Gabe Wyatt except grief and public scorn, a point made clear by the glass sparkling at her feet.

As Gabe bolted through the office door, Cassie ran after him with thoughts of Luke flooding her mind. She wanted to believe the best of her son, but who besides Luke would break a window? She didn't think for a minute it had been an accident. Rocks didn't sprout wings and fly. Boys threw them.

Cassie caught up with Gabe as he trotted down the church steps. "How could he do that!" she cried. "After all you've done for him—"

"Don't jump to conclusions, Cassie."

To her, the evidence seemed overwhelming. Luke had become resentful after cleaning the church and retaliated. Or worse... Maybe he'd seen them about to kiss. Her stomach knotted. How would she explain *that* to her son? Had anyone else seen them? It seemed unlikely. The bright sun would have turned the glass into a mirror. They'd been in the shadows, but perhaps someone had seen them slip alone down the hall and had jumped to the wrong conclusion.

As they crossed the churchyard, Cassie scanned the path to town for Luke but saw nothing, not even dust. She turned to the meadow stretching north and saw only waving grass. To the west lay rolling hills that turned into distant, insurmountable mountains. She felt as if Luke were lost to her forever.

Pastor Hall approached from the side of the building with his black robe billowing behind him. He had his hand on Billy Drake's shoulder. Behind Billy, Cassie saw Maude and her husband dressed in their Sunday best, a black suit for Mr. Drake and a prim gray gown for Maude. They looked as polished as silver candlesticks. Cassie, dressed in a green frock with leg o' mutton sleeves, felt like a peacock.

Maude's gaze shot from her to Gabe and back again. Her lips quirked into a haughty half smile Cassie recognized from their youth. Maude looked ready to accuse her of everything from low morals to being a bad mother.

Cassie opened her mouth to apologize to Reverend Hall for Luke, but Gabe took command of the conversation. He hadn't worn his gun to church, but he had his badge and a natural authority.

He looked straight at Billy. "What happened?"

Billy had a chin as haughty as his mother's. "Luke broke the window. I saw him do it."

Gabe made a humming sound. "That's funny."

"Why?" Billy asked.

"Because I was looking out the window."

Cassie sealed her lips. Gabe had been looking at *her*, though she supposed a lawman was allowed to bend the truth in the course of seeking it.

Billy shrugged. "He threw the rock. You must have blinked or something."

Cassie held back a cringe. *Or something* would include nearly kissing her. His lips had been an inch from hers. She'd seen gentleness in his eyes, then a question and an offering of sorts. She'd been ready to grab that gift and hold tight, but the rock had brought her to her senses. People in Guthrie Corners hated her, especially Maude who looked as smug as a debutante in her new hat. Cassie recognized the haughty look because she'd seen it fourteen years ago in her own mirror. Back then, she'd thought she owned this town. Not anymore. She'd never hold her head high again.

She refocused on Gabe. He was looking at Billy with a flat expression that belied nothing. "What exactly did you see?"

Billy shrugged. "He picked up a rock and threw it."

"I wonder why?" Gabe asked.

"I dunno."

If Luke had spoken in that tone, Cassie would have told

him to answer Deputy Wyatt's question *right now*. Maude, though, glared at Gabe as if he'd called Billy a liar.

Gabe didn't seem to notice. "It just seems odd. When someone throws a rock, there's usually a reason."

"Maybe he was mad."

"At what?" Gabe sounded conspiratorial, as if he were including Billy in a secret. Cassie flashed back to the jail where he'd used silence to break Luke. Billy had a different personality and different motives. Gabe, she realized, had become an expert in setting verbal traps. She'd have to be careful. If she didn't watch her words, she'd end up telling him that she still loved him.

Billy seemed eager to help. "I don't know why he got mad, but I saw him break the window. I told him to stop, but he ran away."

"What exactly did you say?" Gabe asked.

Billy's cheeks turned from pale to pink. Looking down, he played with the grass with the toe of his shoe. "I just said, 'Stop.'"

Cassie knew a half truth when she heard one.

So did Gabe. "Just stop, huh?"

"Yeah." Billy sounded defiant.

Gabe crossed his arms. "So you *saw* Luke throw the rock. And you said 'Stop.'"

"That's right."

Gabe stared straight into Billy's eyes. "You know what I can't figure out?"

"What?" Billy sounded defensive.

"Why would Luke throw a rock when you were

standing right there? Unless *maybe* something else happened."

Billy's face raised his chin. "I *saw* it. I swear it!"

Whenever Luke talked like that, Cassie knew he was hiding the truth. He'd inherited his father's flare for drama. She glanced at the Drakes and saw nothing but pride. Reverend Hall hadn't said a word, but she looked at him now and saw the sad expression of a wise man. He, too, suspected Billy of lying.

Gabe's eyes glinted. "You need to 'fess up, Billy. Now."

Maude broke in with a shrill voice. "My son is *not* a liar, Gabe. You know that!"

The three of them went back a lot of years, but Maude's use of Gabe's first name struck Cassie as out of place in front of Billy. It undercut Gabe's authority. It also put Cassie in her place. *I know him…I belong here.* Cassie no longer belonged in this town, but she'd do anything for Luke. Right now, that included standing shoulder to shoulder with Gabe.

Ignoring Maude, he turned to Mr. Drake. "Sir, I believe your son is holding back."

The man's eyes glinted. "Perhaps you should speak to *Miss* O'Rourke's son—"

"It's *Mrs.* O'Rourke," Cassie insisted.

Maude lifted her chin. "Of course, it is."

Her words dripped like honey, sweet but sticky enough to cause a mess. Cassie wanted to tell Maude to jump in a lake, but antagonizing the woman would do no good. Cassie had made mistakes, but she'd done her best to clean up the mess. Why couldn't Guthrie Corners give her a chance?

Gabe stayed focused on Mr. Drake. "I'll speak to Luke, but I was hoping Billy could provide some information."

Mr. Drake opened his pocket watch, read the time, then shut it again. "Speak to him if you must, but we don't have all morning."

"I do," Gabe said easily.

With those two small words, Gabe had announced he'd do whatever it took to find the truth. Until now, no one had ever believed in Luke or in Cassie. It felt good.

With her chin up, she followed Gabe's stare to Billy. She guessed the boy to be Luke's age, but he was maturing faster. Luke had grown two inches since Christmas, but he still had the stick-like body of a boy. Billy was taller, heavier and far more confident. In a fight, Billy would win hands down. He also looked just like his mother, a fact Cassie tried to overlook.

Gabe kept his voice mild. "Where were you standing when you saw Luke throw the rock?"

"By that tree." He pointed to a cottonwood.

"Why?"

"My mother told me to wait for her. She had to speak with Mrs. Hall about something important."

Cassie heard Maude's arrogance in the boy's voice. There'd been no need to inform them of his mother's importance. Everyone knew Maude ran Guthrie Corners. Cassie felt sorry for Billy. Someday he'd learn that not everyone is impressed by a high-and-mighty attitude. Cassie had learned that lesson herself. In a blink she'd gone from a promising actress to a lowly bookkeeper.

Gabe kept pressing Billy. "Did you two speak at all?"

Billy paused. "Sort of."

Cassie could hardly stand the silence, but Gabe let it build until the tension crackled. Billy looked ready to break, but Maude interrupted. "Boys will be boys. There's nothing more to say."

"*And* we have a luncheon engagement," her husband added.

Gabe's expression went from blank to hard. "I'm done with Billy. You folks go and enjoy your meal."

Right in front of them, he touched Cassie's arm with reassurance. "Don't worry. I'll find Luke."

His eyes met hers with the intensity she recalled from fourteen years ago…from fourteen minutes ago when his mouth had come within an inch of hers. He'd used her first name, too. It was a claiming of sorts, a statement that she belonged as much as Maude did. Cassie wanted to accept that gift, but she feared it. Maude hated her. William Drake owned the bank. They had the power to make Gabe's life miserable.

Looking at Gabe now, she felt the weight of every mistake she'd ever made. She couldn't bear the thought of causing this good man any more grief. For his own good, she had to keep him at arm's length. She stepped back, breaking his touch but not her gaze. "Thank you, Deputy."

The corners of his mouth lifted, but the smile stopped short of a grin. "You're welcome, Mrs. O'Rourke."

Reverend Hall broke in. "Thelma always has refreshments after church. Cassie, you're welcome to join us.

Maude, William…I know you have an engagement, but a cup of tea wouldn't spoil your meal."

The couple traded a look, then Mr. Drake shook his head. "No thank you, Reverend. Not today."

Not today had meant not with *her*. Cassie didn't want to sip tea with Maude any more than Maude wanted to share an hour with her. She had intended to make her own excuses and she still did. She needed to look for Luke.

Reverend Hall looked pointedly at Maude. "Another time, then."

"Of course." Her voice dripped with cool disdain. After a glance at her husband, she slipped her hand in the crook of his elbow and looked at Cassie as if she were dirt. "Have a nice day, *Mrs*. O'Rourke."

The Drakes walked down the path to town with Billy at their side. When they were several feet away, the boy looked over his shoulder with a smirk. Cassie saw red. Gabe and Reverend Hall traded a look but said nothing. The arrogant look on Billy's face reminded Cassie that she had a job to do as a mother.

"I should go, too." she said to Reverend Hall. "Luke might have gone home and the apartment's locked."

"I'll check for you," Gabe said.

"No, I'd rather—"

"Stay here, Cassie." The invitation came from Reverend Hall. If anyone had cause to judge her, it was this elderly minister with yet another broken window. Cassie could hardly look him in the eye. "I'm sorry about Luke and the window. I just don't know what to do."

Gabe interrupted. "I do."

"So do I," said the reverend.

Cassie gave a small laugh. "I'm glad, because I don't know my son at all right now."

Both men chuckled. She didn't see the humor, but the deep rumbling gave her comfort. Reverend Hall smiled at her. "Thelma and I raised three sons. Luke's being a boy. Granted, he's troubled and bitter and can't go around breaking windows, but he's not a bad seed. No child is."

"Especially not Luke," Gabe added. "I'll find him and we'll have a talk. My gut tells me Billy left out a few details."

"Mine, too," said the Reverend.

These men, both strong and honorable, believed in her son. A lump pushed into Cassie's throat. She'd never felt such acceptance. When she looked at Gabe, she saw the man she'd almost kissed. He'd be a good father, but in the next breath she called herself a fool. She had no right to such a thought.

His expression stayed neutral. "I'll find Luke and bring him here. Wait for me."

"All right," she answered.

Gabe bid the reverend goodbye, then strode down the path to town. Cassie couldn't take her eyes off his straight back and wide shoulders. Dressed in his Sunday best, he cut a fine figure of a man. She couldn't help but wonder why he hadn't married. She'd hurt him, but surely he'd healed with time. People learned to live with their scars. Cassie had. Those marks were deep and she'd never marry again because of them, but she'd made a good life for herself and her son.

Reverend Hall touched her back. "Let's have some of Thelma's lemon cake."

"I'd like that," Cassie replied.

As they crossed the yard, Cassie took in the white-washed porch and the pots of geraniums on the steps. It looked picture-perfect, but Thelma had often been candid with Cassie's mother and Cassie had heard their conversations. This house had known the heartache that came with a rebellious child. Thelma's middle son had settled out West but not before running wild. He'd even done jail time in the Laramie Territorial Prison.

Walking with the reverend, Cassie thought of his words about children and bad seeds. He'd voiced her deepest fear. Luke had his father's blood and his looks, even his taste for sweets. Did he also have his tendency to deceit? Cassie's biggest mistake as a woman had been jilting Gabe. Her biggest mistake as a mother had been choosing Ryan O'Rourke to father her child.

She lifted her chin and looked at the reverend's profile. Gray hair crowned him with wisdom. The hint of a smile gave her hope.

"Do you believe what you said, Reverend? That no child is a bad seed?"

"I do."

"Even when they do bad things?"

He chuckled. "That's when I believe it the most. If love covers a multitude of sins—and I believe it does—then the lack of it leaves those sins uncovered. They fester. I don't know what happened to Luke's father—"

"He turned violent," she said simply. "I left him for fear of our lives."

"So Luke's confused and angry."

"I try, but—"

"You're succeeding, Cassie. Believe that."

"I wish I could."

They'd reached the bottom of the porch steps. Instead of going up to the house, he stopped and faced Cassie, waiting in silence until she raised her face and looked into his eyes. They were silver like his hair, faded with time but bright with kindness. "Imagine where Luke would be without you."

She thought of the trash can he'd lit on fire, the day he'd been sent home from school for fighting. Shivering with dread, she took a breath. "He'd be running wild in Chicago."

"But he's not, is he?"

"No." She smiled at the irony. "He's running wild *here*."

"Where we can all watch him," the reverend said. "Luke is missing his natural father's love, but yours is strong. So is the love of the Lord for his children. That love covers everything—Luke's sins, your mistakes. Whatever you need."

"I want to believe that—"

"So do it," he said with force. "God brought you home to us. He's not going to leave you now."

Oh, how she wanted to believe this elderly man… The thought of being home—a place where she had friends and hope, even love—made her eyes sting with unshed tears. Standing by the steps, she smelled Thelma's lemon cake. Grass rippled in the distance and she imagined lying down in it and resting in the sun. She longed to set down the weight on her shoulders but couldn't. She had a store to run and a boy to raise. She'd made a mess of her life and had to live with it.

"I wish I could believe you," she said to the reverend.

"Why can't you?"

"Because I've hurt people. I don't deserve—"

"Pshaw."

He'd come as close to cussing as she'd ever heard a preacher come. Startled, she looked into his eyes and saw a fire she didn't expect. "This isn't about what *you* deserve, Cassie. If God gave *me* what *I* deserve, I'd be staked to an anthill and left to die in the sun. I've hated. I've lied. I've committed murder in my heart."

When she looked shocked, he gave an impish smile. "And that's just since this morning."

"I don't understand—"

"Sin is sin," he said easily. "To God, it's all the same. There aren't big ones and little ones. We *all* fall short and don't you ever forget it. We're also God's children. What keeps us safe is love—our heavenly Father's love—and a mother's love here on earth. You're doing that for Luke."

"Am I?" She clutched her reticule. She needed the hankie but didn't want to acknowledge the tears.

"Absolutely," the reverend said. "Now come sit with Thelma and me. I have a story for you about another mother, a woman in the Old Testament named Rizpah."

"Who is she?" Cassie had never heard the name.

"She was one of Saul's concubines."

As Reverend Hall guided her to a chair, Cassie thought about what that meant. As a concubine, Rizpah could have been used and abused. She wouldn't have had a husband. "Did Rizpah have a son?"

"Two of them." He sat at a right angle to Cassie. "But she saved five others as well as her own."

"From what?"

The door opened and Thelma came out with a tray of refreshments. As she set it on the low table, Cassie stood and they hugged.

"I saw the window." Thelma grimaced in sympathy. "Where's Luke?"

"He ran off," she replied. "Gabe's looking for him."

With a final squeeze, Thelma released her and they both sat, taking chairs that faced the path to town where they'd see Gabe—and hopefully Luke—returning to the parsonage.

Thelma gave an indignant sigh. "They better show up soon. Lemon cake is Gabe's favorite."

Cassie hadn't known. In the days of their courtship, she'd made him an apple pie for a picnic. He'd told her it was the best he'd ever eaten.

Reverend Hall leaned forward, lifted the teapot and filled all three cups. Without a word, he added a spoonful of sugar to his wife's cup and handed it to her. "I was about to tell Cassie about Rizpah."

"That's a hard story," Thelma replied.

"Tell me." Cassie raised the steaming cup to her lips. She didn't think a Bible story could lift her spirits, but she needed a distraction. She wished now that she'd gone looking for Luke herself. Not with Gabe... She could still feel where he'd touched her arm. Sitting with the Halls made her think of the things she'd never have…a husband who knew how she took her tea, someone who'd see her with gray hair.

Reverend Hall set down his cup. "Rizpah gave Saul two sons. Frankly, I don't think he was the best leader. He got into it with the Gibeonites, and it was left to King David to make things right. For retribution, the Gibeonites asked for the death of seven of Saul's sons."

"Oh, no." Cassie whispered.

"That's right," the reverend said. "Rizpah's boys were in the lot. So were the five sons of Merab. The Gibeonites put them to death and hung up their bodies for the buzzards. Do you know what Rizpah did?"

Cassie knew what *she'd* do. She'd have cut down the bodies and given them a decent burial, but Rizpah had lived in a different time. She'd been a concubine, a woman at the beck and call of others.

"Tell me," she said to the reverend.

"For five months, she stayed by those seven bodies. Every minute of every day, she chased away the buzzards until David finally buried the bodies. That's love, Cassie. Those bodies stank. They were repulsive and decaying, but that's what a mother does… She loves her children when they're at their most unlovable."

Thelma spoke in a hush. "When our boy was in Laramie, I wrote him every week. Even when he didn't write back, I sent letters."

The couple shared a sad look, then the reverend smiled. "Those were hard days, but do you know where he is now?"

"California," Cassie replied.

Pride lit the reverend's eyes. "He's in Los Angeles,

married with a couple of kids. He runs a grocery business."

Thelma smiled. "They sent us photographs for Christmas. He's got two little girls who look just like him."

Cassie thought of her worries about bad seeds. Maybe the reverend had a point. "I'm happy for him," she said.

Reverend Hall cleared his throat. "I want to say one more thing about Rizpah and it's this… She didn't protect just her own sons. She protected all seven of those bodies."

He paused, giving Cassie time to think. She flashed to Billy's smirk as he looked over his shoulder. It gave her chills. "You mean Billy."

"That's right," the reverend said. "He's on a crooked road. It looks straight to William and Maude, but it's not. I'm hoping you'll do something for me, Cassie."

"What's that?"

"While you're fighting the buzzards for Luke, say a prayer for the Drakes."

Why should she pray for Maude? The woman had started the untrue rumor that Cassie had never married Luke's father. She'd also insinuated that Cassie cheated her customers. "I'll pray for Billy," she said diplomatically.

The reverend raised his silver brows. "*And* Maude."

Cassie sat in silence. Thelma's cup clinked on the saucer. A bird chirped. The breeze stirred in a low hush until she sighed. "All right, I'll try."

"Good," said Reverend Hall. "Let's eat that cake."

As Thelma sliced into the rounded edge, Cassie

stared down the path to town. A man appeared in the distance and she recognized Gabe. Luke was nowhere to be seen, yet she still wanted to run down the path…to Gabe. She thought of what the reverend had said about love covering a multitude of sins. Thanks to Maude, Cassie's sins were laid bare to everyone in Guthrie Corners. Until she made peace with the town, she had nothing to offer Gabe except a bad reputation, heartache and a boy who broke windows. She'd never succeed as a businesswoman. She'd be dependent on him, a thought she couldn't abide under any circumstances.

If she loved Gabe—and she did—she'd be wise to cover up her feelings until she could stand on her own two feet. Holding back a sigh, she watched as he neared the parsonage. If it weren't for Luke, she'd have excused herself and gone home. Instead she sat straight in her chair. For Luke, she'd do anything…even eat cake with Gabe Wyatt.

Chapter Five

Gabe knew every inch of Guthrie Corners, but he hadn't found Luke. A boy who didn't want to be found could hike a mile in any direction and disappear into the land. Luke had been in town long enough to know about the cave south of town, the one by the stream where Gabe had proposed to Cassie. If he'd gone west, he'd find an abandoned house with a missing roof.

Gabe considered saddling his horse and taking a ride, but then he'd thought of Cassie and had another idea. If he borrowed the reverend's piano buggy, they could ride together. Knowing Cassie, she'd want to hunt for Luke. The ride would also answer the question hanging in his mind. After all these years, did she still love him? Had that near-kiss been about forgiveness alone, or had it been about the future?

Looking at her as he neared the parsonage, Gabe took in the tightness of her mouth and tried to read her thoughts. He couldn't discern them with his eyes, but he knew that a kiss would tell him what he wanted to know. He'd never stopped loving Cassie, but he'd tried. For a while he'd gone to socials and church picnics. He'd kissed his share of women and had courted one with thoughts of marriage. He'd ended it when they'd kissed and he'd found himself aching for Cassie.

His lips hadn't touched hers in Reverend Hall's office, but Gabe had felt the wanting. Did he want to risk the heartache? What would she do if he invited her to supper?

He had the engagement ring she'd left at the house.

He had a kitchen table big enough for eight.

He still had the dreams of a man in love. What he didn't have was a lick of common sense. Crazy or not, he wanted Cassie for his wife. Fourteen years was long enough to wait for the only woman he'd ever loved. As he climbed the porch steps, his pulse rushed at the sight of her stiff shoulders. In the reverend's office, she'd gone soft in his arms. The woman looking at him now had turned hard again. It made him love her all the more.

"You didn't find Luke," she said.

"No, but I have a few more places to look." He dropped down on the chair at a right angle to hers and looked at the reverend. "I'd like to check out the cave south of town. Would you mind if Cassie and I borrowed your buggy?"

"Not at all," he replied.

She let out a sharp breath, a sign that she recalled that spot as well as he did. He'd proposed to her by the rushing water on a day as bright as this one. It seemed like a fitting place to test the waters.

Thelma shoved a plate of lemon cake into his hand.

Gabe accepted it but left it untouched. Instead he turned his head to Cassie. "What do you say?"

She twisted her fingers into a knot. "When Luke comes home I should be there."

Gabe saw her point, but he wanted an answer to his question. He also thought it would do Luke good to be locked out for a while. Being hungry and alone inspired a boy—and a man—to ask himself the questions that made a difference.

"We'll be gone an hour," he said to her.

Their gazes met in an understanding that put them back in the reverend's office. Gabe had made his move by asking her to go for a ride with him. The next step belonged to Cassie. With the aroma of lemon cake tickling his nose, he waited for her to speak. As the seconds ticked by, he counted to fourteen and knew the waiting had just begun.

How long would it take him to win her heart? A lot longer than fourteen seconds or fourteen minutes. Not even fourteen hours would be enough… Fourteen days might do the trick, but it didn't matter. If she kissed him at the creek, he'd wait fourteen months for Cassie to trust him, even fourteen more years. But first she had to say yes to the buggy ride.

Cassie couldn't stand the sight of Gabe holding the plate of uneaten cake. Did he cook his own supper in the house he'd built for her? Or did he take all of his meals at Millie's? Watching him with his favorite dessert, denying himself for her sake, sent fresh waves of guilt from her heart to the tips of her fingers.

It broke her heart to think of that spot by the stream, yet it seemed like a fitting place to address unfinished business. Fourteen years ago she'd left Gabe with a wedding kiss hanging between them. She'd never leave him hanging again. When they reached the stream, she'd tell him the near-kiss had been a mistake. She hoped they could be friends for Luke's sake, but the future held nothing more.

"Eat," she said. "We'll go when you finish."

"I'm done." He set down the plate and stood.

Cassie rose and hugged Thelma. "I should help with the dishes."

"Nonsense."

The older woman released her with a nudge that sent her following the men to the stable. In minutes they'd hitched the reverend's gray mare to the buggy and Gabe had handed her up to the seat.

Neither spoke as they drove down the road behind the church. As they passed the poplar tree, she thought of Rizpah chasing away buzzards from the bodies of her sons. Cassie had the same passion for protecting Luke. Without it, she'd have never accepted Gabe's offer to return to the spot where he'd proposed. Did he really believe Luke would hide in the cave, or had he picked it today for another purpose?

When they reached the bend that put Guthrie Corners out of view, Gabe spoke in a low tone. "Try not to worry, Cassie."

"I can't help it."

"I know," he said easily. "But mark my words. Luke'll show up for supper."

She wanted to believe him, but Luke—like his father, like her—had an impetuous streak. "How can you be so sure?"

"Because he's a growing boy. They get hungry."

So did grown men…hungry for lemon cake and home-cooked meals. Hungry for companionship and the things she'd taken from Gabe when she'd fled to Chicago. In the distance she saw the outcropping of rocks that marked the cave. In spite of rain and snow, ice storms and hot summer days, the spot hadn't changed a bit. Neither had the man sitting next to her, staring straight ahead with a quiet strength she envied.

She could almost believe they were kids again, untouched by mistakes…except she had a wayward son, a heart full of guilt and a tarnished reputation. The buggy rattled over dry earth. The horse snorted and she heard the rippling of the stream as it came into view. Craning her neck, she searched for a sign of Luke but saw nothing.

"Let's check the cave," Gabe said.

He stopped the buggy on a patch of grass that sloped down to the stream, then came around and helped her down from the seat. Side by side, they walked along the rushing water until they reached the pile of boulders that formed a cave of sorts. As she peeked into the shadows, Cassie saw ashes, a whiskey bottle and cigarette butts, but no sign of her son. She didn't know whether to be relieved or dismayed.

She stood straight and looked back down the stream. "He's not here."

Gabe touched her arm. "We'll keep looking."

His touch shot her back in time to the day he proposed. She'd packed a picnic, but he'd been too nervous to eat. Like today, he'd left his dessert untouched. Instead he'd taken her hand and pulled her to her feet. He'd led her to the edge of the rushing stream where she'd perched on a rock. As she'd looked up, Gabe had dropped to one knee. A ring with a milky white opal, her birthstone, had gleamed between his fingers.

I love you, Cassie. Will you marry me?

Yes!

She'd wept as he'd slid the ring on her finger. He'd pulled her to her feet and kissed her until she'd been blind to everything but him. Over the next few months, she'd gotten her sight back and been afraid of what she'd seen. A future like her mother's…forgotten dreams and silent meals.

Cassie was afraid again—not of being hurt or feeling stifled—she feared for Gabe. The Drakes would make his life miserable. People would shun him as they'd shunned her. She knew how much it hurt to be a pariah. She also knew that Gabe valued his badge and the respect it earned. She couldn't take it away from him, so she faced him with the intention of never kissing him again. As his brown eyes searched her face, she almost lost her will. He looked both lazy and bold, as if he could read her confused thoughts and loved her anyway. For the first time in years, she felt beautiful and loved. He touched her arm and she felt weak all over. She didn't deserve this man's devotion, but she wanted it.

When he angled his head above hers, watching her to see what she'd do, she came to her senses. "We can't."

"Can't what?" he said lazily.

"You know *what*." She stepped back to put air between them. "What happened in Reverend Hall's office, it was a mistake."

"Who says?"

"I do." Using all her strength, she raised her chin. "We were caught up in the past."

"I wasn't."

They were two feet apart, nowhere close to touching but she felt pinned in place by his eyes alone. This was the man she'd left fourteen years ago, the one who scared her with his determination. The one who could break her will with a look alone. Not now, she told herself. Not anymore. Ryan O'Rourke had given her both bruises and a backbone.

"I mean it, Gabe. We can't."

"Can't what?" he repeated.

We can't be in love.

Except she'd already fallen for him. She couldn't deny her feelings any more than she could stop being Luke's mother. The stream rushed in the distance. She felt the heat of the sun on her back. She had to stay strong. "My mind's made up. I hope we can be friends, but it would be a mistake to pick up where we left off."

His eyes took on a hard shine. "How do you know?"

"I just do."

The stream chortled over the rocks. She heard the chirp of a bird, then the scuff of Gabe's boot on the dirt as he put his hands on his hips. Dressed in his Sunday best—a dark suit, a starched collar—he reminded her of a picture she'd seen of a gunfighter. He had the same glint in his eye and the same unmoving lips. To stop herself from talking, she turned her back.

An instant later, she felt his hands on her shoulders. Their shadows blended into a gray puddle, but she felt no pressure from his grip to turn around. She could smell his shaving soap and the sun's warmth on his coat. Every fiber in her being cried out for this man. She wanted to rest in his strong arms, but at what cost? She'd lose her independence and he'd suffer the shame of loving a pariah. Eventually he'd resent her. Blinking, she thought of Rizpah chasing away the buzzards from people she loved. Cassie had to chase the town crows away from Gabe, and she had to look him in the eye to do it. In a single motion, she pivoted and stepped back.

"I'm not worth it, Gabe."

His eyes hardened. "Who says?"

"*I* say."

She braced herself for a harsh retort, but the lines around his mouth softened. As his expression shifted from hard to wise, he let his hands fall loose at his side. "You made that decision for us once before. I didn't like it then, and I don't like it now."

"We don't have a future." She had to be firm, but the words had a tender ring.

"Is that what you want?"

"It is."

She'd lied and she'd done it boldly. Guilt flapped its ugly wings. Her neck hurt and she felt heavy all over. Gabe didn't budge. If he'd crowded her, she could have stepped back. If he'd touched her, she could have acted indignant. Instead he stood like an unmovable rock, one that held the heat of the sun and offered shelter from storms. She wanted to weep for all she'd given up and for what they couldn't have. Instead she raised her chin. "What do you want from me?" she said in a hush.

"I think you know."

As much as she hated silence, Cassie hated the truth even more. She knew exactly what Gabe wanted from her. Love. Trust. A future. She still loved him and she always would, but at what cost? After enduring Ryan's abuse, she'd never lean on anyone again. She wouldn't give up her independence for anything…or anyone. The silence spoke for her. What he wanted, she couldn't give.

Gabe let out a long sigh. "I guess that's my answer."

The stream rippled behind her. She felt like a rock buried in the mud, doomed to endure years of drought and flood. She couldn't move her feet.

His eyes faded with disappointment, but he still held out his hand. "Come on," he said gently. "I'll take you home."

Looking at his outstretched arm, she longed for a different future. Today he'd shown her nothing but goodness. He'd defended her son and forgiven her for the past. He'd offered her a future and accepted her rejection without a hint of pressure. Looking at him now, she felt like a sparrow being tempted by bread crumbs. A home… Love… A father for Luke. She'd never known such generosity, but her longing had to be denied. Ignoring Gabe's outstretched hand, she led the way to the buggy where she gathered her skirts to climb in. Gabe touched her elbow, lifting her with an easy strength. Cassie settled on to the leather, then faced him. "Thank you, Gabe. For everything."

"You're welcome."

Their eyes stayed locked. Her breath caught and he gripped her hand for one last time. Warmth seeped into her fingers and flowed all the way to her middle. Gratitude flooded to her heart and she wanted him to know how much he meant to her. With her heart overflowing, Cassie leaned to the side and sweetly kissed his cheek.

She'd kissed him. Eight hours had passed, but Gabe could still feel the tickle of her lips, the brush of silk against his cheek. The spot she'd kissed had grown stubbled as he'd walked around town searching for Luke in the places a boy would hide. Gabe had walked for hours. He wanted to find Luke for Cassie's sake, but mostly he'd needed to sort his thoughts. Just when he'd given up hope for their future, she'd kissed him. It hadn't been the kiss they'd started in Reverend Hall's office, but Gabe had the answer to his question. Cassie still loved him.

So why had she turned cold again? As he checked alleys for Luke, he'd thought about Ryan O'Rourke. The man should have been horsewhipped for beating his wife. He hadn't broken Cassie's spirit, but he'd left scars that ran deep. It made sense that she wouldn't trust easily. He'd have to work to earn it and that meant going slow and respecting her worries. While walking around town, he'd passed William Drake's bank. He'd been reminded of Maude and the ugly rumors she'd spread. If Cassie couldn't make a living, she'd be forced to leave Guthrie Corners…and him.

"Fool woman," Gabe muttered as he neared the sheriff's office. Didn't she realize he'd take care of her?

Worn out and hungry, Gabe went through the door, lit a lamp and saw a napkin-covered tray on his desk. He wondered if Cassie had left it until he raised the linen and saw Thelma's lemon cake and a hearty sandwich. She'd also left a note that said, "We're praying for you both."

"We need it," he said out loud. Twice he'd walked by Cassie's store. Both times she'd been standing in the window and had shaken her head, an indication that Luke hadn't come home. He'd resisted the urge to knock on her door. He could help her most by finding Luke, and he had to respect her request for friendship and nothing more. Once her situation settled down, he'd start courting her. Until then, he'd be wise to avoid the temptation to rush her.

Instead of saying grace over his meal, Gabe bent his head and prayed out loud for Cassie. "Be with her tonight, Lord. Keep her boy safe and guide me in my search for Luke. Grant me wisdom, Lord. And patience."

Gabe groaned at the last word. Patience tested him like nothing else. After a heartfelt plea for Luke's safety and for Cassie to know peace, he said, "Use me, Lord. Amen."

He ate the sandwich in silence, thinking of the hard ways God sometimes used a man. Men died for people they loved. Jesus had suffered a cruel and haunting death. Gabe would have willingly died for Cassie to spare her pain of any kind. He was doing it now…dying to his desire to go to her…dying to his own need for companionship so he could meet *her* needs for time and understanding.

I love her enough, Lord. I'll wait.

As he cut into the lemon cake, Gabe heard a train whistle. He stopped with the fork in midair. The Denver Special arrived every evening at ten o'clock and left after boarding new passengers.

"That's it," he said out loud. Luke wasn't just licking his wounds somewhere. He was planning to run away. Pushing back from his desk, he raced out the door for the train station.

Chapter Six

When the night fell and Luke still hadn't come home, Cassie put a lamp in the window with the hope of attracting him like a moth to flame. It hadn't worked. The mantel clock had struck every hour since dusk, each time adding a chime until it struck nine times. She had to face facts. Luke wouldn't be home tonight.

Shaking inside, she pulled her shawl tight around her shoulders. After leaving Gabe, she had walked through Guthrie Corners herself. She'd asked everyone she'd met if they'd seen Luke, but no one had. She'd even visited Miss Lindstrom, the schoolteacher, to ask about any boys Luke might have befriended. Just as she'd suspected, he didn't have anyone but himself.

Neither did she. She had nothing but the store. If business didn't improve, even that comfort would be taken from her. She'd have to sell the building and move back to Chicago. Her stomach filled with moths beating their wings. To Luke, the noisy city was home. He knew every inch of their neighborhood and had friends, disreputable or not, who'd take him in. Earlier she'd checked Luke's room. Nothing had been touched. She was certain he hadn't come into the apartment, but she hadn't checked the store. Her son knew exactly where she kept the cashbox. It didn't hold enough money for train fare to Chicago, but the contents would feed a stowaway.

Cassie snatched the lamp, hurried down the stairs and went to the desk where she kept the cashbox in the bottom drawer. As the light spread across the floor, she saw that someone had left that same drawer ajar. She didn't need to open the cashbox to know Luke had stolen from her, but she opened it anyway. Instead of bills and coins, she saw a single greenback, as if he'd left it out of concern for her.

Cassie blew out the lamp, then raced to the street. The Denver Special passed through town every night, signaling its arrival with a warning whistle. When she and Luke had ridden the train west, he'd been interested in everything—the route, where the lines switched. He'd have no trouble finding his way back to Chicago. If he hopped on the Denver Special, she might never find him. She had to get to the station *now*.

With her shawl whipping behind her, she sped down the boardwalk to the east side of town. The train station was situated a half mile away if she took the straightest path, but decent men and women drove their buggies down a road that skirted the block of saloons and questionable boardinghouses. Desperate for Luke, Cassie chose the straightest path.

As she neared the first saloon, she heard raucous laughter and women singing bawdy lyrics to the tune of a piano playing "Turkey In The Straw." Cassie crossed the street to avoid the open door, but she couldn't escape the smells of liquor and cloying perfume. Above her the stars burned bright, but she saw only Cassiopeia with her neck bent in shame. Thelma and Reverend Hall believed in God's mercy, but Cassie had her doubts. She desperately needed a break, but between Maude's gossip and another broken window, no one in this town would give her a second chance…except for Gabe.

As her heart cried out, she heard the thud of boots on the boardwalk. Startled, she turned and saw a man striding in her direction. He looked big, tough and mean. He also resembled Gabe, though she couldn't be sure. Guthrie Corners had its share of ruffians, and the shortcut to the train station had taken her to a place she would never have gone. To avoid the man, she picked up her pace.

So did he.

She started to run, but her skirts got in her way. She caught her toe on a warped board and stumbled.

"Wait up," the man called.

Cassie knew that voice, that bossy tone. It belonged to Gabe. He reached her in five strides, clasped her arms to steady her and raked her face with his eyes.

"What are you doing here?" he demanded

What did he think? That she'd come here for fun? "I'm looking for Luke," she snapped. "What else would I be doing?"

"Getting yourself hurt, that's what."

His fingers tightened on her biceps, then loosened to gentle circles of warmth. His eyes held hers, lingered, then filled with a jealous possession that made her feel both loved and lonely. She couldn't lean on this man, but she had to find Luke and he could help.

She stepped back. "Luke stole money from the cash box. I think he's running away."

Gabe's jaw tightened. "To Chicago."

"Yes."

He hooked his arm around her waist and hurried with her down the boardwalk. In the distance she saw the station, a low building with lanterns illuminating an empty platform. Her gaze rose to the train where she saw a man in a derby looking for a seat. The train had already boarded. Any minute it would leave the station.

She wanted to run but couldn't in her long skirt. "Go ahead of me!" she cried to Gabe.

After a squeeze of her hand, he broke into a run. Cassie ran as fast as she dared. A boiler shot a blast of steam into the sky. She smelled hot oil and heard two toots of the whistle. The engine chugged once, twice, then began to move.

She shouted Luke's name at the top of her lungs and ran faster. Instead of climbing the steps to the platform, she veered left and chased the slowly moving train. She saw steps and an open door to a passenger car, but she didn't have a prayer of reaching it. The engine picked up speed and the clattering cars turned into a blur of tears, grit and steam. As the caboose raced by, Cassie fell to her knees and wept.

"I'm sorry, honey."

She felt Gabe's hand on her back, then his arm around her shoulders as he dropped to his knees and pulled her head against his chest. "We'll wire ahead to the next stop. If he's on that train—"

Cassie raised her head. "I want to go after him."

"I know you do, but you can't. We don't know where he is."

She looked into Gabe's eyes and saw an understanding that shot her back in time to another train, another parting. Had he chased after the train that had taken her away to Chicago? Had he watched it disappear around a bend? Had he heard the fading whistle and felt as if his body had been ripped in two? Cassie lowered her eyes in shame.

He lifted her chin. "Luke might not even be on that train."

"He is. I know it."

"Did you see him?"

No, but he had *her* blood as well as his father's. "I just know."

"I don't." His fingers slid off her chin. "Let's go see the stationmaster. He might have seen something."

Gabe stood and offered his hand. Cassie took it and let him guide her back to the station where he opened the door and ushered her into the narrow room with a counter. She recognized the clerk as Carl Martin.

Carl looked from her to Gabe. "Good evening, Deputy. What can I do for you?"

"Mrs. O'Rourke is looking for her son." Gabe described Luke and gave his age.

Carl puckered his lips. "Ain't seen no kids around. It's usually business folks takin' the evening train."

"What about earlier?" Cassie asked. Maybe Luke had gone west instead of east.

The clerk shook his head. "What'd he do? Run off?"

"Yes," she said quietly.

When the clerk grunted with irritation, Cassie read his thoughts. *What kind of mother are you? Why weren't you watching your boy?*

Gabe touched her back, then spoke to Carl. "I'd like to send a wire to the next stop."

The clerk handed Gabe a pencil and paper.

With Cassie watching, he wrote a terse message describing Luke and asking the stationmaster to check the train for stowaways, then he signed it "Deputy Gabriel Paul Wyatt." His badge commanded a respect she couldn't have gotten on her own and she felt grateful. As he handed the paper to Carl, the clerk promised to send it right away. Gabe thanked him, then guided Cassie through the door and into the night.

The air still smelled of steam and hot oil. With her heart aching, she stared up the empty track.

Gabe put his arm around her waist. "I'll walk you home."

"No."

"Cassie, it's late—"

"I have to keep looking," she insisted. "If there's a chance he's here, I have to find him."

She pulled away from his arm, but he tightened his grasp. "Let me."

"But I'm his mother."

"That's right," he said. "For all we know, he could be home right now. You need to be there for him."

She'd never felt so empty in her life, not even when Ryan had hit her. That night she'd had a child to protect. Tonight she had nothing but empty arms. As much as she hated the thought of waiting in her silent apartment, she knew Gabe had a point. If Luke came home, she'd be ready with a meal.

"All right," she said.

"Good."

As they faced each other in the moonlight, Cassie blinked away her feelings. Earlier she'd cried in this man's arms. She'd leaned against his chest and taken the comfort she'd vowed to forsake. For a few brief minutes, she'd shared her load and it had felt good. She couldn't read Gabe's thoughts, but she knew her own and they scared her to death. She loved this man. They belonged together, but she feared the consequences of braiding their lives.

Judging by Gabe's expression, he had no such reluctance. Slowly…carefully…he drew her into his arms until his jaw scraped her temple. She felt the bristle of the whiskers he'd shaved before church, then the pressure of his hand as he tucked her head between his hard shoulder and the flesh of his neck. His breath caught the rhythm of hers. Their hearts matched in perfect time, reminding her of the past and how deeply she'd hurt him.

She'd hurt him again if she wasn't careful. Intending to step back, she raised her head. His mouth was a whisper from hers. If he turned his head, they'd be kissing. The thought made her tremble, but even more tempting was the stillness of his embrace. The man she'd left had been impatient. He'd have already kissed her breathless. The new Gabe had the patience of Job. The future, she realized, was in her hands.

Looking down, he spoke in a rough voice. "I better take you home."

"Yes," she murmured. "Luke could be waiting."

He nodded, but the look in his eyes had nothing to do with her wayward son and everything to do with a man's wayward thoughts. Or worse, the noble thoughts of a man in love, a man considering marriage, children and the holiest of commitments.

They stepped apart and turned toward town. Instead of walking past the saloons, Gabe steered her down the longer road that curved by homes and gardens. Whether he'd done it to avoid the saloons or because he wanted more time with her, she didn't know. Either way, she enjoyed walking at his side, sharing her burdens and worries with a friend... Just a friend, she reminded herself. If Luke had run away, she'd be destined to search for him forever. If—when—she found him, she'd still be unwelcome in Guthrie Corners and unable to support herself. With each step in the direction of her apartment, the future looked bleaker. It looked bleakest of all when they reached the mercantile and the stairs leading to her empty home.

"Go inside," Gabe said. "I'll come by in the morning."

She wanted to stay with him, but instead she climbed the steps, slipped into the dark room and lit a lamp. Like before, she carried it to the window and put it out for

Luke. This time, though, instead of an empty street, she saw Gabe watching for her through the glass. Wordless, she touched the pane with her fingers as she thought of an old Bible verse.

But now we see through a glass darkly. But then face-to-face...

She'd been in the dark for so long... She hadn't dared to pray for herself since the day she'd left Gabe at the altar. She hadn't felt worthy and she didn't feel worthy now, but she could pray for others. With a lump in her throat, she closed her eyes. "Be with Luke, Lord. Keep him safe. And Gabe, bless him, Lord Jesus. He's a good man." In the sudden silence, she recalled her promise to Reverend Hall. "Be with Billy, too, Lord. Help Maude and me to be good mothers to our sons."

As she whispered amen, her heart pounded. She had more to say to God but couldn't find the words. Feeling weak, she opened her eyes and looked down at the street. Gabe hadn't budged. If she motioned to him, he'd come up the stairs. He'd stay until she felt strong again. Somehow she stayed still. Another minute passed, then he tipped his hat and walked away, leaving her with knotted fingers and the knowledge that she didn't want to be alone after all.

Could she have it all? Her business *and* Gabe? Could they make a family with Luke and children to come? If business picked up, she could stay and find out. If it didn't, she'd have to leave. And if Luke didn't come home, none of her plans mattered. Looking at the empty street, Cassie touched the glass. For all her hard work and good intentions, she'd been rendered helpless by her own son. Feeling bereft, she raised her eyes to the stars. She hadn't stopped believing in God, but she'd stopped trusting Him. Tonight she couldn't stand on her own. No matter how hard she tried, she couldn't save her son.

Trembling, she bowed her head so that the crown touched the glass, then leaned enough to feel the pressure like a hand. "I'm sorry, Lord Jesus. I've made so many mistakes… I've failed everyone." Tears welled. The glass grew warm against her forehead, like a touch. "Please help me, Father God. Please bring my son home. I can't do it myself."

A sob broke from her throat. She felt weak all over and more helpless than she had all night. She didn't know if God would answer the prayer of a sinful woman like herself, but she hoped He'd look out for a troubled boy.

After leaving Cassie, Gabe went home. He figured Luke had either hopped the Denver Special or holed up somewhere for the night. Gabe couldn't go looking for him without causing a ruckus, so he slept a few hours, put on fresh clothes and left the house with Cassie's worry coursing through him. He knew how it felt to be left with doubts and questions. Fourteen years ago he'd been in her shoes. *Where did you go, Cassie? What did I do? Why did you leave me?*

He never wanted to ask himself those questions again. That's why he'd left her on the steps to her apartment. Earlier, when she'd tipped her face up to his, he'd almost caved in and kissed her. Now he was glad he hadn't. She needed her son far more than she needed the confusion of an ill-timed kiss, and Gabe intended to find him.

He went first to the train station where he spoke to Carl. The stationmaster at Ellison had already wired to say he'd searched the train and hadn't found Luke. Gabe took the news as a positive sign. If the boy had holed up in Guthrie Corners, he'd be waking up hungry. Gabe thanked the clerk, then headed for Pete Doyle's livery. He'd checked it twice yesterday but not after dark. The barn and corrals sat a quarter mile down the tracks and offered a good place to hide for a boy intending to hop a train. Gabe knew Pete well. The man wouldn't mind a bit if Gabe nosed around.

When he reached the barn, he went around to the back and entered through a side door. Stepping as lightly as he could, he walked between the stalls, looking in each one until he found Luke sleeping on his belly in a pile of straw. With his hair mussed and his arms akimbo, he looked like the innocent child he was meant to be, not the boy who'd seen his mother beaten by his father and felt those fists himself.

Gabe didn't consider himself an emotional man, but his throat went tight. Luke should have been *his* son. They'd have built things together and told jokes. He'd have taken him fishing and taught him to shoot. Looking at the boy with Cassie's hair and a stranger's eyes, he felt so cheated he wanted to smash his fist against the stall. Instead he closed his eyes and prayed.

Lord Jesus, help this boy. He needs a father.

And Gabe needed a son… The answer to the

dilemma seemed obvious. He'd have to win Cassie's heart before he could call Luke his own, but for now he could take the boy under his wing and teach him how to handle bullies like Billy Drake. The three of them could go on picnics and he'd charm Cassie for as long as it took for her to trust him.

Your will be done, Lord. I'm willing to wait, but Luke needs me now and I need Cassie.

As Gabe whispered amen, Luke stirred against the straw. He looked like a child, but the last thing he needed was babying. He got enough of that from his mother. Like most boys, he needed someone to push against so he could build his muscles. Young bucks with new antlers did the same thing. So did yearling mustangs and young bulls. If Luke wanted—needed—to fight, Gabe would oblige.

He planted his boots a foot apart and put his hands on hips. "O'Rourke! Get your butt up *now!*"

Luke grunted. "Go away."

"Not a chance." Gabe hadn't hollered in a long time. He hadn't had a reason but he did now. "You scared your ma half to death. The church has another broken window. And unless Mr. Doyle gave you permission to mess up his stall, you're trespassing."

Luke buried his face in his arms. "Leave me alone."

"I can't do that." Gabe dropped to one knee, gripped the boy's shoulder and rolled him over. Luke struggled, but he was no match against Gabe and his head finally turned.

What Gabe saw told the whole story. Luke had a black eye, a cut below his left ear and a tear in the knee of his pants. He might have broken the church window, but he'd done it after taking a beating from Billy Drake. Gabe hurt for him, but Luke didn't need pity. He needed to get his pride back.

Gabe arched a brow. "I hope the other guy looks worse."

"He doesn't."

The pain of that confession hit hard. No man liked to take a beating. Christ had done it for the sake of all mankind, but He'd had the last word when He'd risen from the grave. Knowing both Billy and Luke, Gabe figured the fight had started with Billy's smart mouth. Luke needed vindication.

Gabe stood tall and offered his hand. Luke looked at it, then at Gabe. "Are you going to arrest me again?"

"Nope."

"What are you going to do?"

"Fix you breakfast, clean up those cuts and take you to apologize to your ma for stealing money. While we eat, you can tell me what Billy said that made you so mad."

"I hate him!" Luke declared.

"I figured that." Gabe waggled his fingers to get Luke's attention. "Let's go. I'm hungry."

The boy's thoughts warred on his face. He had an empty belly and he wanted Gabe's friendship, but he felt guilty about everything he'd done, including stealing from his mother. Running away still appealed to him.

Gabe dropped back to a crouch. "Your ma's worried about you, Luke. But trust me…she's going to forgive you. She knows you took the money. We both thought you were headed to Chicago."

"I was." He sounded forlorn. "But I fell asleep."

"I'm glad you did." He kept his voice neutral. "Billy Drake's been bullying the kids in this town long enough. I'm proud of you for standing up to him."

He pushed to a sitting position. "Really?"

"You bet." Gabe meant every word. "I don't know what started the fight—"

"He called my ma a bad name…the worst one."

Gabe would *never* strike a woman or child, but he'd have leveled a man for throwing that insult at Cassie. He had no doubt where Billy had gotten that foul idea. Maude and her rumors had to be stopped. He gripped Luke's shoulder. "You defended your mother. That was honorable. I'm not saying you did the right thing with the window—"

"I didn't mean to." Luke looked at the straw. "I was aiming for Billy and missed. I'm sorry about the window, but I'm not sorry I threw the rock."

"I can see why."

"I'd do it again."

Gabe believed him. Luke had the instincts of a man but not the judgment. Unless someone taught him how to fight—and when—he'd break more windows.

"How about I teach you a few things?" he said to the boy.

"Like what?"

Gabe shrugged. "For starters, how to throw a punch."

"Really?"

"Sure." He'd buy a fifty-pound sack of flour, hang it

from a tree and show the kid how to put his weight behind a punch. Luke could beat the stuffing out of the flour sack, but that wasn't the only lesson.

"You have to promise me something," Gabe added.

"What?"

"You have to listen to what I say. A man needs to know *how* to fight, but it's more important to know *when* to fight."

When Luke's eyes clouded, Gabe thought of Ryan O'Rourke beating on Cassie. How much had the boy witnessed? Too much, Gabe decided. Luke had ugly memories, but time and God would work for the good. Someday Luke would be a strong defender of the weak because he knew how it felt to be small.

"What do you say?" he said to the boy.

Luke pushed to his feet. "When can we start?"

"Today," Gabe answered. "But first we eat breakfast. Then I'll take you to apologize to your ma."

Luke looked chagrined. "She's not going to like it."

"Like what?"

"She doesn't like fighting. She says I should just walk away." Luke sounded disgusted.

Frankly, so was Gabe. He didn't want to undercut Cassie's authority with her son, but she was wrong about walking away from trouble. Gabe believed in turning the other cheek as much as Reverend Hall. He never started a fight and didn't fight to defend himself alone. But when danger threatened someone else, he stood ready to protect and defend. He'd been in the U.S. Cavalry and took pride in serving his country. As a lawman, he'd promised to keep the peace at all costs.

Three years ago, he'd killed a man and had no regrets. If he hadn't, Betty Woolsey would have been shot dead by her crazy husband.

When it came to boys and fighting, Cassie had a few things to learn. Gabe hoped she'd understand what he wanted to teach Luke. If she didn't, they were headed for a squabble of their own.

Chapter Seven

"No!" she cried.

"But Cassie—" Gabe frowned at her.

"I said no."

She couldn't believe her ears. How dare he promise to teach Luke how to box! She abhorred violence of any kind. She'd felt the power of Ryan O'Rourke's fists and didn't want her son to follow in his father's footsteps.

Twenty minutes ago she'd wilted with relief when Gabe walked into the mercantile with his hand on Luke's shoulder. She'd run to them from the counter and they'd met in the middle of an aisle. Luke had apologized for scaring her, then he'd given her back the money with the most sincere "I'm sorry" she'd ever heard. When she'd started to fetch a beefsteak for his black eye, Gabe had stopped her and Luke had looked proud. The next thing she knew, Gabe was talking about boxing lessons and bags of flour.

Over Cassie's dead body! She understood the desire
to strike back. She'd wanted to slap Maude across the
face when she'd smirked over Luke, but violence begat
violence. She knew, because when she'd defended
herself against Ryan, he'd hit her even harder.

She looked at Luke now and wanted to hug him
again. Earlier she'd tried to kiss the top of his head, but
he'd drawn back from her. Gabe had looked annoyed
and now they were talking about punching bags.

Gabe glanced at Luke. "Go get ready for school."

"But he's hurt!" Cassie declared. "He's tired and—"

"He can do it." Gabe motioned at the door with his
chin. "Get going, Luke. And don't be afraid to look
Billy in the eye."

Cassie frowned. "Stay away from him."

"I can't," Luke muttered. "He sits behind me."

"I'll speak to Miss Lindstrom," Cassie said. "She can
move your seat."

The two males exchanged a look Cassie didn't like
at all. It left her out in the cold.

Luke stared back at Gabe, who indicated the door to
the apartment. "Go on, kid. I'll see you after school."

Her son looked at her with the defiant expression
Cassie knew too well, then followed Gabe's order,
leaving her speechless. When the door closed, Gabe
faced her. They were in the center of the store by the
fancy dishes she loved. The *empty* store…she hadn't
sold a thing in days, not even to a stranger, and now her
son and Billy Drake were wrestling in the dirt.

Gabe looked pained. With the plates on one side of
the aisle and the glassware on the other, he looked too

big for the small space. "You have to trust me, Cassie. Luke needs those boxing lessons."

"I don't want him fighting," she insisted.

"It's what boys do."

"It's what *fools* do!" She turned and headed for the counter. "Nothing good ever comes from people beating on each other."

"This isn't about *beating* on anyone."

She slipped behind the wood, lifted a rag and wiped the spotless surface. Gabe came forward but didn't follow her to the nook behind the counter. She focused on the rag, making half circles until she couldn't stand the silence and threw the rag down. "I give up. What *is* it about?"

"Honor."

To Cassie, honor meant being fair and truthful. It had nothing to do with punching bags. She started to pick up the rag, but Gabe put his hand on hers.

"Do you know why Luke has that black eye?" he asked.

"He and Billy were fighting."

His jaw tightened. "Billy insulted you. Luke defended your honor and took a beating for it."

"Oh, dear."

"That boy stood up for you, Cassie. He did the right thing. *How* he did it is another matter. That's why I need to buy that sack of flour."

Cassie thought of Ryan's fist on her jaw. She thought of his blood coursing through Luke's veins and how her son got the same mean look his father had. She'd come to Guthrie Corners to erase that violent tendency, not to feed it.

"It's just wrong," she insisted.

Gabe opened his mouth to speak, then sealed his lips. Whatever he'd been about to say, he'd thought better of it.

"Spit it out!" Cassie ordered.

"All right," he said, dragging out the words. "You're turning Luke into a sissy."

"I'm *what?*"

"You heard me."

"How dare you—"

"I'm right and you know it." His voice deepened to a growl. "You mean well, Cassie, but you don't understand boys. Luke needs to push against life to build his muscles. Look at him... He's as tall as you and has fuzz on his lip. He's not a little boy anymore."

She'd noticed the fuzz a few days ago and wished it was dirt she could wipe away. She missed her little boy. She didn't want him to get hurt, nor did she want him rolling in the dust with Billy Drake. She had enough trouble with Maude and the rumors.

"My decision's final," she said to Gabe.

"It's also wrong."

As the side door opened, she saw Luke. He'd washed his face and tucked in his shirt, something he hadn't done unbidden in weeks. Cassie swallowed hard. Where had the twelve years gone?

The boy eyed them both, then focused on Gabe. "I'll see you after school, right?"

They'd circled back to the boxing lessons. "Not today," Cassie declared. "You have chores."

"But, Ma—"

"Don't argue, Luke. The store needs sweeping and—"

He looked disgusted. "No, it doesn't. No one ever comes in here. They hate you. They hate me, too!"

"Luke!"

He strode out of the store, slamming the door behind him. Cassie stared in horror. Her son was too tall to be a boy and too skinny to be a man. She might not fully understand boys, but she knew that fighting caused more problems than it solved.

Gabe gripped the edge of counter. "You have to trust me, Cassie. Luke needs a man in his life. He needs a father."

A father for Luke meant a husband for her. She couldn't go down that road, but neither could she force a single word from her lips. She stepped back from the counter until she bumped the stool.

Gabe's knuckles turned white against the dark wood. "He's being bullied and so are you. There's a time to turn the other cheek and a time to stand up. Luke needs to stand, Cassie. Maybe you do, too."

Her insides shook. "What do you mean?"

"Don't hide from Maude like a whipped dog. You're stronger than that. Do something."

Gabe's voice had risen and he looked furious. He wouldn't hit her, but she still wanted to cry and had to bite her lip to keep it from trembling.

He turned away, showing her his broad back with his arms loose at his sides. After two deep breaths, he faced her again and spoke in a quieter tone. "I won't turn Luke into a bully, but there's stuff he needs to know."

"Like what?" she demanded.

"For one thing, how to duck."

Cassie thought of his bruised face. Gabe was right about Luke needing a father *and* about ducking, but she saw another answer. "Why can't you teach him how to fish or something?"

"I will," he answered. "After I teach him how to defend himself."

Everything in Cassie cried out to trust Gabe's judgment, but she wouldn't lean on anyone, especially not a man who thought he knew it all.

"No fighting," she said. "It's not right to hit someone."

"It's less right to be hit."

"I know that."

Instead of pacing back to her, he froze in place to create a wall of air. "Why are you so scared? Is it because of O'Rourke?"

"Of course, it is!" She'd been such a fool. "I'm afraid Luke will turn into his father."

"That's just plain crazy."

Cassie saw red. "You don't have to be insulting."

"I'm not." He held out his hands in surrender. "He's got your blood, too. You're raising him. That counts for more than anything O'Rourke did in the past."

Cassie thought of love covering a multitude of sins. She loved her son enough to stay strong. "My decision is final," she said to Gabe. "Fighting is wrong. *Hitting* is wrong. I don't want Luke learning to box."

"Then you better lock him in his room, Cassie. He's *already* fighting. You can't stop life from happening to him."

"I can try!"

"You're going to cripple him," Gabe said with a rush.

"How dare you!"

"You're so *wrong* I can't believe it." He raked his hand through his hair, leaving furrows of frustration that matched the ones on her heart.

She glared at him. "What gives you the right to criticize me? You don't know what it's like—"

"I know boys!" he said in full voice. "I know how they think, what they need. You don't—"

"He's my son!"

"And he's destined for *my* jail!"

"Get out!" Cassie ordered. She couldn't stand arguing. She felt shaky and weak and afraid.

"Cassie—"

"Leave! And stay away from Luke!"

Fury burned in his brown irises. "That's a mistake and you know it."

He didn't want to go. She could see the reluctance—even pity—in his eyes, but he had to respect her wishes. Without a word, he walked out the door and closed it with a loud click. Cassie picked up the cloth and started to dust her empty store. When she reached the pretty dishes, she wiped them clean with tears streaming down her face.

Whether Cassie liked it or not, Gabe had promised to meet Luke after school. He wouldn't go against Cassie's wishes and neither would he criticize her to her son, but the boy deserved an explanation. Gabe had been thinking all morning about what he'd say and had decided to counsel Luke to be patient.

The irony made him snort. Patience? Yeah, right. Gabe's vow to wait fourteen months, weeks or days for

Cassie to wise up had turned into a hair shirt. He'd been giving serious thought to inviting her to the next church social, but then they'd argued. He couldn't ask her now, not until they squared things over Luke.

Gabe reached the schoolhouse just as the doors opened and children spilled out, young ones first and then older ones. Near the back of the crowd he saw Billy Drake and three boys acting like goofs. One of them was making a face and wailing "waaaa" like a cry baby. Not a good sign, Gabe thought. He looked for Luke, didn't see him and felt a stone drop in his belly. When the last child left, he walked into the schoolhouse where he saw empty seats, Miss Lindstrom at her desk and Luke writing "I will not throw rocks" over and over on the blackboard.

He also saw dust on the seat of the boy's pants. Between the "cry baby" taunts and the evidence that Luke had been shoved to the dirt, Gabe felt certain he'd been provoked into throwing the rock. The boy had also gone to school with a head of steam. He didn't need punishment right now. He needed guidance and Gabe intended to give it to him no matter what Cassie said.

Taking off his hat, he walked past the desks. "Good afternoon, Miss Lindstrom."

Luke stopped writing but only for an instant. As the tap of the chalk resumed, Miss Lindstrom stood to greet him. "Good afternoon, Deputy."

She sounded friendly but not eager. Good, Gabe thought. When she'd first arrived in town, she'd made a point of sitting near him in church. He'd had to move to the back row to break her of the habit.

"I'm here for Luke," he said.

"He has fifty more sentences to go. Then he's free to leave." She spoke in a singsong Gabe found annoying.

Luke slammed the chalk into the tray and turned. "It's not fair!"

Miss Lindstrom raised her eyebrows. "I saw you throw the rock. You could have hit one of the smaller children."

"I was aiming for Billy!"

The "cry baby" chant made perfect sense. The boys had gotten into a quarrel and Luke had ended up in the dirt. His anger had leaked in tears and Billy and his cohorts had seen it. If Luke didn't do something now to redeem himself, he'd have to put up with Billy and his garbage for months.

Gabe directed his gaze to Miss Lindstrom. "It's your schoolhouse, but I'd appreciate it if you'd release Luke to me."

Her mouth wrinkled. "I don't know. I have rules."

"So do I."

She sighed. "I suppose, but just this once."

Luke glared at Gabe but spoke to his teacher. "I won't go with him. He's not my father, so you can't make me."

Gabe had heard enough. "Get your things, Luke."

"No!"

"Fine. I'll do it for you." He snatched up the boy's book bag, gripped his shoulder and manhandled him out the door and down the steps. Luke tried to shake off his hand, but Gabe refused to let go. "I'm not in the mood to chase you down."

"Then don't."

"You're out of luck, kid. I'm in this for the long haul."

Gabe herded him around the corner of the school-house to a spot where they wouldn't be in plain view. A split rail fence marked the border of the schoolyard. A meadow stretched fifty yards to the west, giving the boy no place to hide. Confident he had Luke corralled, Gabe let go of his shoulder and dropped the book bag. "What's this about throwing rocks?"

The boy ran to the fence. Gabe reached him in four strides and hauled him down from the top rail. Luke shouted at the empty meadow. "Leave me alone!"

"No way." Gabe spun him around so they were eye to eye. "We were talking about rocks."

Luke bent down, snatched up a stone and hauled back to throw it at the schoolhouse. Gabe snatched his arm. "Drop it, Luke."

"I'll throw rocks if I want to!"

"No, you won't. Now drop it."

"Make me."

Luke jerked against Gabe's grip, but he couldn't break it. He pushed forward and pulled back. He twisted. He cursed. He struggled like a fish on the end of a line. Gabe had never seen a human being as bitter as Luke. All that hurt and anger…it had nowhere to go except deeper into the boy's soul. Luke had to get rid of it.

Gabe held tight until the rock dropped from Luke's hand, then he released his grip. "You want to fight. Is that it?"

Luke's eyes blazed. "I hate you!"

Gabe figured the boy hated everybody right now including himself, so he didn't mind being a target. He challenged Luke with a smirk. "Well, whoop-de-do."

The boy lunged at him. As Gabe side-stepped, Luke's momentum forced him to his knees. The sting of the fall must have goaded him even more, because he pushed to his feet and charged again. This time Gabe stood his ground. The blow knocked him back a step and he stumbled. As he regained his balance, Luke pummeled his middle with his fists. The boy packed a real punch, but Gabe didn't stop him. Instead he held out his arms to make himself an easy target for the boy's anger. Whatever Luke had to dish out, Gabe could take.

When he landed a particularly hard punch, Gabe grunted. A female gasp came from near the school-house and he turned his head. Instead of Miss Lindstrom looking annoyed, he saw Cassie with her mouth agape. Her expression shifted from shock to outrage.

Not now…not when Luke had a full head of steam.

He shook his head to warn her away. At the same instant, Luke started to cry and shout while throwing punches. He had no awareness of his mother, no sense of anything except the feelings pouring out of him. He needed this release. Surely Cassie could see it. Babying him now would be the biggest mistake she could make. He gave her a hard stare, one full of warning, then focused on Luke. His mouth was still knotted and he'd worked up a sweat. He was walloping at Gabe's torso, but the punches were losing power. Gabe spoke in the voice he'd used as a sergeant. "Keep your fists up, O'Rourke. Protect your face."

Luke seemed to come out of a fog. Gabe didn't want him thinking too much, not until they'd crossed from enemies to allies. "Hit from your shoulder, not your elbow."

Luke's next blow landed smack in the middle of Gabe's chest. He could have stayed still, but he backpedaled as if Luke had knocked him off balance.

The boy's eyes popped wide. Surprised at his own strength, he lowered his fists.

"Fists up!" Gabe ordered as he came at him. "I'm going to swing. You duck, then come at me with your right fist."

Gabe slowed the punch to nothing. Luke saw it coming, dipped his head and socked Gabe smack in the ribs that were already bruised. Air whooshed from Gabe's lungs and he moaned.

Luke looked pleased. "Did that *hurt?*"

"Of course, it hurt!" Gabe wanted to shout with pride. "You're strong."

"I am?"

"Strong enough." Gabe rubbed his side. "The trick is to be smart about it. You can flail around like a windmill, or you can anticipate the other man's moves. I'm not hitting back, but Billy Drake will."

Gabe thought of Cassie and risked a glance at the schoolhouse. He was expecting a quarrel but saw only waving grass. She'd left, though he knew that quarrel would be inevitable. His mind drifted to the line of her mouth, the way she looked in that prim dress…

Whomp!

The next thing Gabe knew, he was on his backside in the dirt. Luke looked shocked and little afraid. "Are you all right?"

Gabe laughed out loud, a real belly laugh, low and deep. As Luke's eyes changed from fearful to proud, a grin spread across his face. Gabe stood and mock punched the boy's arm. "You rascal!"

Luke's face lit up. "I decked you!"

"You sure did, kid."

"And you're big!"

"Bigger than Billy." Gabe stood and brushed off his trousers. He and Luke had matching patches of dirt on their backsides. It struck a chord, one that sounded low and deep and showed up in his voice. "You've got a lot more to learn, Luke, including the most important lesson of all."

"What's that?"

"It's when *not* to fight." Gabe deepened his voice. "Never swing first. Never swing at someone smaller than you. And never, ever hurt a woman."

"Yes, sir."

For the next hour, they wrestled like bears. By the time they finished, the grass had been trampled, Luke's pants had holes in both knees, and Gabe imagined purple blotches on his ribs. It had been a long time since he'd burned off steam and it felt good, especially because Cassie had stoked the fire in his belly. He wanted to win her love and he intended to do it. Spent and happy, he and Luke dropped down to the grass and sat at right angles to each other, each leaning against the trunk of the cottonwood. The sun had dropped in the sky, softening the hard blue of the day but not the knowledge that Cassie would read him the riot act when he showed up with Luke.

Gabe stared across the meadow. "My belly says it's time for supper."

"Mine, too."

Gabe didn't want the day to end, but he shoved to his feet. As he reached down to give Luke a hand, the boy looked up with a peculiar light in his eyes. "I wish my dad had been like you."

Of all the blows Gabe had taken today, that one hurt the most. He answered with the deepest truth of the day. "If I had a son, I'd want him to be like you."

The boy looked chagrined. "Even if he threw rocks sometimes?"

"*Especially* if he threw rocks."

Staring straight ahead, they walked side by side to Cassie's mercantile. Luke heaved a sigh. "My ma's going to know I was fighting."

"I'll speak to her," Gabe said. "If she's going to be mad at anyone, it should be me."

Gabe clamped his jaw. He didn't like to quarrel, but some fights had to be fought.

Chapter Eight

Cassie pounded on the door to the parsonage. As soon as Thelma opened it, she blurted her only thought. "I need help."

"Come in." The older woman opened the door wide. "Tell me what happened."

"It's Luke."

"I figured."

"And Gabe."

Thelma closed the door with a click. "That figures, too."

As Cassie followed her into the parlor, she told the older woman about this morning's conversation with Gabe and the discovery that he'd gone against her wishes. When Luke hadn't come home after school, she'd gone to see his teacher. She'd heard voices behind the schoolhouse, investigated and found Luke attacking Gabe like a rabid animal.

For an instant she'd been angry with Gabe, but then

she'd seen tears on Luke's cheeks. Her son had gone into a blind rage and Gabe had been taking the punches. With his arms up and bent at the elbows, he'd been the picture of surrender, even sacrifice. She'd thought of Christ on the cross and had trembled with the knowledge that she was just like Luke, flailing blindly at life. Gabe had been right about her son needing to become a man, but she didn't know what to do about it. With her business in dire straits, she felt guiltier than ever for her failings as a woman and a mother. That's why she'd run to Thelma.

With her neck aching, Cassie knotted her hands in her lap. "I'm so confused."

Thelma sat on an old cane rocker, picked up her knitting and set the chair in motion. As she lifted the needles, a pink baby blanket took shape and her lips quirked upward. "Are you angry with Gabe?"

"I want to be."

"But you're not?"

"How can I?" Needing an answer, Cassie glanced around the room. Everywhere she looked she saw photographs of the Halls and their three sons, each one as tall or taller than his father. "Gabe was right about Luke."

Thelma twisted the yarn around her index finger. "How so?"

"He says Luke needs someone to push against."

"That's part of it."

Cassie furrowed her brow. "What's the rest?"

Thelma kept rocking. "The boy needs someone to show him what it means to be a strong man. He needs a father."

And the sky is blue. Cassie held in the retort. "I know that."

Thelma stopped rocking and set the knitting in her lap. "So what's stopping you from asking me for that lemon cake recipe? It's Gabe's favorite, you know."

Cassie knew that, too. She thought of yesterday and how he'd set it aside to help her. This morning he'd rescued Luke and this afternoon he'd rescued him again. She owed him more than a cake.

Thelma picked up her knitting and went back to rocking. The wood creaked like old bones, but the gray-haired woman said nothing, leaving Cassie to ponder her question. Why not bake that cake for the man she loved? The answer hit as hard as Luke's fists had pounded Gabe. "I can't lean on anyone, Thelma. Not after what happened with Ryan."

"I see."

"Do you really?" Cassie lifted her arm to indicate the wealth of family pictures. "Reverend Hall's a good man and a good father. Have you ever doubted that he loves you?"

The older woman held her head high. "Not once."

"Did you ever wonder where he was at night? Or smell perfume on his collar?"

"Never."

"Then you don't *see* at all." Cassie pushed to her feet. She wanted to leave, but she had nowhere to go except her empty store. Instead she paced to a window facing a field of tall grass. "Ryan hurt me, Thelma. I'll never put myself in that position again."

"Gabe's not Ryan."

"I *know* that." Cassie scowled at the tall blades. "But people change. They leave. They let you down."

"It's true that I married well." The needles clacked behind Cassie's back. "But I've had my share of trouble. I know what it's like to feel like someone's let you down."

Cassie turned in surprise. "Who?"

"Not Ben."

"Your sons?" The middle boy had run off.

"Not in the ways that matter. Ben and the boys are human beings. They've hurt me on occasion and I've been disappointed in their decisions at times, but they're human and I know that. I never expected perfection from any of them."

As Cassie watched Thelma rocking steadily, she recalled the disappointments in her own life. Her mother's death had been sudden and devastating. Her father had never been one to talk. After her mother's passing, he'd pulled into himself like the tortoise at the Chicago Zoo she'd seen with Luke. Even Luke had disappointed her, though he had the excuse of youth.

"Who let you down?" she asked Thelma.

"The Lord did."

Shivers went down Cassie's spine.

"At least that's what *I* thought." Thelma gave a small laugh. "As things turned out, He knew what was best."

Cassie turned back to the window, holding in a sigh as she stared at the empty meadow. "I've heard that before."

"I imagine so." Thelma's knitting needles kept up a steady rhythm. "You don't know this, but when the boys were little, Ben and I were so poor I worried about feeding them. He'd been pastoring a church in Nebraska and we loved it, but the elder board changed hands. The new men voted us out."

Cassie understood the sting of rejection. "That had to be hard."

"It was." Thelma rocked the chair harder. "For two years we lived like vagabonds. Ben preached wherever people would listen and we lived on offerings. When things ran short, he worked odd jobs. Those years were hard, but I wouldn't trade them for anything."

"Why not?"

"Because they toughened us up. Now when Ben preaches about God's mercy, he knows what it is. When I tell a woman I know how it feels to stretch a bag of flour, I really do."

Cassie had known hardship in Chicago, both the pain of her marriage and the fear of doing without. After the divorce, she'd skipped meals so Luke could have all the milk he wanted. "I don't feel that way about Chicago. I wish I'd never left."

As Thelma lowered her hands, the pink yarn puddled in her lap. "You've lost your faith, haven't you?"

Cassie felt as dry as sand. "I don't ever think about it." Except at night when she looked at the stars. Except when she was worried about her son. Except when she looked in the cash box and worried again. She forced herself to look at Thelma's face and not the baby blanket. "I just want a roof over my head and food and clothing for Luke. That's enough."

"Oh, Cassie."

"What?"

"*Things* will never be enough. In the blink of an eye, they can be lost forever. Only God is enough. That's why I'm so worried about you."

Cassie thought about what "enough" meant, both to herself and others. She'd taken Gabe's "enough" when she'd run away. She'd taken her son's "enough" when she'd chosen Ryan O'Rourke for a husband. Her neck hurt as she stared out the window. "No one took my 'enough.' I gave it away."

"You made mistakes."

"I did more than that." Cassie had no patience for sugarcoating. She knew how it felt to be the victim of a mistake. After hitting her, Ryan had apologized with trinkets, but she'd still had the bruises. She couldn't let Thelma excuse the wounds she herself had inflicted on others. She had to take responsibility.

"I ruined my life, Thelma. I hurt Gabe and Luke, too. I should never have left this town and I shouldn't have married Ryan O'Rourke. I knew he drank and chased women, but I married him anyway because I wanted a part in a stage play."

"That's still a mistake," Thelma insisted.

Cassie turned back to the window. A bee buzzed on the other side, hitting the pane over and over. It reminded her of Ryan's hand slapping her face and she felt the sting of tears. She turned back to the room, but she couldn't stop her feelings. They came out in a rush. "When Ryan hit me, I thought I deserved it. Now I'm a divorced woman and my son breaks windows."

Thelma lowered the knitting. "Sit down, Cassie."

"I'd rather stand."

The old woman's features hardened with determination. "That's pride talking. It's my house, and I asked you to sit."

Cassie resented Thelma's bossy manner, but she positioned herself on the divan. When the woman's eyes shone like silver, Cassie thought of swords and tea sets, the playthings of children that turned them into adults.

"Your mother's gone," Thelma said. "But I'm here and I'm taking her place. Someone has to chase those buzzards away from you."

Cassie thought of Rizpah. "What buzzards?"

"The ones that have you convinced God doesn't care about you because you've made mistakes, that He doesn't love you just as you are. Those thoughts are black and ugly and evil. God sent his son to die for you, Cassie. He knows all about your flaws. He knows about mine and Ben's, Gabe's and even Luke's. You said you wanted enough. Here it is… God's love. His forgiveness is all you need. He's promised you eternal life. Lift up your eyes and you'll get a taste of it now."

Everything in Cassie cried out with need. "I want to believe you, Thelma. I do, but…"

"But what?"

"The town hates me. Maude's spreading rumors. If business doesn't pick up, I'll have to leave. Where's God now?"

"He's right here." Thelma gave her a hard stare. "He's in Ben and me. He's in the grass and the sky. He's in the sun and the stars. You just have to look."

Cassie thought of the stars bearing her name, the

queen chained to a chair with her neck bent and her spirit broken. What would it be like to look up and see glory instead of guilt? *Oh, Lord... Help me.* A cry pushed into her throat, but she choked it back.

Thelma bowed her head. "Father God, Cassie needs you right now. She's tired and afraid and she's lost her way…"

A lump pushed into Cassie's throat, then tears welled. When Thelma asked the Lord to heal her wounds, the moisture spilled down her cheeks. Still praying, Thelma crossed from the rocker, dropped to her knees and took Cassie's hands as she lowered her head. "Dear Jesus, you love your children. You love Cassie. Chase away the buzzards, Lord, every one of them. Amen."

As Thelma looked up, Cassie thought of all the buzzards in her life. Guilt topped the list by a mile. Fear came in second and it still had its claws in her. If business didn't improve, she'd be forced to leave town. Maude had been circling Cassie for weeks now, watching her struggle and waiting to pick the flesh from the bones of her store. That buzzard needed to be chased away and Cassie knew how to do it.

When she raised her face to Thelma, she felt a fire in her belly for a new challenge. "I'm going to have a sale."

"That's a fine idea," Thelma replied.

Still holding the old woman's hands, Cassie pushed to her feet and lifted Thelma with her. "I'll mark everything half off. Let's see if Maude can sabotage that!"

"She'll try, I bet."

"Let her." Cassie thought of Gabe teaching Luke to defend himself and others. She'd just learned the same lesson. "I have a boy to feed and I intend to do it."

Thelma's eyes shone with pride. "Good for you, Cassie. When is the sale?"

"Saturday. I'll advertise in Friday's paper." She had no money to spare, but her future depended on the size of the crowd. If she could support herself, she could stay. And if she stayed, she could bake that cake for Gabe. She could even invite him to supper. She took a breath. "Thelma?"

"Yes?"

"Could I have that recipe for lemon cake?"

"You sure can." Thelma headed for the kitchen with Cassie behind her. As Cassie wrote down the ingredients, she thought about Gabe. Knowing his integrity, he'd come home with Luke and confront her. Instead of a quarrel, he'd get a supper invitation. She couldn't do more until her business succeeded, but she hoped that day would come.

She finished copying the recipe, hugged Thelma goodbye and hurried to the grocer where she bought lemons. They'd been shipped from California and were expensive, but she wanted the cake to be perfect. If she hurried, she could have it baking when Luke and Gabe arrived at the apartment.

An hour later, Cassie had put the pan in the oven and her apartment smelled sweet. She'd just put her hands in the dishwater when Luke came through the door.

"Ma, I'm home. Can Gabe stay for supper?"

A deep voice came from the landing. "Hold your horses, son."

Son...eating supper as a family. Cassie's heart thumped with longing. It was too soon to encourage Gabe. First the store had to succeed, but for tonight she could show her gratitude with a home-cooked meal. It would be plain, but Gabe had always liked simple food.

She reached for a dish towel and headed for the door. "Please, Gabe. Come in. You're more than welcome for supper."

He arched one brow. "I am?"

Her cheeks flushed. "I'd love for you to stay."

He lingered in the doorway, giving her time to change her mind. Cassie flashed to another time he'd lingered... He'd come into her father's mercantile and bought a set of spoons. He hadn't needed the spoons at all. They'd been an excuse to chat with her. Smiling, she motioned for him to come inside. "Supper won't be fancy, but we have dessert."

His eyes twinkled. "I smell Thelma's cake."

"I hear it's your favorite." Her cheeks turned rosy.

He looked over her shoulder at Luke. "Go wash up. I need a word with your ma."

"Yes, sir."

Luke padded down the hall, leaving Cassie agape at his good manners. As Gabe stepped over the threshold, she closed the door. Turning, she looked into his eyes. "I'm sorry for what I said. You were right about Luke."

"I didn't intend to go against your word."

"It's all right." She thought of the blows he'd taken. "You must be bruised. I've got liniment—"

"It's nothing."

"It was *something* to Luke." She wanted to touch his

shirt sleeve but didn't. "Thank you isn't enough for what you did today, but it's the best I can do."

"It's plenty." He touched her cheek with his thumb. "Cassie, I—"

"Not yet," she murmured.

With their eyes locked, she stepped back and smiled shyly. As Gabe lowered his hand, Luke came down the hall. He'd changed his shirt, combed his hair and was carrying a box that held toy soldiers, the ones he'd spent hours painting on wintry days. After a final look at Cassie, Gabe followed the boy into the front room.

She went alone to the kitchen, a cramped room meant for a single adult and not a family. As she sliced ham and potatoes, she listened to Gabe telling stories about his cavalry days. She'd first heard them on her parents' porch, sitting with him in the swing while the sun set and the stars came out. Normally she'd have asked Luke to set the table, but she didn't want to break the mood. Instead she put out utensils herself, then dished potatoes, ham and beans from the stove.

"Supper's ready," she called.

Luke gave his usual seat—the one across from her—to Gabe, and sat between them, making Gabe the head of the table.

As he lowered himself on to the chair, he sought Cassie's gaze. "I'd like to say grace."

"Of course." For the first time in years, she bowed her head with sincerity. So did Luke.

"Father in Heaven," Gabe began. "We thank You for this meal and for the loving hands that fixed it. Amen."

Direct and honest, that was Gabe. As Cassie lifted

her knife and fork, excitement bubbled inside her. "I have news about the store."

Gabe's brows lifted. "Oh, yeah?"

"I'm going to hold a sale," she said. "Everything will be marked half off for one day only. If that doesn't draw customers, nothing will."

Gabe looked pleased. "Sounds smart."

"I'll help," Luke added.

For the next half hour, they made plans. Gabe offered to paint a sign for the store window. Luke said he'd pass out handbills. By the time Cassie served the cake, they'd become a team. They also had a common enemy, one that couldn't be ignored. Gabe mentioned her first. "Do you expect trouble from Maude?"

"Probably," Cassie answered. "But I'm ready for it."

"Me, too," Luke added. "I *hate* Billy."

Gabe lowered his fork. "Hate's pretty strong, Luke. Especially when it's aimed at someone as bad off as Billy."

"I don't think he's bad off at all," Luke countered.

"I do." Gabe lowered his chin. "Billy's a bully. One of these days, he's going to get his clock cleaned and he won't have anything left. No friends. No pride. Mark my words, that day's coming."

Cassie wanted to cheer for Gabe. He'd directed her son from hate to charity while protecting the boy's pride. She gave him a look full of admiration.

Gabe countered with a look of his own. "Maude's a bully, too. Sometimes you have to fight."

"I'm going to." In addition to holding the sale, Cassie

would pray for Maude and Billy when she prayed for Luke. She might not see any changes, but she would do her best. "Guthrie Corners is home. I want to stay here."

"Me, too." Luke added.

Gabe pushed his plate away. "The sale's a good idea, but there's another way to fight."

"What?" Her nerves prickled.

"The Civic Association's having a social on Friday night. Come with me."

Needing time to think, Cassie raised her napkin to her lips and pressed. The Friday night social was a long-standing tradition of the Guthrie Corners Civic Association. For many years her father had served as president. William Drake now held that position and Maude would be the hostess. The event took place in the town hall, but it might as well have been the Drakes' parlor. Buzzards flapped and cawed in Cassie's mind. The time had come to shoo them away for good. "I'd like that," she said, smiling.

Gabe's brows shot up. She'd surprised him. She also knew that men brought their wives and children, so she turned to Luke. "We'll both go, all right?"

"Do I have to dress up like Billy?"

Gabe interrupted. "Only if you want."

"No way!" Luke declared.

But Cassie would… If she could triumph on Friday, she'd be back in business on Saturday. She could attend church on Sunday with her head held high. She smiled at Gabe, then sliced a second piece of cake and handed it to him. Years ago they'd danced at socials like this one. He'd taken her for moonlight walks and they'd stolen kisses. Her heart pounded with memories, then dreams.

"Does Pete Doyle still bring his fiddle?" she asked.

"He will this time," Gabe said with a glint in his eye. "I'll see to it."

Chapter Nine

Gabe slipped six bits into Pete's hand. "Play 'Beautiful Dreamer,' will you?"

"Sure thing, Deputy." The livery owner wedged the fiddle under his chin, then warmed up the strings with a fancy scale. As the harmonies filled the hall, Gabe strode to where he'd left Cassie with Dale Archer, owner of the feed store, and Betty Lou Baines, the best seamstress in town.

The night had been a resounding success, though he and Cassie had both been nervous when it started. Three hours ago he'd arrived at her apartment. She'd been stunning in a royal blue gown, but her cheeks had been as pale as moonlight. He knew how much tonight meant to her. Over the past five days, they'd become close again. He'd kept up Luke's boxing lessons and he'd muscled cabinets into new places for Saturday's sale. Every night she'd cooked him supper and they'd talked on the divan while Luke did his homework in his bedroom.

He hadn't kissed her for only one reason. She'd made it clear that her future in Guthrie Corners depended on the store's success. If she couldn't make ends meet, she'd be compelled to return to Chicago where she could support herself. Gabe didn't see the need. He could provide well for Cassie, Luke and babies to boot, but she had strong feelings and he had to respect them.

Tonight Cassie would sink or swim. So far she'd been swimming like a fish. In spite of Maude's cool looks, Cassie had held her head high. With Gabe at her side, she'd approached businessmen and their wives, inviting them to the store to look at her fine things from Chicago. Gabe thought of the opal ring he'd kept all these years. If the night stayed as bright, he'd be slipping it on her finger in no time.

He reached her side just as Pete played the first notes of the song. Cassie looked up and smiled at the same memory that had prompted him to ask for it. "Beautiful Dreamer" had been playing when they'd danced for the first time in this same room. He put his hand on her back, then spoke to Dale. "I believe Mrs. O'Rourke promised me another dance."

Dale laughed. "It looks like she promised you *all* her dances, Deputy. Enjoy yourself." He looked at Cassie. "I'll tell my wife about the draperies. She'll be there tomorrow."

"So will I," Betty Lou added. "I'm from Chicago, you know. I loved browsing at Russell's."

Cassie smiled like a gracious queen. "I'll see you all at the store. We open at 9 a.m."

As they turned to the dance floor, Gabe saw a glow

in her eyes he'd missed for fourteen years. She'd triumphed tonight. He'd waited long enough. Before the night ended, he'd ask her—again—to be his wife. "Let's dance," he said in a gravelly voice.

"Yes."

As she swayed into his arms, he swept her into the swirl of colorful dresses and tapping feet. The way her face lit up was worth every cent of the money he'd paid Pete. He'd never seen her so happy, so alive. The blue dress matched her eyes and reminded him of a twilight sky. The sparks between them snapped like the fireflies he recalled from his southern youth. He drew her closer. "You look beautiful."

"I'm happy." Her fingers tightened on his shoulder. "Everyone's coming tomorrow. My father's old friends…women like Betty Lou. I just needed to open the door."

Gabe tightened his grip on her waist, drawing her close as he looked into her eyes. "I can think of another door that needs opening."

He meant the door to his house. He wanted it to be *their* house, but first she had to marry him. The question formed in his heart and rose to his lips. Before he could ask it, Cassie swayed fully into his embrace, keeping time with the music *and* with him, matching their steps in the slow, sweet rhythm of the song. When he looked into her eyes, he saw stars of light. He also saw fear. Before he proposed, he had to chase it away. "I love you, Cassie."

"Oh, Gabe—"

"I think you love me, too."

Her eyes glistened with hope, but she looked down at her feet. "I do, but I'm frightened."

"Of what?"

"Everything."

He didn't want to hear a protest. With the music rising and the crowd swaying, he kissed her tenderly on the lips, tasting the sweetness of their tomorrows without a hint of the bitter past. He didn't care who saw them. The kiss felt good and right, pure and so full of promise that he didn't notice when the music stopped and the crowded shifted. Nor did he hear two boys shouting from out on the street. He didn't come to his senses until Cassie pushed out of his arms.

"That's Luke!"

She lifted her skirt and ran for the door. The crowd had the same idea. Gabe elbowed through the throng and caught up to her as she raced down the wide steps. He heard shouting in the alley, thumps, bumps and a thud that sounded like a fist on a flour sack. As they rounded the corner, he saw Billy sitting in the dirt with a bloody nose and Luke looking proud.

Gabe pushed ahead of Cassie. "Wait here."

"But he's my son!"

Yes, but Luke didn't need his mother right now. He needed a father, a man who'd skinned his knuckles and knew about battles and war and honor. As he strode ahead of Cassie, he glimpsed Maude approaching from the opposite side of the alley.

Gabe reached Billy first and hauled him to his feet. "What's this about?"

"He hit me for no reason!"

Luke shouted back. "It was *too* for a reason!"

"You started it!" Billy countered.

"Both of you," Gabe bellowed. *"Knock it off!"*

The boys stopped hollering, but Cassie and Maude had reached the edges of the crowd. He could get to the bottom of this mess if the women stayed out of it, so he froze Cassie with a look. He tried the same glare on Maude, but she burst through the crowd and pulled dear, precious Billy into her arms. "How dare you question my son!"

Gabe spoke in a voice just for Maude. "Someone has to. The boy needs discipline."

"How dare you!"

Gabe scanned the crowd for Mr. Drake but saw only onlookers. "Where's your husband?"

"He's speaking to the mayor."

"I see," Gabe answered.

Judging by the pained look in his eyes, so did Billy.

Gabe spoke to Maude. "Step back now. I'll handle this."

The woman's face twisted with disgust. "No, you won't! You're all wrapped up with Cassie. You'll take her side. She's trash and everyone knows it!"

Gabe's blood ran cold. "That's uncalled for, Maude."

"It's true!" She pointed at Cassie, who'd stayed on the periphery as he'd asked. "You're cheap and foolish, Cassie Higgins! You treated me like dirt. Now you know how it feels. I promise you, *no one* with an ounce of class will ever set foot in your store. If they do, they'll pay."

Using only his eyes, Gabe urged Cassie to speak her

mind. *Fight! Stand tall!* Instead she wilted like a flower with a broken stem. He couldn't stand there and say nothing, so he faced Maude. "Cassie's a good woman. This town needs her."

He scanned the crowd, matching eyes with each man and each woman, daring them to speak on Cassie's behalf. One word of support would change the tide. Instead the edges of the crowd peeled back like the skin off an orange. Dale Archer turned his back and headed down the street. So did Mary Lou, Millie and other folks who'd earlier been friendly. Tomorrow the store would be empty, but Gabe clung to a single hope. Cassie had already told him that she loved him. Surely she wouldn't leave him again.

When the crowd dwindled to the three of them and the two boys, Maude hooked her arm around Billy's shoulders. With a smug look, she dabbed at his bloody nose and made baby talk. Gabe felt sick for the boy. As she led him away, he wondered what had happened to cause the fight. As much as he needed reassurance from Cassie, Luke needed him more and so he turned to the boy. "I figure you had a good reason."

"Yes, sir." Luke had a boy's shoulders but a man's glint in his eyes. "He was pestering Margaret."

Everyone in town knew Margaret and felt sorry for her. Her mother had died six months ago and her father had fallen apart. Still a child herself at the age of eleven, she was raising her younger siblings, two boys and a girl who missed their mother. She also had curly hair and freckles. Someday she'd be a beauty, but not today. If Billy had been harassing the girl, Luke had done well to protect her.

Gabe clapped him on the back. "You did the right thing, son. Let's go home."

He looked to Cassie for agreement, but she had eyes only for her son. They were misty and wide and full of love. Then she looked at Gabe and he knew… Maude had shattered her hope. Unless he could persuade Cassie to lean on him—to let him protect and provide—she'd leave.

Expecting the fight of his life, Gabe guided them both down the street to Cassie's apartment. Luke chattered every inch of the way, describing how Billy had pulled Margaret's braid and called her "Freckle Head." Luke had told him to stop. He'd warned him twice, but Billy had ignored him and cornered Margaret, chanting the mean name.

"That's when I pulled him back," Luke said. "He tried to push me, but I dodged just like you taught me."

"That's good." Gabe was only half listening. He put his hand on Cassie's back and she stiffened. He lowered it and felt lonely.

Luke kept chattering. "He swung first. I ducked, then I swung back. I hit him square on the nose. I don't remember what happened next, but everything you taught me, it worked really well."

"As long as you fought fair, I'm proud." Gabe glanced at Cassie. She hadn't said a word since Maude's lambasting. He'd have preferred tears to silence, but anger would have been best. They could have fought for the future together. Instead she looked as pale as a dead body.

When they reached the stairs to her apartment, she

spoke for the first time. "Luke, go wash up. I need to speak to Deputy Wyatt."

The formality made his blood boil. Luke, standing straight and proud, climbed the stairs. The instant the door closed, Cassie sighed. "I'm sorry, Gabe. I can't stay in Guthrie Corners."

"Why not?" He ground out the words.

"This town hates me."

"So what?"

"If I can't make a living, I can't feed Luke."

"I can." He touched her cheek, then leaned forward to kiss the spot where a tear had trickled.

Before his lips tasted salt, she stepped back. "I can't lean on you like that."

"You mean you won't."

"I can't!" she cried. "I leaned on Ryan and he cheated on me—"

"I'm not Ryan O'Rourke!"

"Of course not," she murmured. "But I know what it's like to not have enough. You could die. You could lose your job—"

"Or we could have fifty glorious years," he insisted. "You can't let fear stop you."

She squared her shoulders. "It already has."

"Cassie—"

"If even a single person comes tomorrow, I'll stay." Moonlight shimmered on her cheeks and turned them pale. "But if no one comes, it'll mean it's time to go. This town hates me, Gabe. It'll turn on you, too. Luke will struggle every single day. I can't stand the thought!"

He saw her point but from another angle. "Luke can take it. So can I."

"*I* can't." She hung her head.

Instead of cupping her chin, Gabe kept his hands at his sides. "You have to fight, Cassie."

She raised her head but only enough to look at his chest. "Maybe people will come tomorrow. Maybe this won't be a problem."

"It already is."

Her eyelashes fluttered up. "What do you mean?"

As much as he wanted to hold her close, Gabe stood tall. Cassie had to win this fight on her own. "It's like before," he said. "You're making decisions for both of us, but not this time, Cassie. I've got a say in the future."

"Yes, you do."

"I don't care if you run your own business or not. I'm all for it," he said with complete sincerity. "What I won't do is marry a woman who doesn't trust me to take care of her. I'd take a bullet for you. I'd dig ditches to see that you had enough."

"I know." She looked at her toes. "It's just not…"

"Enough," he finished for her.

She said nothing.

Gabe felt a fury that went back to the day she'd jilted him. "I've never been enough for you, have I?"

"That's not it."

"Then what is it?" he demanded.

"I don't know." Her voice wailed.

"When you figure it out, let me know." He turned on his heels and walked away. If she called to him, he'd go back in a heartbeat. He'd take her in his arms and be strong for them both. He'd do anything for her…except be a doormat. With the silence echoing, he headed home to his empty house where he kept the Bible with Cassie's name as his wife and the ring she didn't want. Alone in the dark, he went to the bedroom that should have been theirs and sat on the mattress, worn more on one side than the other. Bereft and alone, he dragged his hand through his hair.

"She needs help, Lord," he murmured. "Show me what to do."

Thoughts tumbled through his mind. He imagined dragging in customers at gunpoint. He considered pounding on doors and making threats. *Buy from Cassie or you'll answer to me!* But she didn't need that kind of support. She'd said she'd stay if just one customer showed up. Gabe would have gladly been that customer—he'd buy the dishes she favored—but the thought smacked of disrespect, even manipulation.

"Please, Lord. Send someone to her shop." He slid to his knees. "I'd die for her. I'd do anything—"

As he hit the floor, his boots slipped beneath the bed and nudged an old valise. His next thought lit up the moment, the future and everything in between. He'd used that valise to bring his things to Guthrie Corners. He could use it to leave with Cassie on an eastbound train.

If the sale flopped and she left, he'd be going with her. He'd lost her once to foolishness and he wouldn't do it again. He wanted to go to her now and tell her he'd buy the train tickets, but the thought of Cassie leaving with her tail between her legs didn't sit well. He understood about shaking the dust off his feet, but he also knew how the Lord felt about Pharisees and Philistines. Someone needed to put the Drakes in their place and Gabe intended to be that man. But how? The thought that came struck him as both simple and fitting.

Cassie went up to the apartment and saw Luke sitting on the divan, waiting for her with a question in his eyes.

"Are you mad at me?" he asked.

Cassie sat next to him. "No, Luke, I'm not. You were helping Margaret."

She wished someone had helped *her*. Gabe had, but the town had turned against him, too. Sitting with Luke in the shadows, she imagined the brush of wings on her face and the peck of beaks. Maude had eaten her alive tonight. Cassie had wanted to fight, but Maude's first words had wounded her so fiercely she'd lost the will. If she stayed in Guthrie Corners, she'd face that scorn every day. So would Luke. So would Gabe. She couldn't bear the thought. She simply didn't have the courage. Nor could she stand being dependent on anyone, even Gabe. At least in Chicago she'd have her pride.

"We need to talk," she said to her son.

"About what?"

Cassie resisted the urge to smooth his hair. "What do you think about going back to Chicago?"

"I don't want to."

"I don't either, Luke. But I have to be able to support us."

His voice rose to a little boy whine. "What about Gabe? You like him, don't you?"

"I do, but I'm worried about money."

Luke had heard about money trouble all his life. He took the news with a quiet dignity he'd never before possessed. When had her boy started thinking like a man? Since he'd known Gabe, that's when. Was she wrong to leave? Cassie called out to God in the dark of her soul. *I need help, Lord. What should I do? I can't stand the mockery, but neither can I bear the thought of leaving.*

"I have to send a payment to Mr. Russell," she said quietly. "If nothing sells tomorrow, I can't do it."

"It's because of Mrs. Drake, isn't it?"

"She's been angry with me for years."

"I don't want to go, Ma." He stood up. "I want to stay and fight."

Gabe's influence…again. Cassie felt both proud and scared. "We need to pick our battles, Luke. I don't think I can win this one. And I have to take care of us. I have to buy food and clothes—"

"I'll work."

What a change in her little boy… She didn't want to discourage him, but who in Guthrie Corners would hire him? What did a mother do? Cassie needed to chase the buzzards away from her son, but he was becoming a man who needed to stand on his own. She'd learned from Gabe that she needed to respect Luke's pride, but she found it hard. She found it harder still to think of Gabe. She wouldn't leave without saying goodbye, but if she had to leave town to protect her son, she'd do it. She didn't doubt that Gabe would provide for their basic needs, but she couldn't bear the thought of public scorn. Gabe could lose his position, a job he loved. He'd blame her like Ryan did…

Cassie turned to Luke. "It's best that we leave."

He looked at her with wide, vulnerable eyes. "What about Gabe?"

Cassie didn't say a word.

"You like him, don't you?"

"Yes."

She watched Luke's expression, a mix of confusion and daring. Twelve-year-old boys didn't go down the road marked love, but they knew it existed. Luke raised his head higher. "Gabe wouldn't care about the store. I know it."

"No," she answered. "But I do."

"Gabe wouldn't run," Luke said forcefully. "Neither will I. Billy's a bully. I'm not sorry I hit him. He was being awful to Margaret."

"I know, sweetie."

Luke scowled. He didn't like being called "sweetie" but it had slipped out and he took it. Cassie forced herself to sound stronger, more respectful of him. "We'll have to see what tomorrow holds, okay?"

"All right," he mumbled. "I'm going to bed."

He walked down the hall, leaving Cassie to bow her head and pray for God to chase away the buzzards from her store, Gabe and especially her son.

Chapter Ten

The next day, early in the afternoon, Cassie lost all hope. She locked the door to Higgins Mercantile for the last time, then surveyed the merchandise she'd been looking at for a month. Not a soul had come to the sale, not even the Halls, though Thelma had sent a note saying they were under the weather. For a moment Cassie wondered if they'd heard about the ugliness at the social, but she decided they hadn't. If Thelma had gotten word, she'd have dragged herself to the store to show support.

Gabe hadn't shown up, either. She'd half expected him to pressure her by being that one customer she'd mentioned. Instead he'd kept his distance. The gesture made her love him all the more, but it didn't change the facts. She hadn't sold a thing and she owed Mr. Russell a payment. The buzzards had won.

Awash in despair, she headed for the back room to fetch a shipping crate. As she passed the dishes she loved, she heard a timid knock on the front door, turned and saw Margaret peering through the window. The girl probably wanted Luke, but Cassie hadn't seen him all morning. At breakfast he'd asked if he could visit Gabe and she'd said yes. The silence in the store had driven her crazy, but she'd been glad to spare Luke the humiliation of no customers.

Sighing, Cassie went to the door and opened it. Margaret always looked a little pale, but today her freckles stood out like strawberries on her ashen face. "Are you all right, sweetie?"

"I'm okay."

"Are you looking for Luke?"

The girl glanced down the street as if she was worried she'd been followed. Seeing no one, she looked back at Cassie. "I came to buy something."

Cassie wrinkled her brow. "You did?"

"Yes, ma'am."

As she motioned for Margaret to come inside, Cassie pondered the peculiar nature of her visit. Had her father sent her? But why wouldn't Ian Glebe come himself if he'd decided to show his support?

Margaret headed for the counter and the jars holding penny candy. She looked at the peppermint and licorice, the butterscotch and the gumdrops that would be dry by now, then she reached into her pocket and set two pennies on the counter. "I'd like candy for my brothers and sister."

"Sure," Cassie answered. "You'll need some, too."

"I only have two cents."

"That's more than enough." Cassie filled four brown

bags with as much candy as they'd hold. When she finished, she slid the purchase across the counter.

"There you go," she said brightly. She wouldn't let her gloom show to a child.

"Thank you." Margaret started to leave, then turned back with a solemn expression. "My father told me to stay away today, but I heard him talking to Deputy Wyatt and Luke. They said you needed people to buy things or you'd have to leave town. That's why I came."

Cassie stood speechless.

Margaret looked even more ashen. "I know two cents isn't enough, but it's all I have."

Her one customer…a child with two pennies who'd mustered her courage to help someone else. Cassie felt a sudden, humbling rush of shame. Last night Luke had chased a buzzard away from this girl. Today she'd risked everything to repay his kindness. She'd brought the best gift she had—as little as it was—to honor him. Luke was her hero, because Gabe had taught him how. Looking at the pennies, Cassie saw the biggest buzzard of all coming straight at her. Black and ugly, the vulture had a name and its name was Pride. *Her* pride. Never leaning… Never trusting anyone… Not even Gabe when he'd waited fourteen years out of the purest love she'd ever known. She hadn't trusted God, either.

Especially God, she admitted to herself. Today, in spite of her lack of faith, He'd sent that one customer. Two cents wouldn't pay Cassie's bills, but it was enough to keep her in Guthrie Corners. If Gabe would still have her, she'd stay forever.

As soon as Margaret left the store, Cassie hurried out

the door. She had to get to Gabe. Three steps down the street, she recalled something Margaret had said about her father. *I heard him talking to Deputy Wyatt.* While she'd been hiding in the store, Gabe had been fighting for her. So had Luke. She sped to the sheriff's office and went inside. Blinking, she flashed on the day she'd found her son in jail. Gabe had set the boy free to be a man. He'd set her free, too. Free to love… Free to trust.

Instead of seeing him behind the desk, she saw another deputy. "I need Gabe," she said.

"He's not here."

"Where is he?"

The man shrugged. "Dunno. He's off today."

She sped out the door and ran to the house that would soon be theirs…if Gabe would have her. She banged on the door but no one answered. She considered running through the streets of Guthrie Corners in search of him, but he could have been anywhere. He could be eating lemon cake at Thelma's or fishing at the stream. He could be at Millie's or…the list went on and on. Desperate to spill her feelings, Cassie went back to the store, selected the finest stationery she stocked and penned a letter to Gabe… A love letter that told her deepest feelings. She sealed it with white wax, then took it to his house and slipped it under his door, just as she'd done fourteen years ago. This time, instead of pain and rejection, the letter held the sweetest of invitations.

"That was awful!" Luke whined to Gabe.

Gabe had to agree. They'd spent the day calling on

anyone in Guthrie Corners who might have supported Cassie. People had been friendly until he'd stated the purpose of the visit. When he'd suggested Millie could use new table linens and that Cassie had them on sale, the café owner had given a firm shake of her head.

"It's not about Cassie," Millie had said. "I admire the woman for trying. But if I tick off the Drakes, I'll be hurting for business, too."

Next he and Luke had visited Dale and Jenny Archer. Mrs. Archer had looked sympathetic, even irked, but Mr. Archer had given a firm shake of his head and insisted on staying out of the tangle with the Drakes.

Betty Lou's dress shop had been locked up tight.

Pete Doyle didn't have time for fancy things.

They'd visited Ian Glebe, Margaret's father, last of all. Gabe had told the man what had happened and how Luke had come to his daughter's defense. Mr. Glebe acknowledged Luke with a curt "Thank you," then he'd been blunt regarding Cassie. "I can't help her, Deputy. You know the Drakes. I'll be next on their list. With four children to feed—and no wife—I can't risk it."

Gabe had no right to judge the man, but the decision struck him as gutless.

Last of all, they went to the bank to speak with William Drake. "Wait here," he said to Luke.

As the boy lingered on the boardwalk, Gabe walked into the building. No tellers were at the counter, so Drake himself came out of his glassed-in office.

"Good morning, Deputy," he said. "What can I do for you?"

"I'm here about Billy."

Drake looked bored. "What about him?"

Gabe deliberately kept his hands relaxed and his tone low. "Last night wasn't as simple as you might have heard. Your son was bullying Margaret Glebe. Luke stopped him."

The banker huffed. "I hardly think you're objective."

"Then speak to Margaret."

"Is there anything else, Deputy?" His tone reeked of sarcasm.

"I've done my duty," Gabe countered. "The rest is up to you and Mrs. Drake. But be warned, sir. Your son is headed for trouble."

Drake's hair, slick with pomade, shone in the light. "Boys will be boys. It's not a problem."

"It is if no one teaches them right from wrong." Gabe didn't have time for the man's nonsense. He'd said his piece and he wanted to get to Cassie. He wished the attorney well and left. Outside he found Luke and they headed for Cassie's shop. The moment of truth had come. The mercantile would be humming with customers, or it would be dead quiet.

When they reached the front of the store, Luke tried the knob. "It's locked."

Gabe peered through the window. Not a spoon had moved. The bolts of cloth sat untouched and uncut. He didn't see Cassie anywhere.

"Go on up," he said to Luke. "I need to do something before I speak with your ma." Later today he'd hand her the train tickets with the opal ring.

After Luke slipped inside, Gabe headed for the depot. He bought the tickets for two weeks' time, long enough for Cassie to close up the shop and for Gabe to give notice that he'd be leaving his job. If he couldn't sell his house, he'd rent it out. With the tickets in his shirt pocket, he headed home.

As he opened the door, he saw an envelope on the rug, face up bearing his name in Cassie's curly writing. Fourteen years turned into a mist and burned away with the heat of anger. Another goodbye… Another rejection. He relived the humiliation of standing alone in church. He felt the burning in his gut. Once again, she'd lacked the courage to face him.

Gabe stared at Cassie's handwriting for a long time. Did he really want to marry this woman? Looking at the curls of his name, large and bold and in Cassie's hand, he thought of her stubborn pride, her irritating ways… and he knew. He could stand anything except another "Dear Gabe" letter. What she had to say, she could say to his face.

He set the letter on the side table without reading it. Tomorrow after church, he'd call on her and speak his mind.

Cassie waited all afternoon and long into the evening for Gabe to come to her. She'd poured her deepest feelings into the letter and he'd chosen to ignore it. She didn't blame him. From Luke she'd learned that they'd made calls and been rejected by everyone except Margaret. Gabe had come face-to-face with the scorn Cassie had predicted, and he'd changed his mind about marrying her. She didn't blame him a bit.

By morning, she'd lost all hope that he'd come to her.

She wanted to go to church, but she also wanted their next encounter to be in private. Later today she'd go to his house, but right now she had work to do. The unsold merchandise had to be shipped back to Chicago, so after breakfast she and Luke went downstairs. Together they hauled the crates from the storeroom and began clearing the shelves.

Feeling bereft, she looked at the dishes she treasured. Fragile and pretty, she'd pack them last with extra care. She and Luke worked in companionable silence, each lost in thought until someone pounded on the door. She opened it and saw Gabe. He'd worn his dark suit to church and had pulled his hat low to shield his eyes, either from the sun or from her, she didn't know.

"Hello, Gabe."

"Cassie."

She couldn't stop staring at his jaw. Clean shaven and hard-set, it reminded her of oak and marble.

"May I come in?" He'd issued an order.

"Of course."

She opened the door just enough for him to slip inside, then closed it. Luke saw him and stood straight, but he didn't speak a greeting. Instead the men—Luke had that air today—traded a look of silent understanding.

Her son headed for the door. "I'm going upstairs."

Cassie knew what the next minutes held. Gabe would tell her that he'd changed his mind about marrying her. She'd force a smile and say she understood. They'd part with a handshake and a promise to stay in touch for

Luke's sake. She'd do all those things with her head high.

As Gabe took off his hat, she looked into his eyes. "You must have gotten my letter."

"I sure did." He spat the words.

Cassie didn't understand. She'd expected a hard goodbye, but it wasn't like Gabe to be cruel. "I'm sorry."

"Why, Cassie?"

He'd asked her that question in Reverend Hall's office and she'd confessed the truth. This time she didn't understand it. She'd said everything in the letter. She wrinkled her brows. "Why what?"

Gabe reached between the pages of his Bible, took out the envelope and held it out with disgust. "You could have at least told me in person."

Looking down, she studied the crisp folds of the paper and the unsmudged ink. With her fingers trembling, she took the envelope and felt the wax seal, still unbroken, against her thumb. The fool man hadn't read the letter! He'd taken it for another rejection. Her heart soared with hope, but she didn't let it show.

"You're right," she said.

His eyes stayed hard, challenging. "Read it out loud. We can both hear the foolishness."

Cassie popped the wax with her fingernail, removed the two pages and began to read.

My Dearest Gabe,

For fourteen years I've wandered this earth without you, yet you've lived in my dreams and dwelled in my heart. In those secret places where a woman keeps her truest treasure—her love, her family—I've kept those memories of you. Today they're more alive than ever. I love you. I always have and always will.

"Cassie—" his voice broke and he reached for her. She stepped back. "Let me finish." He'd waited a long time for this moment and so had she.

"Last night you told me again that you loved me. In a moment of selfish pride, I said I didn't trust you to take care of Luke and me. This morning, with the help of a child, I came to my senses. Your love is more than enough. It's everything a woman could want. If you'll still have me, I'd be honored to be your wife. Nothing would give me greater joy. I know that Luke loves you, too."

She heard his breathing, heavy and unsteady. Her own matched it with a ragged cadence. She wanted nothing more than to go into his arms, but she had to finish reading.

"I'll be waiting for you, my love. Tonight and always.
Love, Cassie."

With her heart pounding, she looked into Gabe's eyes. They had a sheen of love and a spark of possession. Knowing that she'd treasure this moment as much as he would, he kissed her with a tender vengeance. "You scared me to death!" he whispered between breaths. "I thought you were leaving again."

"Never."

With their cheeks touching, she felt him smile as he murmured into her ear. "I have a surprise for you, too."

"What?"

"I've got three train tickets in my pocket. If you want to leave town, that's fine but I'm going with you."

"Oh, Gabe."

"We'd get married first, of course."

Cassie grinned. "Today?"

"Sure."

She wanted to jump and clap like a child. "Let's tell Luke. He'll be so happy."

Grinning, he hooked his arm around her waist and kissed her again. Just as their lips touched, the front door opened. A month ago she'd have jumped to make a sale. Today she called to the customer from across the room. "The store's closed."

Gabe's eyes twinkled. "Go on. Make a last sale."

Chuckling, Cassie broke from his arms, looked down the aisle and saw Ian Glebe. After a glance at Gabe, he spoke to Cassie. "My daughter came home yesterday with enough candy for a year. It seems she has better manners than I do, Mrs. O'Rourke." He held out his hand. "I've come to say thanks to you and your son."

While Cassie stood in shock, Gabe called up the stairs for Luke. The boy raced down, saw Mr. Glebe and stopped.

Margaret's father held out his hand. "Thank you, Luke, for helping Margaret."

As they shook, the door opened again. Dale and Jenny Archer strolled in. After a friendly nod to Cassie, they ambled to the drapery display. The Halls walked in next, then Millie and a dozen old friends of Cassie's father. Cassie was back in business, but at that particular moment, she wasn't happy about it. Gabe came to her side. "What's wrong?"

She wanted to shoo everyone out of the store. "I thought we were getting married this afternoon!"

"We are."

"But—"

Gabe grinned. "Enjoy it, Cassie. We waited a long time. A few minutes won't hurt."

After two hours the shelves had noticeable holes and she had four invitations to have tea with old friends and new ones. Even Millie had come by. She'd purchased a dozen tablecloths and ordered red-checked napkins. Everyone except the Drakes had called on her today. Cassie knew what she had to do. Unless she forgave Maude, the buzzards of unforgiveness would peck at them both until they had another argument. Silently, Cassie thought a prayer. *I forgive her, Lord. I hope she can forgive me.* Tomorrow she'd visit Maude and do her best to wipe the slate clean.

Before the thought left Cassie's head, the front door opened and she saw Maude with her husband and Billy. The women studied each other from across the room. Instead of steeling herself for animosity, Cassie approached her rival with an outstretched hand. "I know we've had our differences, Maude. I was terrible to you all those years ago. If you can forgive me, I'd like to be friends."

Maude looked into Cassie's eyes, then gripped her hand in both of hers. "I'm sorry, too. I've been horrible to you. I've spread lies—"

"It's over," Cassie said.

"I came to make it right." Maude glanced at her husband, then at Billy. "Before we leave, my son will be apologizing to Luke. Thanks to Gabe, my husband had a talk with him."

Cassie squeezed Maude's fingers. "It's not easy raising a boy, is it?"

"No!" Maude laughed and so did Cassie. As mothers of sons, they had a lot in common. As the women stepped apart, Maude glanced around the shop. "You have lovely things. I need to do some shopping."

"Take your time," Cassie said, smiling.

For the next hour, people came and went. When the last customer left, Gabe touched her elbow. "I spoke to Reverend Hall when they came by. He and Thelma are waiting at the parsonage."

"What for?" Luke asked.

Cassie didn't think Luke would object, but twelve-year-old boys could be unpredictable. He didn't have a say in this matter, but his acceptance would mean a lot.

Gabe looked at Cassie, then spoke directly to the boy. "I love your mother, Luke. I always have. I've asked her to be my wife and she's agreed."

The clock ticked. Dust settled in a shaft of light, then

Luke stood tall and looked hard at Gabe. "You'll be good to her, won't you?"

"Yes, son. I will."

A lump pushed into Cassie's throat and wouldn't slide back. With tears welling, she watched as Luke kept his eyes on Gabe. "Does this mean you'll be my father?"

"I'd like that," Gabe said. "But you're almost grown. I respect that."

"I still need a dad."

"Good, because I need a son."

Grinning, Gabe held out his hand to shake. Luke took it, squeezed hard, then turned to Cassie. In his eyes, she saw the boy who'd always live in her heart and the man he'd soon become.

Gangly and awkward, he put his arms around her. "I love you, Ma."

"I love you, too."

As her son hugged her tight, Cassie looked over his shoulder at Gabe. Tall and strong, he filled her heart with joy, peace and the hope of children. Laughing out loud, she thought of the set of dishes she'd always wanted. They'd look lovely on Gabe's table, especially when their family grew. She'd love a brother for Luke, and she'd always wanted a daughter of her own. With her heart full, Cassie whispered a prayer of thanks.

* * * * *

Dear Reader,

If I'd had a few more pages, I'd have written an epilogue for Cassie and Gabe. I'd have given them two more children, a girl and a boy, and I'd have given Luke the brightest future I could imagine. He could grow up to be anything. An inventor? A doctor? Even president of the United States.

Mothers work hard to give their children opportunities. We want them to develop strong wings and to fly high. We build nests. We feed them and teach them. Eventually we set them free to find their own way. I've had some experience with children leaving the nest. My sons are both grown and living amazing lives far from home.

Just as poignant is the memory I have of leaving the nest where I grew up. Several years ago, my husband accepted a job that required a cross-county move. I'll never forget telling my parents. "We gave you wings," my mom said. "We expect you to use them." I know it broke her heart (my dad's, too) when we moved three thousand miles away, but she smiled through it and stayed strong.

That's what moms do. They love unselfishly. They do what's best for their kids. I am blessed indeed to have that kind of mom.

Best wishes,

Victoria Bylin

QUESTIONS FOR DISCUSSION

1. Cassie O'Rourke has a son who's on the verge of serious trouble. She's desperate to protect him from the influence of his "friends." Do you think leaving Chicago is the right decision?

2. Deputy Gabe Wyatt takes a tough but loving approach to Cassie's rebellious son. How does Luke respond to Gabe's discipline? Why are Gabe's efforts effective when Cassie's efforts aren't?

3. Cassie feels guilty for her past and how her choices affected her son. Is this guilt legitimate? What lessons does she learn about forgiveness? Why is she finally able to forgive herself?

4. Gabe wonders if Cassie still loves him. Cassie believes herself to be a pariah and puts distance between them. Is her decision noble or selfish? Who is she really protecting, and why?

5. Do you agree with Gabe's belief that boys need to learn how and when to fight? What character traits mark the difference between boyhood and manhood?

6. Disturbed by events between Gabe and Luke, Cassie goes to Thelma, a minister's wife, for help.

What does Thelma do for Cassie? How do Thelma's actions relate to the Old Testament story of Rizpah?

7. Cassie O'Rourke is a prodigal daughter with a prodigal son. Have you had a prodigal child in your life? Have you been one? How did God work to bring you and a loved one into a new place of peace?

Turn the page for a sneak peek of Shirlee McCoy's suspense-filled story,
THE DEFENDER'S DUTY
On sale in May 2009 from Steeple Hill Love Inspired® Suspense.

After weeks in intensive care, police officer Jude Sinclair is finally recovering from the hit-and-run accident that nearly cost him his life. But was it an accident after all? Jude has his doubts—which get stronger when he spots a familiar black car outside his house: the same kind that accelerated before running him down two months ago. Whoever wants him dead hasn't given up, and anyone close to Jude is in danger. Especially Lacey Carmichael, the stubborn, beautiful home-care aide who refuses to leave his side, even if it means following him into danger….

"We don't have time for an argument," Jude said. "Take a look outside. What do you see?"

Lacey looked and shrugged. "The parking lot."

"Can you see your car?"

"Sure. It's parked under the streetlight. Why?"

"See the car to its left?"

"Yeah. It's a black sedan." Her heart skipped a beat as she said the words, and she leaned closer to the glass. "You don't think that's the same car you saw at the house tonight, do you?"

"I don't know, but I'm going to find out."

Lacey scooped up the grilled-cheese sandwich and shoved it into the carryout bag. "Let's go."

He eyed her for a moment, his jaw set, his gaze hot. "*We're* not going anywhere. You are staying here. I am going to talk to the driver of that car."

"I think we've been down this road before and I'm pretty sure we both know where it leads."

"It leads to you getting fired. Stay put until I get back, or forget about having a place of your own for a month." He stood and limped away, not even giving

Lacey a second glance as he crossed the room and headed into the diner's kitchen area.

Probably heading for a back door.

Lacey gave him a one-minute head start and then followed, the hair on the back of her neck standing on end and issuing a warning she couldn't ignore. Danger. It was somewhere close by again, and there was no way she was going to let Jude walk into it alone. If he fired her, so be it. As a matter of fact, if he fired her, it might be for the best. Jude wasn't the kind of client she was used to working for. Sure, there'd been other young men, but none of them had seemed quite as vital or alive as Jude. He didn't seem to need her, and Lacey didn't want to be where she wasn't needed. On the other hand, she'd felt absolutely certain moving to Lynchburg was what God wanted her to do.

"So, which is it, Lord? Right or wrong?" She whispered the words as she slipped into the diner's hot kitchen. A cook glared at her, but she ignored him. Until she knew for sure why God had brought her to Lynchburg, Lacey could only do what she'd been paid to do— make sure Jude was okay.

With that in mind, she crossed the room, heading for the exit and the client that she was sure was going to be a lot more trouble than she'd anticipated when she'd accepted the job.

Jude eased around the corner of the restaurant, the dark alleyway offering him perfect cover as he peered into the parking lot. The car he'd spotted through the window of the restaurant was still parked beside Lacey's.

Black. Four door. Honda. It matched the one that had pulled up in front of his house, and the one that had run him down in New York.

He needed to get closer.

A soft sound came from behind him. A rustle of fabric. A sigh of breath. Spring rain and wildflowers carried on the cold night air. Lacey.

Of course.

"I told you that you were going to be fired if you didn't stay where you were."

"Do you know how many times someone has threatened to fire me?"

"Based on what I've seen so far, a lot."

"Some of my clients fire me ten or twenty times a day."

"Then I guess I've got a ways to go." Jude reached back and grabbed her hand, pulling her up beside him.

"Is the car still there?"

"Yeah."

"Let me see." She squeezed in closer, her hair brushing his chin as she jockeyed for a better position.

Jude pulled her up short. Her wrist was warm beneath his hand. For a moment he was back in the restaurant, Lacey's creamy skin peeking out from under her dark sweater, white scars crisscrossing the tender flesh. She'd shoved her sleeve down too quickly for him to get a good look, but the glimpse he'd gotten was enough. There was a lot more to Lacey than met the eye. A lot she hid behind a quick smile and a quicker wit. She'd been hurt before, and he wouldn't let it happen again. No way was he going to drag her into danger. Not now. Not tomorrow. Not ever. As soon as they got back to the house, he was going to do exactly what he'd threatened—fire her.

"It's not the car." She said it with such authority, Jude stepped from the shadows and took a closer look.

"Why do you say that?"

"The one back at the house had tinted glass. Really dark. With this one, you can see in the back window. Looks like there is a couple sitting in the front seats. Unless you've got two people after you, I don't think that's the same car."

She was right.

Of course she was.

Jude could see inside the car, see the couple in the front seats. If he'd been thinking with his head instead of acting on the anger that had been simmering in his gut for months, he would have seen those things long before now. "You'd make a good detective, Lacey."

"You think so? Maybe I should make a career change. Give up home-care aide for something more dangerous and exciting." She laughed as she pulled away from his hold and stepped out into the parking lot, but there was tension in her shoulders and in the air. As if she sensed the danger that had been stalking Jude, felt it as clearly as Jude did.

"I'm not sure being a detective is as dangerous or as exciting as people think. Most days it's a lot of running into brick walls. Backing up, trying a new direction." He spoke as he led Lacey across the parking lot, his body still humming with adrenaline.

"That sounds like life to me. Running into brick walls, backing up and trying new directions."

"True, but in my job the brick walls happen every other day. In life, they're usually not as frequent." He waited while she got into her car, then closed the door, glancing in the black sedan as he walked past. An elderly woman smiled and waved at him, and Jude waved back, still irritated with himself for the mistake he'd made.

Now that he was closer, it was obvious the two cars he'd seen weren't the same. The one at his place had been sleeker and a little more sporty. Which proved that when a person wanted to see something badly enough, he did.

"That wasn't much of a meal for you. Sorry to cut things short for a false alarm." He glanced at Lacey as he got into the Mustang, and was surprised that her hand was shaking as she shoved the key into the ignition.

He put a hand on her forearm. "Are you okay?"

"Fine."

"For someone who is fine, your hands sure are shaking hard."

"How about we chalk it up to fatigue?"

"How about you admit you were scared?"

"Were? I still am." She started the car, and Jude let his hand fall away from her arm.

"You don't have to be. We're safe. For now."

"It's the 'for now' part that's got me worried. Who's trying to kill you, Jude? Why?"

"If I had the answers to those questions, we wouldn't be sitting here talking about it."

"You don't even have a suspect?"

"Lacey, I've got a dozen suspects. More. Every wife who's ever watched me cart her husband off to jail. Every son who's ever seen me put handcuffs on his dad. Every family member or friend who's sat through a murder trial and watched his loved one get convicted because of the evidence I put together."

"Have you made a list?"

"I've made a hundred lists. None of them have done me any good. Until the person responsible comes calling again, I've got no evidence, no clues and no way to link anyone to the hit and run."

"Maybe he won't come calling again. Maybe the hit-and-run was an accident, and maybe the sedan we saw outside your house was just someone who got lost and ended up in the wrong place." She sounded like she really wanted to believe it. He should let her. That's what he'd done with his family. Let them believe the hit-and-run was a fluke thing that had happened and was over. He'd done it to keep them safe. He'd do the opposite to keep Lacey from getting hurt.

* * * * *

Will Jude manage to scare Lacey away, or will he learn that the best way to keep her safe is to keep her close…for as long as they both shall live? To find out, read
THE DEFENDER'S DUTY by Shirlee McCoy
Available May 2009
from Love Inspired Suspense.

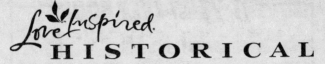

REQUEST YOUR FREE BOOKS!

2 FREE INSPIRATIONAL NOVELS
PLUS 2
FREE
MYSTERY GIFTS

Love Inspired.
HISTORICAL
INSPIRATIONAL HISTORICAL ROMANCE

YES! Please send me 2 FREE Love Inspired® Historical novels and my 2 FREE mystery gifts (gifts are worth about $10). After receiving them, if I don't wish to receive any more books, I can return the shipping statement marked "cancel". If I don't cancel, I will receive 4 brand-new novels every other month and be billed just $4.24 per book in the U.S. or $4.74 per book in Canada, plus 25¢ shipping and handling per book and applicable taxes, if any*. That's a savings of over 20% off the cover price! I understand that accepting the 2 free books and gifts places me under no obligation to buy anything. I can always return a shipment and cancel at any time. Even if I never buy another book, the two free books and gifts are mine to keep forever. 102 IDN ERYA 302 IDN ERYM

Name	(PLEASE PRINT)
Address	Apt. #
City	State/Prov. Zip/Postal Code

Signature (if under 18, a parent or guardian must sign)

Mail to Steeple Hill Reader Service:
IN U.S.A.: P.O. Box 1867, Buffalo, NY 14240-1867
IN CANADA: P.O. Box 609, Fort Erie, Ontario L2A 5X3

Not valid to current subscribers of Love Inspired Historical books.

Want to try two free books from another series?
Call 1-800-873-8635 or visit www.morefreebooks.com

* Terms and prices subject to change without notice. N.Y. residents add applicable sales tax. Canadian residents will be charged applicable provincial taxes and GST. Offer not valid in Quebec. This offer is limited to one order per household. All orders subject to approval. Credit or debit balances in a customer's account(s) may be offset by any other outstanding balance owed by or to the customer. Please allow 4 to 6 weeks for delivery. Offer available while quantities last.

Your Privacy: Steeple Hill Books is committed to protecting your privacy. Our Privacy Policy is available online at www.SteepleHill.com or upon request from the Reader Service. From time to time we make our lists of customers available to reputable third parties who may have a product or service of interest to you. If you would prefer we not share your name and address, please check here. ☐

LIH08R

Love Inspired.
HISTORICAL

TITLES AVAILABLE NEXT MONTH

Available May 12, 2009

GIFT FROM THE SEA by Anna Schmidt
The Great War took more from nurse Maggie Hunter than just her fiancé—it also claimed her faith in God and in love. Then an injured man washes up on the shores of her Nantucket home, and to save him, Maggie must learn how to believe in hope again.

COURTING THE DOCTOR'S DAUGHTER by Janet Dean
A dedicated healer working beside her doctor father, widow and mother Mary Graves has no time for nonsense like Dr. Luke Jacobs's "elixir of health." But there's more to Luke than meets the eye. He's got a lifetime of love he's willing to share, if he can convince Mary to let him into her home, her family—and her heart.